I0586028

THE

SISTER

TRIP

Being sisters doesn't mean
they're friends

MEL A ROWE

Also by Mel A ROWE

ELSIE CREEK SERIES:

The ART of DUST

DIAMOND in the DUST

CAKED in DUST

XMAS DUST

MUSTER in the DUST

ROLLED in DUST

WRITTEN in DUST

OASIS OF THE OUTBACK DUOLOGY:

The Station - Volume I

The Station - Volume II

Standalone Stories:

Avoiding the Pity Party

Unplanned Party

The Football Whisperer

USA Bestseller—Winter's Walk

Run Beautiful Run

The Sister Trip

Receive exclusive insights, and news on upcoming releases by joining: https://melarowe.com/newsletter/

COPYRIGHT

**Caveat: As a courtesy, since there may be some sparse language choices in this story that may represent an obstacle for the reader, I am offering this warning. Please note this language and cultural references are purely for fictional purposes only and not designed to offend any individual persons, culture, or religions implied.

*The Following Is Written in Australian English

For those sisters who are friends

& for those friends

who are like sisters.

Mel A Rowe

One

'I'm your sister!'

'That doesn't mean I have to like you,' Teà said to Little Miss Lottie Voss, the younger sister who ruled this tiny, somewhat claustrophobic empire, from the front seat of dear old Dad's 1970 XY Ford Falcon 500, with a big view of nothing. She couldn't believe the car still existed—and right now, she hated it.

What kind of father demands that his two daughters take an ancient, yet immaculately shiny, dark blue beast through the outback without any air conditioning? It didn't even have a decent stereo. And they were well out of phone range, heading north with Alice Springs hours behind them.

Teà tried to get comfortable on the bench seat, but the stupid bulky jar her sister insisted on keeping between them was annoying. 'I'm sick of this thing taking up all the room in the front seat.' She unclipped her seatbelt and hoisted the jar to the back seat, where the rest of Lottie's junk lived. Which was a lot of luggage, all in plaid. They matched Lottie's dress.

'You can't put it there.' Lottie reached back, keeping one hand on the steering wheel.

'Well, I can, and I did.'

'Oh no, you can't. It should be here. I'm driving and it's my rules.'

'Get a grip, princess, and keep two hands on the steering wheel at all times.' Turning around again, Teà pushed the ceramic jar further onto the middle of the back seat. 'It can sit there.'

'It's unsecure.'

'It's—*watch out,* Lottie!'

Lottie slammed her little feet on the brake.

Teà was flung against the dashboard. The tyres squealed as the car's chunky square body swerved on the deserted road.

The engine stalled.

Smoke filled the air.

A tick-tick-tick came from the beefy six-cylinder engine.

'Did I hit it?' Lottie asked in a soft voice, leaning over the steering wheel. A sweat bead trickled down her temple. 'Oh, I can't look. I just can't.'

'So now you want me to play the big sister?' Teà wiggled free from her wedged position between the car seat and dashboard, with her bum almost touching the floor.

She hoisted open the heavy passenger door to roll onto the tarred road. Hot stones embedded in her hands and she jumped to her feet.

The heat was horrendous, hitting her with laser precision from a sun that hung like a lonely globe in a sky completely clear of clouds. They'd left the land of rain and lush green hills for this sunburnt world of red dust. Welcome to the Northern Territory outback.

She rubbed her tender spine. 'Does my back have a welt?'

It could've been worse, considering how slow Lottie was driving. Snails would win this epic road race.

'You shouldn't have taken off your seatbelt. This is all your fault. Go check the front of the car. We're on a deadline.' Lottie tapped her wristwatch.

Teà's boots were the only sound on the road washed with a glistening heat wave that disappeared like a mirage on the curve of the horizon.

She didn't want to peek at the front of the Ford either. But they were in the middle of the road surrounded by nothing but red dirt ranges and lots of scrub. Purple pockets of wildflowers splashed like paint spilled on a red carpet, but the green on the spindly trees was an icky army-olive green.

'What is it?' Lottie called out from her safe space behind the wheel, straightening up her blonde ponytail. She grimaced at the sun, then sat back in her seat and slathered on more sunscreen, which would sweat off into milky streaks in a matter of moments.

Teà swiped at a fly.

The flies were a pain.

Small. Black. Sticky flies.

Teà took a deep breath and forced herself to inch forward. *Please be nothing. Please be nothing.* She wasn't in the mood to drag away any roadkill. Nor was she a fan of this road trip, constantly bickering with Lottie. If Lottie wasn't her sister, Teà would've left this party back in South Australia days ago.

The good thing is they only had four days left, then they'd never have to see each other again. She just had to remember, there was a big pot of gold at the end of this dusty rainbow.

There was a flapping noise at the front of the car, accompanied by a squealing mewl that sounded like a baby lion cub.

Teà cringed as her stomach squeezed tight. *No, it wasn't still alive. Was it?*

She peeked over the car's long bonnet, sparkling under the relentless outback sun, and spotted feathers. Not the scattering you'd expect from hitting a bird, as they were still attached. Stuck in the car's grill.

'It's a duck.' A white-bodied duck, with pink webbed feet, and a chestnut band. Its wings a vibrant dark green, so rich they seemed black.

'Grab my gloves from my daypack, Lottie.' Teà

squatted beside the duck. 'Hello, little fella, I'm sorry my sister's driving sucks.'

'I heard that.' Lottie came up beside her and held out the gloves. 'Why do you have such thick gloves in your bag?'

'For work.' As Teà slid on the gloves she felt the ground rumbling beneath her boots. She peeked around the car's boxy body, the outback scrub reflecting off the car's deep navy-blue paint. 'Lottie, there's a truck coming.' The car stood barely off the road, with a long, swerving line of black rubber laid out in a crazy-crayon trail.

'Oh, I'll move the car.' Lottie headed for the open driver's door.

'No, you can't. You'll kill it.'

The large truck went down through the gears, then there was a hiss of its brakes.

'Lottie, wave him through.'

'I did, but it's obvious he wants to stop.'

'Or your waving skill is as bad as your driving, and he thinks we need help.' Teà turned away from the wave of red dust stirred up by the road train. The gravel crunched and popped under the massive tyres as the truck and its three trailers came to a halt.

'Are those helicopters on your trailers?' Lottie asked the driver, who was jumping out of the truck.

Teà double-blinked at the dream-like vision of a male swaggering towards them on the deserted outback highway.

'Yeah, muster choppers. Three of them.' Heel toe, heel toe, his boot stride was sure and steady. His well-worn denim jeans hugged a set of sturdy thighs that made his lazy hip-rolling stride perfect in those jeans. His wide-brimmed cowboy hat sat low on his brow, shading sunglasses that hid his eyes, but showed his deep outdoorsy tan. 'You girls all right?'

Girls! Teà rolled her eyes, dragging her gaze away from the fantasy cowboy to return her focus on the duck. Had she been drinking enough water? Her imagination seemed to be running away with her.

'We hit a duck. And it's stuck.'

'*You* hit the duck, Lottie. I'm trying to save it.' Teà ever so gently wrapped her hands around the duck's tender body, positioning herself.

'Here, let me help.' He didn't even wait for a response, removing his sunglasses, perching them on the brim of his Akubra. 'I'll hold the body; you get its wings. Try to keep its feathers straight so it can fly away.'

'Sure.' The sweat trickled down her temples, and her shirt stuck to her skin, as she carefully pulled back the trapped feathers, one by one. Some were severely twisted, making her heart fall for the poor little thing that seemed astonishingly calm. 'I'm Teà, that's Lottie.'

'Devin.' His brown eyes were a rich coffee caramel, with his eyebrows a deeper brown, the same colour of his hair barely seen beneath the hat's brim. Damn, he was handsome. Too handsome.

Teà licked her lips, suddenly parched, yet also salivating, as her blood pressure headed into boiling billycan territory. *It's just the weather*, she told herself— which was hotter than a thousand ovens someone forgot to switch off. 'What type of duck is this?'

'Burdekin duck. A juvenile. There are some grey patches on the side. They're a protected species in this area.'

'What does that mean?' Lottie's shadow spread over them, offering some relief from the relentless sun.

'You get a year's jail and a massive fine for hurting one of these fellas.'

'Lottie did it.' Teà grinned, using the back of her gloves to wipe at the sweat.

Devin's lips barely curled in the corners, as the sun-kissed creases deepened around those brown eyes. They were more than just a plain brown.

'But-but—' Lottie, already pale, dropped to a shade of

glow-in-the-dark kind of pale.

Teà carefully removed the last of the wing's tip, successfully pulling it free from the Ford's grill. 'Do ducks live in the middle of nowhere?'

Devin shrugged. 'Stretch out its wing to see if it's broken.'

As Teà gingerly straightened the wing, it bellowed a mewling, screeching honk that echoed into the wilderness. She cupped her mouth, waiting for the last of those horrific cries to cease.

'Did I break it? Oh no, I'm going to jail, aren't I?' Lottie, the drama queen, pressed her hand to her forehead and turned to face the sun. 'Destined for a life behind bars, I'll miss Mother's Day, Sophie's first day at big school, and Pip's first day of kindergarten. And my husband will divorce me and marry some hussy from the schoolyard.'

Devin arched an eyebrow.

'I think it's sprained?' He carried it to the side of the road, putting the duck gently on the ground. Its white body and pink webbed feet were a stark contrast to the red soil. The chestnut stripe hung like a necklace around its feathery chest, reminding her of a mayor's golden livery chain worn as part of their ceremonial robes. It was a pretty duck. Until it fell over to its side, like a dead duck.

'Did it have a heart attack?' Lottie asked.

'Probably gone into shock.' Devin adjusted his hat. 'You can leave it here.'

'What are its chances of survival?' Teà asked.

His gaze was steady, with his thick lashes highlighting eyes that weren't just brown. They were a dark caramel blended perfectly with rich roasted coffee beans. It came with a stare that punched a burst of pure caffeine through her veins, making her pulse jack hammer. She lifted her hair off the back of her neck, desperate for a breeze.

Again, Devin shrugged a set of square shoulders that made his T-shirt stretch over a very fine muscular torso. He gazed up at the sky where a lone kite was circling above, then returned his unflinching gaze to her. 'Not good.'

'Is duck good to eat? In case we need to hide the evidence.' Teà winked at Devin. Caramel and coffee were fast becoming her favourite food groups.

His lip barely curled for a fleeting second. But it was there. 'Never had Burdekin before. But I've tried Peking duck.'

'I don't mind Szechuan duck.'

'Got a ringer back home who does a decent smoked goose. He could do a duck.'

'I tried duck à l'orange once.'

'Isn't pate made from duck?' Devin kept a straight face, but his eyes were shining.

'So it is.' Teà pushed her tongue to her cheek, struggling to keep up the game. She was used to bantering like one of the boys. Flirting for her was foreign. She didn't flirt. Ever.

But then the duck wheezed. Struggling to sit up, it staggered like it was drunk.

'Look who's coming around.' She'd never been happier for a duck. It was cute.

Devin squatted down beside her as the duck limped towards him.

'You should take the duck.'

'I'm in a truck. You take the duck. Take a few photos and make yourselves famous on Instagram or something.'

'Can we do that? If it's a protected duck.' Teà's smile softened as the duck limped towards her, using her arm to prop itself up and to coo like a pigeon. 'Is that a wheeze?'

'They whistle, wheeze. Rarely quack. Strange ducks.'

'How do you know about them?'

'We've got a couple of billabongs full of 'em back home.'

Lottie stood by the car, wringing her hands. 'If you have places full of them, why are they so protected?'

Devin shrugged. 'They mate for life. I think they got

hunted to near extinction.'

As the rugged cowboy tenderly patted the injured duck, it brought up some extinct emotions Teà hadn't felt in ages. She didn't want to either. That tender warmth brewing on the inside to fill her with a serene calmness — was not real.

'*Hello! Peoples,*' screeched Lottie.

'Shh, Lottie, you're upsetting the duck.' It shifted closer to Teà for protection. *Aww.*

'Don't you mean your lunch, the way you two carnivores are carrying on?'

'Steady on.' Devin stood to full height. A tower of raw masculinity, so much taller than the dainty Lottie.

'Why don't you take the duck back to your billabong, Devin?' Teà said.

'Can't. I'm on a job.' He inspected the car's front grill. 'Nice car. Luckily, there's no damage. Where are you two headed?'

'The next town, I believe?'

'Wauchope?'

Lottie pulled out her carefully regimented itinerary, a map covered in highlights and sticky notes. 'Aren't the Devil's Marbles next?'

'Two hours that way. And being this late in the day,' he said, again gazing up at the sky, 'you'll be camping at Rusty's Roadhouse, too.'

'You guessed right. Is there someone we can give the duck to at the roadhouse? Like some wildlife rescue?'

'Teà …' He turned and faced her, poking up his hat's brim. But the way he said her name in that voice, with a stare that went beyond a look, it felt so intimate. 'That's a protected duck. No one is going to touch it for fear of getting pinged. You and Lillie—'

'My name is Lottie. It's short for Loretta.'

'Hmph.' He didn't even gaze at Lottie, just kept those eyes on Teà. The unwavering attention was unnerving.

The duck tapped on Teà's leg, gratefully allowing her

to drag her eyes away from Devin. The poor thing was so helpless.

With no thought she picked it up, tenderly tucking it under her arm, where it cooed. How was this duck so tame? 'He deserves a second chance at life. I can't abandon him out here. He'd get lonely, and nobody deserves to be left alone and defenceless against the elements ...' She'd know.

There were now three kites circling above them. *The vultures.* 'What if we dropped it off at some billabong, somewhere?'

'Oh, good idea.' Lottie nodded so fast it should have brought on a case of whiplash as she spun to face Devin. 'Where is the nearest billabong?'

'It's the dry season,' Devin said to Teà, tenderly stroking the duck's neck. 'There's no water around for miles. So how that duck got out here ...' He let the words hang, his fingers barely brushing her arm.

She swallowed, stepping back from the dishy cowboy in denim. She tried not to watch him—honest to God, she did—but he was the only place her eyes wanted to travel. Slowly. From hat brim to boot heels.

His eyes remained on her, in a quiet look. A look that lasted for so long it unnerved her, forcing her to look away.

'We'll find a waterhole or something. Or until the duck flies away. Come on, Lottie, we're on a deadline.' Her face was flushed as her T-shirt clung to her sticky skin. 'Um, thanks for your help, Devin,' she stammered out. 'Maybe Lottie will release the moths from her purse to buy you a beer for saving the duck and her neck.'

Devin's chuckle was low as he turned to walk away.

Hot damn, he was throwing off some sexy vibes.

'Hey, what do ducks eat?' She opened the back door, but couldn't help pausing to watch his sexy hip-rolling swagger and that beautiful behind that was hugged perfectly in those well-worn jeans. She was so tempted to tap his butt just to see how soft that denim was and how tight those buns were.

Not. Gonna. Happen.

He shrugged at her, sliding on his sunglasses, as he kicked at the front tyre of his truck. 'Google it when you get into phone range.'

'When will that be?'

'Not for another two hours, *thataway*.' He tossed his thumb over his shoulder as he walked along the side of the truck, checking the ropes strapping down the three helicopters. One for each trailer.

Good. She didn't need that in her face.

'Lottie, we could take the duck back to Alice Springs. I'm sure we could find a park ranger or a vet to help it.' Teà stroked the soft feathers of the duck settling in her arms. It was probably still in shock.

Lottie faced the direction they'd come from, then down at her map of many colours. 'Nope.' She rolled it up with a snap. 'I have to do this. You could hitchhike back to Alice, but then we'd both be breaking the rules, and we'd both lose. I have my family to think of, which is far more important than you and that dumb duck.'

They were both committed to this road trip from hell, whether they liked it or not. There was too much to lose.

Teà looked down at the duck. 'Ready to join our road trip, Quacker?'

'You named it! You can't eat it now.' Again, Devin's chuckle carried from the trailers, making her grin like a schoolgirl. She was everything uncool around this guy.

'Let's go, Lottie. You drive.' Teà clambered into the back seat. The car was an oven.

'I'm not having that feathery thing in Dad's car—'

'It's that or jail? Remember, we're on a deadline, Lottie.' Teà dumped the urn back onto the front seat. 'And you can share the front seat with Dad.'

Two

Steering the car, Lottie glared at the rear-view mirror reflecting her sister, lounging across the back seat with her stylish lace-up leather boots resting on the front seat. With a dumb duck. 'Have some respect.' She thumped at the seat to force those boots off.

'To you or the car?'

'I don't even let my husband put his socked feet on our coffee tables.'

'Why not?'

'Excuse me?'

'Isn't home a place where you chill? Or does he trek a trailer-load of mud through the house, while ponging of sheep dung. To plonk his butt on the couch, slapping down a sweat-stained hat on the floor, as he cracks open a beer?'

'Adrian would never do that.'

'Oh, wait. I was talking about Dad.'

'Dad never did that.'

Teà arched an eyebrow at her.

'In the end, he didn't.' Lottie glanced at the urn seated beside her. 'Dad was good.'

'Sure, he was. To you. Always to his *little mate, Lottie.*'

Lottie sat straighter with chin raised. 'Because I was the dutiful daughter. I was there for him. Not like you, who ran away.'

'Well, Daddy dearest must have loved me enough to include me in this stupid road trip of horrors we're on.' Teà shoved a suitcase off the back seat. 'You really have a thing for plaid. Not only are you wearing it, but your luggage is all plaid.'

Lottie frowned, her knuckles whitening as she gripped the steering wheel. It still irked her that after seventeen years Teà got to swan in and act like the queen of the car, hogging the back seat, shoving Lottie's precious plaid luggage around.

Lottie never travelled, so it was the first time she'd used her luggage. Unlike her husband, Adrian, flying in and out for the mines. Leaving her to manage the farm, house, two small children, a hundred sheep, crops, leases, and a cranky father—all while maintaining the dressmaking business her mother had started.

She didn't have time to be stuck in a vintage car playing another one of her father's map games. And she certainly didn't have time to play nice with her older sister, Teà.

Teà. The taller sister. The fun sister who didn't have a care in the world. Who got to traipse freely around the world with a backpack full of excuses for not coming home sooner. She hadn't come back for Lottie's wedding, didn't send flowers for Lottie's mother's funeral, and hadn't even fronted for their own father's funeral.

The only way Teà Eliza Voss had finally deigned to grace them with her presence was for Lottie to file a missing person's report with the police. She hadn't wanted to—she'd *had to*, or the whole inheritance deal was toast!

It was part of the rules.

The only problem was, Teà popped up looking like the sister she remembered. With her dark hair, so much longer now, in sleek black pants and long black coat. Complaining of jet lag and carrying a suitcase that magically turned into a backpack.

How dare that over-dressed backpacking female turn her nose up at Lottie for packing four cases and a beauty bag. No way was Lottie leaving home without her hairdryer!

'We're going to the outback, you won't need many clothes,' so said toffee-nosed Teà, dumping her black bag into the boot.

Black. Everything was black. Black socks, black underwear — the superfine kind of black lace underwear that made Adrian pause over his morning cuppa while staring out the window like he did most mornings — when he was home. Only to see Teà's fancy underwear swinging on the clothesline like some stripper doing a horizontal pole dance.

Those five days, waiting to leave to start this road trip, were torture — especially with her sister hanging around the house.

Ugh. It sucked more than misaligning the princess seams on a bride's bodice.

Especially when the kids loved their Aunt Teà. Not to mention how Adrian got all gawky around Teà. Then the lawyer had to speak with Teà in private, to re-explain the rules of this road trip. How come Teà got all the attention?

Victor Voss was Lottie's dad, too. She was a grieving daughter who deserved the attention. After all, it was Lottie who doted over her father. Who washed, ironed, fed, and fetched for her father, nearly her entire adult life.

All while they never heard from Teà again.

Gone. Just like that. Without any explanation.

It was soon followed by Teà's room getting cleaned out, all photos taken down, successfully removing all traces of Tea's existence from their household.

Yet, her parents never gave Lottie an explanation. Nothing. It was as if her older sister had died, and no one dared mention Teà's name again.

Until Daddy put Teà in the will.

So of course, the money-hungry Teà showed up.

Who wouldn't, when over four hundred acres of prime farmland was on the line?

It's what was driving them to follow a breadcrumb trail

of hand-written notes across the country. They were like love letters, without the love, from their father! Leaving them with no clue as to where they were going.

The lawyer had merely handed over an envelope, along with a cheque to cover their travel expenses. The first set of instructions found inside that sealed business-sized envelope, contained a note and map drawn by their father. It came with a list of items to stock up at Port Augusta. Then on to Coober Pedy, to then aim for the Devil's Marbles.

But there was a whole lot of nothing in the Northern Territory—home to the harshest, remotest regions of the Australian outback. It scared her being this far from home.

Did Sophie lock up the chickens when she collected the eggs? Did Adrian help their daughter mark the dates on them? Sophie wasn't good with numbers. Did her dear baby boy, Pip, have enough warm clothes on? Did her husband remember to warm up the hot water bottles for Pip's bed? She didn't trust their son with an electric blanket yet. Were they eating right? Were they—

'Quack.'

Teà giggled, hand feeding that stupid duck in the back seat like the cold queen of broken hearts being carted around in her vintage carriage.

The duck Lottie could do a year in jail for.

'Dad would kill us for having a duck in his car.' Lottie glowered at the dumb, damaged duck. 'No pets were allowed in this car.'

'Dad used to let Spot lie in this car all the time.'

'Who?'

'Spot. The ginger cat who had an oil-stain spot on its back. He'd lie across the front dashboard in winter for the sun.'

'I don't remember Spot.'

'You were young when he died.' Teà lifted a plaid ribbon as if measuring it up for size. 'Dad said Spot was the best mouse catcher he ever had. No mouse messed with the electrics of this car with Spot on the job.'

'Is that my ribbon?' Lottie frowned, peeking over her shoulder for just a second. If she dared to take her eyes off the road for too long, she might hit something again.

'You are the only one I know who wears plaid.'

'What are you doing?'

'Bandaging up *your* duck.' Teà wrapped the plaid ribbon around one of its legs, like a splint, allowing the duck to stand steadier.

'It's not my duck.'

'It is now. It's wearing plaid. He's very stylish.' Teà giggled. 'Considering how old this car is, it's in great condition. Where's it been, same car shed?'

'No, we moved it to the back shed. Only brought it out for weddings.'

'Weddings?'

Lottie smiled, rolling her shoulders, her grip loosening a little on the steering wheel. 'I used to drive this in weddings.'

'So, you and your mum not only made the wedding gowns, but you also drove the bride's car, too?'

'I loved it. We had to be there anyway, to ensure their bridal gowns and bridesmaids' dresses were perfect for the ceremony. It was Adrian's idea about using this Ford for weddings. He even drove it a few times, too. That's how we met — at a wedding, when I was busily repairing a small tear the bride had made with her heels.'

'Was it love at first sight?'

'Oh, yes.' Her heart just bloomed, as her hand grip loosened on the steering wheel. 'I was like Cinderella with pearl-headed silk pins hanging from my mouth and tucked up along my sleeve. On my knees, mending a bride's gown, and in walked Prince Charming himself.' She sighed, her shoulders relaxing.

Teà sat forward, hooking her arms over the back of the seat. Her delicate perfume was so fresh, considering they direly needed a shower from sitting in a hot car. 'Really?

Prince Charming?'

'Adrian's my kind of prince. Pushing up his clunky glasses, stuttering as he spoke, with his tie all skew-whiff, and shirt all wrong. I had to help him.'

'And you, being a fixer, found your fixer upper.'

For the first time since they'd met again, they shared a smile. A half smile.

But Lottie couldn't afford to make friends with the enemy, so she returned her attention to the long road ahead that brought promises of a big golden egg. 'Adrian was the bride's younger brother. He had to drive his sister to the ceremony, and they were already late. They were worried the groom was going to do a runner.'

'Why?'

'She was pregnant.'

'Did the bride tell you that?'

'She didn't have to. I had to keep letting out the darts in her bridal gown. And most brides plan their wedding a year in advance, but not this one. It was quite the scandal. Adrian said his father demanded they get married, and Adrian was supposed to be the muscle.'

'Your husband, Adrian?'

Teà's giggle made Lottie's back straighten.

Oh, bless him, Adrian wasn't perfect, but he was her husband. Hers.

But truth be known, Adrian was terrified of that brother-in-law. 'It doesn't matter now. They got divorced and Adrian's sister remarried this nice sheep farmer in Tumby Bay. But that first wedding, where I met Adrian, had the town talking of the early baby.'

'Weren't you a shotgun bride yourself?'

'Excuse me!' Lottie's eyelids fluttered, as if washing away some imaginary grit. Momentarily distracting her from the never-ending tarmac road, with its white line and occasional sign. There was nothing else out here to keep her entertained.

Teà counted on her outstretched fingers to hold up six

digits on two hands. 'Sophie, your eldest daughter, is six and you've been married for six years.'

Lottie lifted her chin so high her neck was tight. 'I got pregnant on our honeymoon, thank you very muchly! It's what married people do.' A honeymoon that was an overnight stay at the nearest seaside town, following a disastrous ceremony. They never got their honeymoon to some fancy vacation spot, what with shearing to be done, crops to be harvested, and her mother passing, it threw out all her plans of a perfect wedding.

She scowled at the mirror, reflecting the cretin in the back seat. This was all Teà's fault. They wouldn't need to do this road trip if Teà hadn't shown up. 'Thanks for coming to my wedding, by the way.'

'Did you invite me?'

'I didn't know where to send the invite.'

Teà sat back, stroking the duck sleeping beside her on a plaid towel.

'Is that my towel?' Lottie asked.

'You had four of them.'

'You could have used a newspaper, or *your* towel?'

'I only have the one and it's in the boot. You really have a thing for plaid.' Teà gave an evil laugh that made Lottie's neck tingle.

'I like plaid.'

'I'm not judging.'

'Oh, yes, you are. I can hear it in your tone.'

'Tone? Ha. Have you heard yourself speak to human beings lately?'

'At least I speak to people, not like you.' Teà never got involved, not in conversations, except with Lottie's children, while Lottie was busily getting ready to do this trek. Teà did nothing to help them on this journey. No way in hell was Lottie going to hand over the car keys to a stranger.

'Did Dad drive this car at weddings?'

'No.'

'Why not? It sounds like fun. Dad always called this the family car.' Teà patted the interior with a wistful expression on her face. 'Remember those Sundays? We'd get dragged out of bed, bundled into the back seat, to follow a map.' Teà pointed at Lottie's map spread over the front seat. 'His lucky two-up coins, a compass, a tank of fuel and an esky full of food and drinks, and away we'd go at sunrise.'

Lottie's lips inadvertently released a smile.

She remembered those days, sitting in the middle between her big sister and her dad, to give her mother a day off.

She side-glanced at the urn. Now it was her father's turn to sit in the middle of the front seat of the car that had taken them on some extraordinary adventures.

The best times were when they'd go fishing by a stream, where she'd squeeze her toes in the soft grass, making daisy chains under dappled sunshine. Teà would share her fishing line and help teach Lottie to lace up her shoes, or plait her hair with wildflowers.

But that all stopped when Lottie was ten.

Even Teà's bedroom, with its ceiling coated in posters of boy bands, was gone. Once, there stood a thick luxurious off-white looped rug at the end of Teà's bed, where plush purple cushions lived. It was the perfect spot to lie down while Teà read her stories, or where she could do her colouring while Teà did her homework. It's where Teà spoke to some friend on her hamburger phone, twisting her fingers on the long twisty cord. All of it gone, when Teà left. Like a big black hole with a trap door slamming it shut, locked tight with a thick industrial padlock.

'The Sunday family drives stopped when you left. Dad rarely drove this car after that.' She glared at her sister in the back seat as a hot ball of fire raged between her shoulder blades.

Her sister left them.

That thing didn't deserve to sit inside this car.

And Teà certainly didn't deserve to be included in her father's will.

'We're here.' Teà pointed to the bug-splattered windscreen.

The roadhouse's roof shone ahead, with a few cars and trucks parked out front, including a row of motorcycles. 'Oh no, bikies.'

Teà lifted her sunglasses. 'Nice bikes. Low riders.'

'Oh, right, so you're a bikie's chick, are you?'

'I was only a backpack for one biker.' Teà's words were barely heard as she faced the window. 'Until he made me ride my own saddle.'

'I have no idea what you just said. Saddle? Do you ride horses, too.'

'No. The seat of a road bike. And a backpack is the nickname for their passenger.'

Lottie parked the car, twisting around in her seat. 'You were a bikie?' Her sister wore enough black to be one.

'Lottie, we grew up riding dirt bikes as kids.'

'You did, not me.'

'I taught you to ride a motorbike as soon as your toes could touch the ground. You were six?'

'Seven.'

'What happened to that old motorbike?'

'Dumped it.' Like everything else that belonged to Teà.

'Probably a good thing, too. It was barely held together with string and duct tape. Your mother hated me letting you ride it.'

'You should have listened to my mother. As a parent — a mother of two children—I'd say no to them riding that motorbike too. My children's safety is everything to me.'

Teà laughed. One of those annoying, know-it-all, irritating laughs that made Lottie grit her teeth.

'You wouldn't stop badgering me until I let you ride that bike,' said Teà. 'Do I get the keys to our room, or do you?'

'I'll get it. The lawyer said it was pre-booked. I want to make sure it's in our budget.'

'Ah, yes, the budget. What is our meal allowance with this budget?'

'Fifty dollars each.'

'Per week, or per thousand kilometres?'

'We have enough food in the car.'

'We have ten grand for travel allowances. We could have caught a plane, then hired a car with air conditioning—'

'We have to drive Dad's car. It's part of the rules.' Lottie held up the notes she took from the lawyer, tempted to use them to swat at the dangerous buzzing, stinging wasp of a sister hogging the back seat! 'We don't know how far we're travelling, or what to expect or—'

'So, a big dinner it is, then. I'm starving. I wonder if they do room service or have something decent on cable?'

'This is *not* a holiday.' Her voice was louder than expected, with her words ringing in the eerie quietness of the outback. 'I don't do holidays. I don't have time for holidays. Not when I'm needed back home. Except now I'm out here in the middle of Woop Woop, stuck with you.' She slammed the driver's door shut and marched to the roadhouse.

'Dad's gonna kill you for slamming his car door like that.'

'He's dead. I doubt he'll care.'

'Finally, something we agree on.' Teà's laughter tinkled in the air.

Hussy! She-devil! Vixen!

No one got under Lottie's skin like Teà did. Her sister's comebacks stabbing at her like a bunch of rusty sewing needles, grinding deep into her bones to dredge up all the heartache and resentment of the past.

What did she do that was so wrong for her father to torture her like this? Stuck in a car with a stranger. Not a sister. A complete, cruel, cold-hearted stranger.

Teà was nothing like the supporting sister she remembered. As far as Lottie was concerned, her sister died seventeen years ago. And her father should have left it at that.

Three

'Well, well, well, of all the gin joints in all the outback roadhouses of the world, he had to walk into mine ...' Teà leaned her elbow against the front bar of the roadhouse.

Devin paused with his beer glass halfway to his lips. '*Casablanca*, right?'

'You know the movie?' Teà tried to catch the attention of the barmaid casually chatting to the bikers gathered at the other end. It was a small bar, with glass-front fridges containing assorted beverages. A large TV hung on the wall above various historical images of the roadhouse's humble beginnings. Small tables and stools ran along the exterior wall below simple old-fashioned windows made of small square panes of coloured glass. A pool table took up space at the other end where the bikers were playing, and where the barmaid continued to ignore Teà.

Devin took a deep mouthful of his beer, the Adam's apple in his tanned throat moving up and down with surety. 'Where's the duck?'

'We've got him under lockdown in case of the duck police.'

His chuckle was low, deep, and dreamy. 'In your room?'

'Back seat of the car. Quacker's claimed it as his own, cuddling up to a bowl of watermelon, wearing plaid. I'm thinking of going bug catching for him, to release them in the car later.'

'Your sister's going to love that.'

'I know, right? Can you imagine Lottie going nuts searching for some rogue cricket chirping under the foot pedals?' Teà giggled, waving her cash at the barmaid, hoping to get served. 'If I'm lucky, Lottie might actually let me drive for once.'

He shook his head before taking another deep mouthful, plonking his empty beer on the bar.

'Another one, Devin?' The busty barmaid with the British accent was front and centre as quick as lightning.

Devin just nodded. With a grunt.

'And I'll have the same, thanks.' *Rude, much!* Yet the barmaid was all over Devin. Sure, the guy was good looking, but this bar was overloaded with so much male testosterone it was breaching its walls. The only reason she sidled up to Devin was he felt safe somehow. Besides, she could control her desires because she was used to being treated like one of the boys. 'My shout, Devin.'

'Devin doesn't let anyone buy him a beer,' said the barmaid. 'He doesn't do shouts.'

Teà grinned, a full Cheshire Cat grin at Devin. 'Your barmaid's very protective.'

Devin rubbed at one eyebrow that matched his dark, messy excuse for a haircut. But his coffee caramel eyes were captivating as they caressed her with his gaze. And those hard lines around his mouth were daring to soften into something that wasn't a smile, but hinted at amusement. 'I don't do rounds, because I drink at my own pace.'

'Well, I'm just shouting you a beer for the help today. Or you don't like women buying you a drink?' She didn't once look away from him, she couldn't, even while speaking to the hovering barmaid. 'Save yourself the drama, hon. I'm not picking Devin up. You can have him for your own nocturnal activities *after* you get me a beer. Please.'

Devin plonked his elbow onto the bar to groan into his

hand. 'Can't a fella have a quiet beer?'

'Easily done.' Teà swiped Devin's fresh beer, exchanging it for some cash. 'Thanks for your help, Devin. And for the record, hon,' she said to the barmaid, who was scowling so deep it threatened to dislodge her thick false eyelashes, 'this guy was not only a hero today, but he was also a thorough gentleman. Now, he's all yours because I don't fight for scraps.'

'Bugger me,' Devin muttered.

Teà nodded at the bikers as she carried her beer past them. Once upon a time she'd have a chat, talk about bikes and perhaps the road ahead. But that all stopped two years ago when her world collapsed.

Lottie was right, this wasn't a vacation to chinwag with locals in the bar. She preferred a quiet corner in the outside beer garden with a magnificent view of the outback and the sinking sun. It was just gorgeous.

Devin plonked three beers down on the table, then dragged a chair across the concrete as he sat next to her and stared at the scenery.

'Well, pull up a pew, why don't you?'

'It's this, or you'll be fobbing off twenty bikers inside trying to buy you a beer, because that barmaid will never serve you again.'

'Does the barmaid have a name? Because she sure knows you and your drinking habits.'

Devin shrugged. 'Are you going to talk my ear off?'

'No. I don't want to talk to anyone.'

'Good. Me neither. That's why I brought two.' He pushed one of the extra glasses of beer in front of her, settled back into his seat and they both faced the sunset. His eyes reflected the curve of the endless horizon overshadowed by an enormous sky filled with orange and yellow broad paint strokes stretching across the outback plains. It was such an inspirational display of colour that kept unpacking itself the lower the sun dropped to the earth.

'That was beautiful.' It had been a long time since she'd shared a sunset with someone. She appreciated his silence. It was soothing. But that gaze …

She licked her lips as his eyes dropped to her mouth before connecting with her eyes again.

'Yeah …' He looked away, clearing his throat. His strong profile the perfect silhouette against the sky's palette.

'Oh, there you are,' said Lottie, coming down from the path that led to the accommodations. 'And with Devin, I see.'

'I might go order some tucker.' Devin moved, but Teà grabbed his arm.

'Good idea. It's Lottie's shout.' After all, Lottie was holding their travel budget to ransom.

Devin frowned. 'Huh?'

'Consider it hush money as part of our bribe to keep quiet about the duck we're trying to smuggle to the nearest billabong.'

That chuckle was deep and low, making her grin as her heart bloomed in ways it shouldn't. 'Just a meal.' *I'm just one of the guys.*

'Fine. Do I get another beer with that meal?'

'You don't come cheap, do you?'

'Do you mind?' Lottie just stared at Teà with wide eyes.

'Lottie, shout the guy a meal, two beers for us and whatever you drink? Do you drink? I've never seen you drink alcohol. Just be sure to drink more water. You're not drinking enough.' Especially driving across the outback, they needed to keep up their fluids.

'You don't need to remind me about drinking water. I'm a mother with many responsibilities.' Lottie stood with the tip of her nose aiming for the stars that had yet to shine.

Sure, Lottie had a beautiful family—a doting husband, and two wonderful children—but to hear about it every ten minutes was a bit much.

'I'm not going inside with those bikers.' Lottie pointed

at the bar.

'You're telling me that the fearless Little Miss Lottie Voss is too scared to go into a roadhouse because of men wearing riding leathers.' Teà grinned. 'They won't do anything.'

'How do you know?'

'Because they're just guys who ride bikes. That's it. They're like any other normal guy who drives a truck, or a car, or flies a helicopter.' Teà pointed to the truck with three trailers hauling three helicopters. 'Can you fly those, Devin?'

He nodded.

'All three yours?'

'Nope. Just one. I'm being paid to deliver the other two.'

'Well, then ...' She leaned over her beer, squinting at the machines. 'With you driving the other two, that would've covered your freight costs. Obviously, you scored yourself a sweet deal.'

His face was flawless, but his eyes flared for just a moment. 'How—'

'That's smart business.' She sat back to check out the amazing scenery, not the guy beside her. 'You're blocking our view, Lottie. Our father wasn't a glass maker.' She bit her tongue to not giggle like a schoolgirl at Devin's deep chuckle.

'What will you have for dinner, Devin?' Lottie asked in such a sweet voice it made Teà's eyebrow twitch. Her sister never smiled, not like this.

'Tell them the usual.'

'Devin's girlfriend works behind the bar; she'll take good care of him. Just be sure to tell her that Devin sent you. Hey, what's good here? Besides backpacking barmaids.'

'It sounds like you're jealous,' butted in Lottie.

'Pfft.' As if. She didn't do jealousy, or form any emotional attachment to men, people, or pets. Wild animals were excused.

'Don't worry, I know what you want. You've been talking all about it since you kidnapped that duck.'

'Only because you hit the duck.' Teà snickered behind her beer glass.

'Ugh, you're incorrigible.' Spinning on her sandals, Lottie headed for the bar, her ponytail swinging, exposing the line of prickly heat spreading across the back of her neck.

'You stirred your sister up to forget she was scared to walk into that bar full of bikers, huh?'

She blinked in slow-motion at Devin, then back at her ponytail swinging sister strutting through the bar like she owned the place. 'You guessed right. You're a lot smarter than I figured.' Too smart for her liking. And he was so much hotter off the outback highway. This guy was ticking all the right boxes.

Hot as hell in looks. Check.

One smouldering eye-locking stare that didn't flinch. Check.

Knew enough to shut up and enjoy the moment. Check.

Watched sunsets, saved ducks, and didn't interfere with their sisterly bickering. Biiig check.

Shame it would never happen.

She inhaled deeply, tearing her eyes away from the smouldering, sexy demi-god of dust beside her to stare at the wilderness. It spread out like a picture hung on the biggest wall on the planet in some priceless big-name museum, that people paid good money to stare at. It was seriously gorgeous.

Lottie returned with a tray of beer and cutlery. 'There you go. *Bon appétit*. The barmaid said it'd be about forty minutes. Kitchen's busy.'

'Where are you going?'

'To call my husband and have a shower.'

'What about your dinner?'

'I might eat in my room.'

'But—'

'You stay here and, I dunno, watch the stars with Devin.'

Teà sat back, watching her sister walk away.

'Is your sister trying to set us up?'

Teà arched an eyebrow at him. 'No offence, but I'm not looking for anything.' After all, she was barely coping with the realisation that she was destined to walk this planet alone forever. Why risk what she'd finally accepted.

'Did I say I was?'

'You're a guy.'

'What's that supposed to mean?'

'And you're probably on a first-name basis with a busty blonde barmaid.'

'I'm a friendly guy,' he grumbled.

She threw her head back and laughed so hard, happy tears squeezed out of the corner of her eyes.

Devin frowned. But he never once stopped looking at her. Truth be told, his hard, determined glare made her mouth drier than the outback dust, suddenly forgetting if it was day or night, let alone what day of the week it was. Wait? It's Wednesday.

'What's the joke?'

'You don't smile. You've got this sullen look happening …' That so went with that hard sultry mouth of his. 'And your communication is barely a grunt at a barmaid for more beer.' However, Devin was the type of guy who, if he patted his chest like an animal skin–wearing caveman, he'd still get the attention.

'And we've only just met.'

Teà grinned coyly behind her beer glass, which was cool against her cheek. 'I used to get told off for guessing things about people.'

'Huh?'

'People watching. Checking out strangers while guessing their story. Did it for fun. You ever do that?' It used to amuse her for hours, with each new batch of airport passengers.

'I live where there are no people.'

'So you're not used to talking to people?'

'I don't like people.'

'Well then, I'm in the winner's circle tonight, aren't I. It won't be long now before we start making each other friendship bracelets, swapping email addresses, sending each other annual Merry Christmas messages. And let's not forget the mandatory bad singing we'll do to each other on our birthdays.' Hey, she could banter like one of the boys. This wasn't flirting. Because she didn't know how to flirt.

Devin shook his head, swearing under his breath as surprise flashed over his face with its solid brow and rigid jaw line. And then he did something truly marvellous. He smiled. It was a glorious smile that completely transformed his features. She forgot to breathe.

Hot damn, she was in trouble. Where was her sister?

A man on the wrong side of sixty strolled towards them, carrying a bottle of rum and a handful of shot glasses. 'Hey, Devin. Good to see you out and about.'

'Rusty.' Devin shook hands. 'Teà, this is Rusty. It's his roadhouse.'

'Hi. You have a nice place, Rusty.' Teà shook his hand. Did the barmaid mention Teà's brusque conversation in the bar earlier? Was she going to get kicked out?

'Are you one of the Voss sisters?'

'I'm Teà—'

'*Teà and Lottie Voss.*' Rusty read from the face of a white business envelope. 'I've got this letter to give you. Only after Victor's gone. Is he …'

Teà nodded. 'We're taking him somewhere to scatter his ashes.'

'Thought so.' Russ sat and efficiently unstacked the shot glasses, as if sorting chips at a blackjack table.

'How do you know my dad?' Teà looked at her name

on the envelope. It was the same spidery handwriting, like the other breadcrumbs they'd gathered on this trek.

'Once upon a time, I knew Victor Voss very well.' Rusty expertly poured three shot glasses of rum without spilling a drop. 'Victor wasn't the type of man you'd easily forget. We did a couple of bangtail musters together. Old-school style. With none of those fancy helicopters they use today.' Rusty tossed his thumb towards the silent choppers on the back of Devin's truck. 'We did it with packhorses carrying our tucker, water and swags, in a country that used to get its supplies by camel train.'

'Where?'

Rusty pointed to the wilderness where the sun was long gone, and the dust was settling in for the night. 'The Murranji Track.'

'Sheez.' Devin rubbed his forehead. 'That's a tough gig.'

'What's the Murranji Track?' she asked Devin.

'A stock route. It's the old shortcut for carting cattle from the Kimberly to the markets in Queensland. How long ago was this, Rusty?'

'I was a young lad then. Your dad, too. And Victor was a courageous bastard, I'll give him that. We had this lightning strike stir up the mob, and they made a rush for it.'

Teà looked at Devin. 'Rush?'

'Stampede,' relayed Devin.

'And your father was a bloody good ringer,' continued Rusty. 'Victor didn't think twice about galloping ahead of the herd to wheel them around and pacify them.'

'How big was the herd?'

'The first time a thousand head.'

Devin's eyebrows lifted as much as Teà's did.

'Fearless, I tell you.' Rusty placed a loaded shot glass in front of them. 'Victor never complained once about watching a sea of cattle backs, swinging that stock whip like it was an extension of his arm.'

'Really?'

'Victor gave me this …' Rusty stroked the scar on his chin.

'Brawling' Devin asked.

'Nah.' Rusty chuckled, shaking his grey head of hair. 'Belly full of rum and bad manners, not even at a legal age to drink when we made this dingbat bet. I bet Vossy couldn't light a match, held between my teeth, by cracking his stock whip.'

'Dickheads.' Devin chuckled behind his beer glass.

Teà grinned, but on the edge of her seat. 'Did Dad do it?'

'Yeah, lit the bugger, burnt my lip, and left me with a scar.' His belly laugh was infectious. 'Damn, we did some dumb bullcrap together.' Rusty's smile faded as he stared at the letter. 'We were so young and bulletproof back then.' He slid the letter across the table, letting it rest in front of Teà. 'Vossy may have been a rogue with the ladies, and a masterful ringmaster in two-up, but your father was a good man. I'm honoured he's left this here.' He raised his shot glass to Teà. 'To Victor Voss. A bloody good bloke from the outback.'

They clinked their glasses together.

Rum wasn't Teà's drink of choice; it burned its way down her chest, making her gasp.

'Careful.' Devin patted her back.

'I'm not used to rum.'

'Well, I won't force another one down your gullet,' said Rusty, putting the cap back on the bottle.

'Rusty, can you give us a hand?' called out a robust woman, carrying loaded plates from the kitchen.

'Righto.' Rusty stood from the table. 'If it wasn't so busy tonight, I'd be happy to share more stories about my ol' mate Vossy.'

Teà nodded. 'You're on. Probably not with the rum.

But can I borrow a cup of cornflour from the kitchen?'

'No worries. Any daughter of Victor Voss is a friend. You too, Devin, if you weren't such a grumpy bastard.' Rusty gave a hearty pat on Devin's strong shoulder, and with the rum bottle tucked under his arm, he carted their empty glasses back to the bar.

'So, what's the letter about?' Devin asked.

'It's the reason we're here. Breadcrumbs. But thanks to Rusty, I get why we're here.' She stood from the table. 'I'd better go find Lottie so she can micro-manage this trek. Save our seats, huh?'

'Do you do any of the planning?'

'Me? No. I'm just the passenger, babysitting Lottie so she doesn't get hurt.'

He sat back. 'You're protecting her. Even though you two are bickering like children, you care about her.'

'She is my sister … Just don't tell Lottie.'

'Secret's safe with me.' He winked at her.

That wink was like an arrow to the heart, causing her to stumble on the path. The heat radiating from her face was hotter than a serious case of sunburn, she had to be glowing in the dark. Fanning herself with the letter, desperate to cool herself down. She was only here for Lottie—not for any hook ups—it had always been about Lottie.

Four

Cradling her mobile phone to her ear, Lottie paced the deserted car park. The blue Ford stood nearby, unfortunately being guarded by a ribbon-wearing duck, hogging the back seat.

A duck that could take her away from her family.

The male voice on the other end of the phone line spoke. 'Hello.'

'Finally! Adrian, it's me.'

'Hey, me.'

She frowned, so not in the mood.

'Where are you?'

'At the roadhouse near the Devil's Marbles. I know I marked it on the map I left on the fridge.'

'The kids took that down. I don't know where that map ended up.'

'What? Why?' She'd spent ages making sure Adrian had their itinerary—as much as she could work out, considering she didn't really know where they were going. The lawyer couldn't tell them anything else, except to hint at the Northern Territory, that was a big place with very few towns.

'The kids wanted to put their latest paintings on the fridge. I think one is a dog, or a pony?'

'Did Sophie draw it?'

'Yeah.'

'It's a pony then.'

'Cool. So how's it going? Bonded with Teà yet?'

She tossed her arm in the air. 'Ugh! Teà is the most irritating know-it-all. I lost count of the many times I wanted to kick her out of the car.'

'She is your sister.'

'She's mean. Cruel. Vindictive. Forever bringing up the past. And now she's forced me to carry a duck across the outback.'

'A what?'

'A duck!'

Adrian laughed. 'In your dad's car?'

'Not funny.'

'It is. Your dad would roll over in his grave—if he had one.'

'It's not a pet, it's a wild animal.'

'Why do you have a duck in the car?'

'Oh, um …' She cupped the phone to whisper, with her eyes darting around the deserted carpark. 'I accidentally hit it while arguing with Teà over putting Dad's ashes on the back seat.' She'd wanted that urn sitting in the middle of the front seat, just like Dad and Teà would strap her in when she was younger. Giving her another reason to scowl at the interfering toffee-nosed Teà.

'Why didn't you just leave the duck there?'

'Because some nosy trucker in a cowboy hat showed up, telling us it's protected.'

'Is it?'

'It is. Teà confirmed it while searching for the kind of food it likes. Oh, Adrian, I'm scared.'

'Why?'

'It's a year in prison for accidentally damaging this duck.'

'What will you do with it?'

'Teà says we'll take it to a billabong. But where? When we're standing in a freaking outback desert.'

'Okay, honey, take a deep breath. It'll all be okay. You'll get through this. You've only got four days to go.'

'I'm not sure I'll make it, not with Teà. She's

incorrigible. A delinquent in a grown-up body. I'm so worried that this inheritance deal will leave us shackled to the evil sister for life.' She huffed, pacing in the red dust behind the car.

'Why not make a deal with Teà?'

'To buy her out?'

'To sell the place.'

She scowled at the night sky. 'No way. That's our home, Adrian. I wouldn't be torturing myself by sitting in a stinking hot vintage car, travelling through the outback without an air conditioner. I'm suffering with prickly heat where the bra wire sits.' The need to scratch was insatiable.

'Sounds painful.'

'It's hot and itchy, and my dress lining irritates it, and—'

'What do you want me to do?'

'Call Dad's lawyer.'

'To ask about protective duck laws?'

'No.' Oh, bless him, Adrian could be so slow. 'I want to contest the will. Teà hasn't been around for seventeen years, but you and I have been working that farm.'

'You have. Your father wouldn't let me touch it.'

'Dad did so.'

'No. Only to drive the truck occasionally. Victor wouldn't let me near the shearing shed. It's why I work in the mines. That way I didn't have to dick around with your dad's stupid alpha-a-hole macho contests.'

She gasped, hand to her chest. 'Dad never—'

'Victor just never did it in front of his *little mate Lottie*. Your mother saw it. It was Lauren who told me to hang in there, and suggested I work away on the mines.'

'How come you never told me?'

'Come on, Lottie, this is your father we're talking about. You worshipped the ground Victor Voss walked on.'

'I did not.'

'Yeah, you did. Your father always came first, the

family second.'

'Not true.'

'Look at where you are, Lottie. You're in the Northern Territory when you've never strayed out of your own electoral area. Yet, you're there because your father told you to go, stuck in a car with a sister you haven't spoken to for seventeen years.'

'I'm doing this for us!'

'Are you? Because to me it looks like you're still running around after Victor.' Adrian inhaled deeply. She could picture her husband pushing his glasses higher along his nose. 'I'll call the lawyer about contesting the will for the property. In the meantime, I hope this road trip will help you let go of your dad and his influence.'

She shook her head in disbelief at what her husband was saying. 'And to do what?'

'Really let go. Of everything. So you, me, and the kids can start fresh, somewhere away from the power of Victor Voss.'

'What? Leave the farm?' She was stunned speechless. Hand to her throat she struggled to swallow. This was her home they were talking about. It was her everything. It's the only reason she was here! The frustration churning in her chest like heartburn, she inhaled so deeply her nostrils pinched. 'I. AM. Doing this for *us*.'

'Are you sure?'

She frowned fiercely at the darkness. 'I am. Now, listen up. Be sure the kids brush and floss before bed.'

'Already did that. They're asleep. You were late to call them.'

'I forgot about the time zones.'

'You're human, Lottie, not a robot.'

Ha! When some days she wished there were two of her. 'Write this down … Greta's coming to pick up the Timber's wedding gown tomorrow around nine. Mick Hamilton is dropping off a cheque for the agistment fees. The keys for the back paddock are on the desk. You can deposit that cheque on Friday when you do the food shopping.'

'I've got this, Lottie.'

'Be sure you do. That's our livelihood. The farm still has to run—'

'I know. The kids and I have got this. Goodnight, honey.'

She scowled at the silent phone in her hand.

But she didn't trust Adrian. Oh, bless him, he could only do one thing at a time.

'Jeez, I'm surprised you're still married, talking to your husband like that.'

Lottie whirled around to face Teà, leaning her hip against the car.

How much did her snooping sister overhear?

'How I talk to my husband is none of your beeswax. He's my husband. Not yours. You don't have anyone.'

'You talk to your husband like he's the hired help.'

'Do not.'

'Do too. I'd never talk to my husband like that.'

'That's *if* you had a husband. Who'd be dumb enough to marry you?' Because Teà didn't do relationships— certainly not ones that involved family.

Teà's shoulders slumped as she dumped a small takeaway container of white powder on the boot of the car. 'This is for you.'

'Don't scratch the paintwork.' Lottie ripped off the lid. 'Why did you give me flour?' What cruel joke was Teà playing now?

'Cornflour. For the prickly heat. I spotted it on the back of your neck. That plaid dress and lining is the wrong type of clothing for this weather.

'I made this dress.' She brushed down the plaid material, even with its layer of dust and sweat ingrained in the fine weave, it still remained stiff with its perfect pleated lines.

'Of course, you did. Just wear something pure cotton, bamboo cotton or linen's good too. Pat on the cornflour after you've had a shower tonight and in the morning. It'll clear up that prickly heat in no time. I use it all the time in my job.'

'Oh ...' The fight inside cooled to a simmer, her finger running through fine flour. Did she dare say thank you?

Not unless it worked.

'How are Adrian and the kids?'

'I missed saying goodnight to my children. I forgot about the time zones.' She missed her children terribly, and the routine of home. This world was so foreign to her. There were no fields of crops, no fences, no sheep. Nothing but a road and this roadhouse.

'Well, this'll get your mind off your troubles.' Teà held up a white envelope.

'Where did you get that? That barmaid said there wasn't any mail for us when I ordered dinner.'

'She must have passed a message along because Roadhouse Rusty delivered it with a shot glass of rum.'

'Who?'

'The owner of this place. Rusty knew Dad when he was a teenager. I forgot Dad was a ringer out here.'

'Dad never told me.'

'Yeah, he did. You must have forgotten.'

No, Lottie was too busy to sit around and listen to stories.

'Coming? Dinner will be ready.' Teà pocketed the letter and headed back to the bar.

'Um, yeah.' Lottie cleared her throat, hungry and curious where the next leg of their journey would take them with only four more days to go. Lord help them.

Five

Devin wished he'd stayed by the front bar, instead of getting stuck between two warring sisters who were like light and dark, fire and ice.

The blonde one was full of spite. She may be short, but she had a knack for looking down her nose at everyone, as if the world was full of morons. Which he happened to agree with. But he wasn't a moron and was in fact well known for coming out swinging at anyone who called him that.

It's why no one talked to him.

And he liked it like that. Minding his own turf, doing his job, watching sunsets with a cold beer in hand was his thing.

But he'd never shared a sunset with a woman before. Not like Teà. They'd just sat back, sipping beers, as if watching a movie of that big flaming fire ball getting doused into the dust for the night.

Most women yakked about things he'd just ignore. Yakked about hair, clothes, and who knows what else. But not Teà.

He'd never bantered so easily with anyone, not like he did with Teà. And he'd never been able to pick up the signals from a woman like he could with Teà. She had the uncanny ability to look straight through him—like really look through to the heart he didn't know he had.

She was doing his damn head in. The way her dark eyes took in everything, holding her ground the way a cunning cattle dog would read the scene before tackling the herd. Not quite predatory, but like she was measuring his value as a worthy competitor.

And then the body that came with the brains was a double bonus. Her toned legs and sweet ass should be part of a national monument to women who walked with the grace of a feisty feline. Sure. Confident. And graceful as a ballerina in lace-up boots. And that cleavage in the vee of her T-shirt was a temptation so severe, he struggled to sit still and not peek down her top. Her hair was a true blue-black, and when she lifted it like a sheet of fine black silk off the back of her slender neck to chase the breeze ... *Can you spell s-t-r-u-g-g-l-e, son?*

He shifted in his seat, his fingers twitching to tease the wispy curl at her nape, and licked his lip that thirsted for the taste of her skin.

The woman said she wanted nothing. Upfront and in his face with a determination that said she meant it. So he backed off.

He should back right off and go back to the bar.

But he was still here.

Was it the fact that she seemed disinterested that had him wanting more?

He didn't play games with people. Especially women.

He needed to back off.

Gripping his beer glass tighter, he took a deep slug. It was killing him sitting here, but he couldn't leave. Not yet. Not until he learned what was going to happen next. 'Are either of you going to open that letter?'

Teà grinned. The girls were in a stand-off, eating their meals while staring at the envelope that was burning a hole in their table.

'Do you want me to leave?' He shouldn't be this invested in something that was none of his business.

'Yes,' said Lottie.

'No. Stay, Devin.' Teà's slender fingers rested across his forearm, like warm ribbons against his skin. He crumbled. Bloody hell, he crumbled like a little boy being ordered to stay, all from the tender touch of a woman. This was not happening.

'Why?' Lottie demanded. 'I think Devin has better things to do. Like entertain the barmaid.'

'Huh?' He scowled at the bar, and there was that blonde British backpacker waving at him. He'd had enough of blondes, brunettes, and all forms of females. His brother teased him about being a bachelor for life. And that suited him just fine.

'Devin can help us.'

'I can?' He looked at Teà, who had done something to his brain. He just couldn't think straight. Or Rusty had laced that nip of rum with a hallucinogenic. *Yee-haw*, how long before the unicorns and bunyips joined this party trip-out under the stars?

'I'm sure your knowledge of this area will be a big help to us, once we find out where we're going next.' Teà tapped on the map full of scribbles, different coloured markers, fluorescent sticky notes, and girlie stickers. They'd ruined that map.

'Go where? I'm confused?' Would Teà give him a load of lip for asking? Normally people didn't like re-explaining themselves when he asked questions. It's why he asked no one for anything, if he could help it.

But Teà didn't seem bothered by his questioning. Casually pulling a seriously sharp pocketknife from her bag, to slice open the envelope.

'Our dearly departed daddy liked to drive his big old blue Ford to visit unknown places and mark them on a map. Victor Voss never liked a clean map. He always believed in leaving his mark on a place, so he'd mark it off on a map. Like how Lottie has reconfigured the entire South Australian coastline on this map—she's even colour-coded designated toilet stops.'

'Did not.' Lottie sat back, brushing down her Scottish schoolteacher chequered dress. She was definitely not his type. Neither were backpacking barmaids, only chatting him up to gain a husband for a visa or a job away from the bar.

Yet, a smart-mouthed brunette—with a smoking-hot body that'd set off smoke detectors—was triggering all his internal alarms, making him want to bolt for the truck and leave. *Can you spell r-u-n, son?*

But how could he? Not while his legs were tree stumps, deeply rooted to the floor of the beer garden. 'What's that got to do with that letter?'

'Lottie, if you please.' Teà matched her sister's frown. 'If we want Devin's help, we should answer his questions. It's the right thing to do.'

'*Fine.*' Lottie sat up like a toy, wound up so tight she'd run in circles that'd dig a hole all the way through to China. 'When Dad passed away, he left a set of instructions in his will for us to search for maps in various places.'

'The breadcrumb trail, I call it,' said Teà.

'Anyway, each place tells us where to find the next part of the map, to eventually find the place our father wants us to scatter his ashes.'

'You have his ashes, on you?' Devin sat back in his seat, looking to Teà for answers. The same way she'd looked to him for muster interpretations when talking with Rusty earlier.

'Oh yeah, we've got him all tucked up in this fancy urn in the car's back seat, being babysat by the duck dressed in plaid.'

His laugh, matching Teà's, surprised him. 'And you're doing this road trip as some final farewell?'

Teà nodded. 'After what Rusty said earlier, I remember Dad telling me about his time in the Northern Territory. My parents met out here, somewhere.'

'They did?' Lottie asked.

'Yeah, my mother was a jillaroo for a season. Dad followed her back home.'

'Not your mother?' He had to ask because they didn't

look like sisters.

'No. Teà's mum died before I was born.'

'I'm sorry.' And he was.

'Thank you.' Teà remained expressionless, but he saw the sorrow in her eyes. And it was crushing. This trip was obviously bringing up all sorts of emotional baggage for both sisters.

Come on, what sort of father would do this? What happened to getting buried and being done with it to move on? 'What's the catch?'

'Excuse me?' Lottie swallowed hard, scratching her neck. That schoolteacher's dress looked hot and uncomfortable, especially with the small lumpy rash festering along her pale neck. Prickly heat was a bugger.

'You must be doing it for a reason. Stuck in that old car, arguing the way you are.'

'It's a race for the family farm,' Teà said to him straight up, no fancy language, nothing. He liked that about her, completely ignoring the scowl on Little Miss Uppity on the other side of their table.

Black and white, they were as sisters. The only problem was, the one wearing black was the shiniest star in his galaxy, with dark eyes that could drown a man.

'What do mean, race for the family farm? You're a farmer?' He pointed at a woman who was as white as an office worker who'd get their suntan from a bottle.

Unlike Teà, who looked like someone who'd get their hands dirty as a badass female in charge of her destiny. He hadn't realised how much he liked that in a woman. Until today.

'Tucknott Flats on Dog Fence Road is my home,' so said Little Miss Uppity, tugging on that ponytail that made her face tighten, pushing her nose in the air. 'Four hundred and five acres of pristine farming land in South Australia.'

Big. Deal. Plenty of local cattle stations had paddocks bigger than that. 'What does it produce?'

'It does sheep and crops,' replied Teà. 'But they've been

leasing most of the land these past few years. Adrian said it was more profitable and less work.'

'Who's Adrian? Your husband?' He peeked at Teà's hands again. He hadn't spotted any wedding rings earlier; her slender fingers were free from jewellery with short nails bare of any polish.

'Adrian is *my* husband, thank you very muchly.' Little Miss Uppity flicked some imaginary dog hair off her dress.

'We have to get to some unknown destination to scatter Dad's ashes, and we have seven days to do it. Dad was very specific about us being in a particular spot in seven days. Only it's taken us three days to get this far,' explained Teà. 'Lottie drives so slow.'

'Hey! I stuck to the speed limits.'

'Barely.'

'It's a vintage car. Not a sports car.'

Devin interrupted their bickering. 'Your father must have given you more than some blind leap of instructions?'

'The lawyer gave us a list of what to pack for the trip. One of our stops was to shop for provisions to camp for a week in the Northern Territory. We get told where to drive, where to fuel up, and where to find the next letter. Like, this spot ...' Teà tapped on the map. 'Rusty's Roadhouse is where we had to be, today, ending day three of seven.'

'And if you refuse?'

Lottie winced, as Teà replied, 'Everything owned by Victor Voss goes up for auction and all proceeds get donated to charity.'

'Ouch. That's harsh.' He looked between the sisters. 'Would your father really do that?' Because *his* old man certainly wouldn't.

The girls didn't say a word.

'What an arsehole.' He mumbled behind his beer.

'Hey! That's my father you're talking about.' Of course, Little Miss Uppity would be quick to defend her father.

Yet, Teà sipped on her beer as if it was another day at

the office.

'Just open the letter already, Teà. I want to know where Dad's sending us next, so I can tell my husband and we can prepare.'

Teà removed a sheet of paper from the envelope, unfolding the crisp white paper to reveal a small map. They all leaned closer as she laid it flat on the table.

'What does it say?' The lettering was too small and spidery for his taste.

'*Fuel up at Dunmarra before turning left for the Buchanan Highway. Then aim for the windmill at Bore 13 on the Murranji Track.*' Teà pointed to a spot on the hand-drawn map that was nothing more than a simple thick black line representing the Stuart Highway. It started with an X for the Devil's Marble's. Then it displayed a sharp left, running in a broken line like ant tracks through the dust, for the Buchanan Highway ending at Bore 13.

'X marks the spot.'

'I know, right?' Teà's eyes and smile were full of mischief. 'We're like land pirates following a treasure map. We don't have a talking parrot, but we do have a damaged duck. And we might not have a wooden leg to dance across the deck with, but I wish Lottie would find some lead in her legs to drive faster.'

He chuckled, sprouting a smile he just couldn't stop. Who was this woman?

'I can't see this Bore 13 on our map.' Lottie leaned over her colour-coded detailed map spread across the table.

'You won't.' He sat back, wiping away his smile. 'You don't want to go there.'

'We *have* to,' Lottie whined. 'All the years I've sacrificed working that place. My family is expecting me to save their home.'

'What's wrong with that track, Devin? You and Rusty said it was a stock route. Hey, Lottie, did you know Dad used to drove cattle on that stock route. I bet we're tracing his old trails, reliving the good ol' days.'

'According to Google Maps, it's part of the Buchanan Highway. Easy as.' Lottie held up her phone with its screen shining brightly.

He inhaled deep, as a trail of icy spiders raced up his spine. 'It's not that easy.'

Lottie leaned in closer, smelling of spearmint and the old-lady shampoo his grandma used to use. 'Listen, buster, we just drove nineteen hundred kilometres to get here. This small Murranji Track's gotta be easier than teaching a bride how to walk down the aisle without tripping on her train.'

He arched an eyebrow at her. 'Huh?'

'It's only about 230 kilometres.'

'On one of the toughest stock routes in the country, Linda.' His voice was low and commanding, forcing Miss Know-it-all back in her seat.

'My name is *Lottie*.' She huffed, crossing her arms over her chest.

'Devin?' Again, Teà gave a small touch to his arm, and he was drowning in a set of cool dark eyes. 'How tough is it?'

'Tough. It's not safe to do it in a vintage car. I wouldn't do it. What was your father thinking, sending you out there without a bull bar and a high-clearance four-wheel drive?'

'We have to.'

'The Murranji Track is not for the fainthearted. It's rugged. Your old man knew that track. So there must be another reason he's making you do this.'

'To test us. It's what he did.' Teà sat back, wearing the same stern expression as her sister.

Can you spell d-e-t-e-r-m-i-n-a-t-i-o-n, son?

It was obvious the Voss sisters were doing it, no matter how much he tried to talk them out of it. No wonder he normally never bothered to talk to anyone.

Goddammit!

He threw down the last of his beer, shuffled his chair

closer to the table, dragging the maps towards him. 'Okay, you'll want to stock up on food, fuel and water here. Then again at the next roadhouse. You'd better have two spare tyres and a decent working jack in that car of yours, because the Murranji is known to shred tyres like cheese.'

'We do.' Both sisters nodded.

'You're lucky I'm going that way.'

'To where?'

'Topp Springs. It's at the other end of the Buchanan Highway. So, I'm in, okay?' He didn't want to be, but it's what the job demanded.

'You are?' Teà looked at him with questioning eyes. They were pretty, with a dainty curl to her lashes accentuating her natural beauty. Her hair wasn't too long or too short, with none of that sticky gel or hair spray in it. She wore no make-up, where some wore it like bandaids to hide their scars. And Teà wasn't model perfect, or magazine flawless, but she was pretty damned perfect. He struggled to look away.

'I'm not making any promises …' He never did, except when it came to family. So he understood Teà's reasons for following through and wasn't going to interfere. She was on her own path that didn't involve him—too much—he hoped. 'But I'll give you a hand as much as I can, without detouring too far from my route. I've got choppers to deliver.' He also wasn't the type of bloke to leave two women alone in the outback. Especially on the Murranji Track, it made his guts churn for the Voss sisters.

But he had to respect their resolve for following through with their father's wishes. Victor Voss was lucky to have such fine daughters—not many people would go to such extremes to scatter ashes, driving an old car along the Murranji. It was the Highway to Nowhere!

'Well, aren't we lucky to run into you?' Teà's smile was like pure sunshine that matched the sparkle in her eyes. He didn't realise he'd been holding his breath until he let it go. This was not what he'd signed up for.

Six

'I think you should make the duck a tailored waistcoat out of plaid,' said Teà, with the duck sitting in her lap in the passenger seat of the blue Ford.

Hunched over the steering wheel, Lottie drove slower than electric mobility scooters favoured by the elderly around shopping centres. 'I'm not sewing for a duck.'

'Ooh, imagine a duck in a wedding dress? You could tap into a whole new market here.'

'Stop it, I need to concentrate.'

'Do you want me to drive?'

'No. And stop asking me.'

'Okay, okay.' Teà fiddled with the plaid cloth she'd made into a triangular scarf and gently placed it over the duck's head. 'Aww, isn't he pretty?' She grabbed her phone to take a photo. The duck was so placid. 'At this speed, you're going to lose Devin's dust trail.'

'Why did you insist on letting him go before us?'

'The way you drive, little sis, Devin would've gotten frustrated and overtaken us eventually. And he's been good to us.' A proper gentleman, waiting on the other side of the rocky creek beds to ensure they crossed safely. Helping to drag them out of the bulldust that was suffocating pits of fine red dust. Even giving Lottie some decent driving tips. At least Lottie listened to Devin, while completely ignoring everything Teà suggested. 'We wouldn't have made it this far without him.'

'Where did he go?' Lottie's voice rose a pitch. With a white-knuckle grip on the steering wheel, she dodged large holes. But there was no way to miss the never-ending abundance of corrugation rows that dug into the dirt road, only accentuated by the vintage car's sucky suspension. It made their teeth rattle.

'He's gone. How can a big truck disappear like that?' Lottie's sweaty brow wrinkled at the wide track that made up the Buchanan Highway. 'How can this dirt road be a highway?'

'It must be a Northern Territory thing. There it is …' Teà nodded at the road ahead. 'Devin said to turn down the track after Cattle Creek.' A simple black and white sign displayed *Cattle Creek*. It stood near a floodway depth indicator that measured over two metres above the red dust. 'I can't imagine this place flooded.'

They drove past towering red ant mounts, then down into stony gorges, passing more floodways, causeways, and dips. They'd been on the road for hours, driving an average of forty kilometres an hour.

'There he is.' Teà's heart rose as she pointed to the waiting road train, not realising she'd been shallow breathing from the anxiety of not having him in her sights. Or was that from Lottie's driving?

And there he was, with that sexy cattleman's swagger, making her mouth water at that whole dusty cowboy thing he had going on. No wonder the roadhouse's female workers smiled wider and toyed with their hair when Devin strolled inside, greeting them with just a nod. It was hot.

Not that she would touch Devin with a sparked-up welding rod, but she could peek. Right? 'Would it be breaking the rules of this inheritance challenge, if we hitched the car onto Devin's trailers and jumped in the cab with him?'

Lottie just glared. Her face a ripe pomegranate red, with beads of sweat streaming down her face to saturate her plaid dress. Her shoulders were tight as she peered over the steering wheel, watching the road for large rocks and dips.

Devin was right, this was a rough road.

'No way.' Lottie's eyes were enormous.

A red sign loomed before them, warning that there was no fuel for two hundred kilometres.

'Where is Devin taking us?' Lottie's voice cracked with strain. It woke up the duck.

Teà pointed past the truck, dragging three trailers, carting muster helicopters with their rotor blades neatly folded. 'We made it, Lottie. There's the windmill at Bore 13.' She could hug Devin, standing there in the sun with his Akubra on low as he guided Lottie to park the car in front of his truck, under the shadow of an old windmill.

The windmill was one of the oldest she'd seen. Surprisingly, despite its age it had a complete circle of all eighteen aluminium blades, designed to harness the power of the wind for water. The same principle used in those windmills they'd spotted on their drive through South Australia.

Devin opened her door. 'Are you okay?'

'Here, say hello to your feathery friend.' She dumped the duck into his arms.

'Why is the duck wearing plaid?'

'I got bored.'

'Lorna still not letting you drive?'

'My name is Lottie,' Lottie said, slamming the driver's door.

Devin ignored her, putting the duck on the ground. 'I see you made a leg bandage for it.'

'I think you're right, it's only a sprain. I've been massaging his wing for a bit and felt nothing broken.' But the duck lapped up the attention. 'Maybe I missed my calling and should have become a nurse for ducks.' Playing her part as one of the guys, who could talk nonsense with the best of them. In her world there was no room for girlie feelings. So, whatever she was feeling for this guy, it wasn't real.

'You got that bored, playing passenger?'

'I'm trying to convince Lottie to make the duck a waistcoat. Out of plaid, of course.' She grinned at the man watching a limping duck wearing a plaid scarf.

Lottie scowled while craning her neck up at the windmill. 'Where would Dad hide it?'

'What are you looking for?' Devin asked Teà.

'Nothing simple. Dad wouldn't leave it in a place where it could get pinched. How busy does this road get?'

'It doesn't. Only road trains hauling cattle use this road.' Devin kicked over some flat rocks among the shoal resting at the base of the windmill.

'You have a shadow.'

He turned to frown at the duck waddling behind him, shook his head, and went back to scrounging around the windmill.

'I don't see anything,' whined Lottie.

'I bet it's up there.' Teà pointed to the heart of the windmill where the rod, holding the blades, ran to the engine and the down rods.

Standing next to her, Devin's masculine odour was so fresh and divine, as they craned their necks at the rusty windmill.

'Why is there a windmill out here?'

'This was part of the government bores set up for this stock route,' Devin replied in his deep tone. It was so soothing, she could listen to him speak for who knows how long, especially with her head resting against his naked chest to fill that gap in her heart, putting all her insecurities to bed.

This wasn't right. It shouldn't be like this. Devin shouldn't be here, sending erratic shots of heat running up her spine. She had to step away from the guy.

'They'd hire blokes to check these bores and troughs were working. Back then, those bore runners saved a lot of people out here.' Devin inspected the frame, the way a naval engineer inspects the hull of a ship for its seaworthiness.

'What do you mean save people?' There was no one out here.

'This is the start of the dry straight. A lot of cattle and men died on this stock route, mostly from thirst.'

Teà swallowed, suddenly parched. 'Is that why you made sure we carried all that water?'

'A person can't survive without water. You can go weeks without food, but without water, out here …'

The wind blew a gust of dust that swirled in a pattern, going faster and faster, stirring up leaves and dust like a dry tornado. Its intensity grew in mere seconds.

'*Willy-willy.*' He snatched up the duck from the ground, dragging Teà with him towards the truck, while Lottie nosedived for the front seat of the car.

Devin shielded them against the truck as the air rushed in a powerful spin of fury and fiery red dust, forcing ferocious wind gusts of over eighty kilometres an hour. It was a whirlwind of raw power reaching over five metres wide and half the size of the windmill. The more it sucked in the hot air, the higher it danced in a zigzag pattern until it smashed into the thicket of trees to dissipate into a wall of raining red dirt.

'That was strong.' She'd never been trapped by such a force, one of wind and dust — the other deliciously male.

'Good place for a windmill, huh?' He gazed down at her, his body pressed against hers with the duck between them. 'Are you okay?' He removed leaves from her hair.

'Your hat?' She raked a finger through his tousled hair to release a layer of powdery red dust, feeling the layer of red grit over her skin and under her clothes. It was worse than beach sand.

'Here?' He pulled his wide-brimmed hat out of his pocket, effortlessly slapping it back into shape before placing it on his head.

'Not your first rodeo, huh?'

'Nope.' He opened the truck and pulled out two icy cold bottles of water.

She drank thirstily, spilling water into her cupped hand for the duck to drink.

'You know the duck shouldn't be here.'

'Where?'

'Out here. There's no water where you found him.'

'Do they migrate?'

'For water, usually after the rains. But we haven't had rain for months. It's the middle of the dry season.'

'But it's possible that he fell out of the sky, going from one waterhole to another.' Their eyes locked in one of those long lingering stares. She could see the layered colours of coffee and caramel that made up his irises. The smooth skin, the stubble along his jawline and the powerful rise and fall of his chest. The surrounding air crackled and sparked as if he were a magnet drawing her towards him as a tornado stirred a haze of lust inside her.

Never had a man been able to spark pure heat that punched straight through to her core, while melting all her inner defences with just one look.

'So, who's climbing the windmill? Because I'm not.' Lottie closed the car door, then straightened her ponytail.

Teà found it easier to breathe stepping away from Devin. Her emotions were in a freefall, with her pulse so unpredictably fast. It wasn't right.

It wasn't real.

Even if just the touch of his fingertip, paired with a smile, was like happiness and home wrapped in a warm blanket, he shouldn't be affecting her like this. She was supposed to be immune to men, swearing to never let anyone get close to her again.

Not. Like. This.

'I'll do it.' She needed to ground herself and get high into the fresh air, well away from the spell of Devin. 'You babysit the duck.' She reached into the car for her daypack, to dig around for her trusty pocketknife and gloves.

This should stop all her feminine fantasies because she wasn't that type of girl. No siree. Normally, she was seen as one of the boys. But not the way Devin looked at her.

'Why do you have welder's gloves?' Devin asked.

'How do you know what kind of gloves they are? They're just gloves.' Lottie shrugged.

'They look like heat-protective welding gloves,' said Devin. 'I've never seen them that small before.'

'I had them specially made during a layover in Singapore.' Teà slipped her pocketknife into the back pocket of her jeans, tied up her hair and slid on her baseball cap, then slipped on the gloves she carried with her everywhere. *Just one of the guys.*

'You're a welder?'

'First-class senior maritime welder.' She expected him to balk, to make some snide remark like the many other men in her past. After all, she was used to playing in a man's world, not one of lace and wedding gowns like her sister.

But you'd think Devin would stop staring at her like that. Watching her as she grabbed the rope from the boot of the car, to sling it over her shoulder.

'Where do you work?' Devin casually perched the duck on his bulky shoulder as if he'd been doing it all his life.

'Anywhere, and everywhere they'd send me. I'll be dropping a safety rope. Can you keep it secure down here?'

Devin nodded. 'Good idea. This thing hasn't worked in years, so who knows how rusty those joints are the higher you go, especially as this wind tunnel sends a daily sandblast against the windmill's frame.'

'Excuse me, *peoples*, what are you talking about?' Lottie screwed her face up, using her hand to shade her eyes. 'What does a maritime welder do?'

'Fixes ships,' replied Devin as Teà climbed. 'Is that

where you worked, Teà?'

'I did offshore oil rigs, freighters, and ocean liners, working the ports from the coast of Mexico through to Alaska, Hawaii, then Europe for the Royal Navy.' Hand over hand, she effortlessly climbed the ladder, as the sweat trickled down her spine. 'Our specialised team would get flown everywhere. Doing all sorts of jobs, squeezing into tight spots, even underwater welding too. But I prefer deserts these days. I just did a four-month stint in the middle of the Kalahari Desert.' It was so good to get out of the car, the freedom as she climbed was exhilarating, with a smile spreading across her face. She loved her job. Good thing, too, as it was all she had in the world.

'So, heights and the remote wilderness don't bother you?' Devin's voice seemed so far away.

Men normally didn't bother her either, but Devin did. *Concentrate!* 'I learned to handle heights when I was young. It came in handy when I did this welding gig hanging off the side of a freighter on a deadline to Delaware. It was on the open seas, on this supertanker that's as tall as a high-rise building.' She threw the rope over the windmill's top horizontal beam, testing it for sturdiness, and let one end trickle into Devin's waiting hands.

She was putting an awful lot of trust in a guy she'd just met.

'How did you get into that? For a woman?'

It was a typical question she was used to answering. 'My dad. I used to do the repairs around the farm. Dad had me climb the rainwater tanks, troughs, and the guttering, to fix them while hanging off the roof.' It was one of the few times her father gave her a pat on the back for a job well done.

Confined in a boxy car these past three-and-a-half days, her muscles were relishing this moment of freedom the higher she climbed. The thick gloves protected her from the steel frame that was radiating a lot of heat from soaking up the relentless outback sun. It would easily burn her skin.

She got to the top; ten metres in the air with a bird's-eye view of her surrounds. Using the rope around her waist, she secured herself with the loose line.

The windmill's structure was old and rusty. She was crazy to do this climb. What was her father thinking? No way Lottie could've done this.

But her father knew Teà wouldn't hesitate.

Even after all these years, it scared her at how well her father knew her.

With the safety rope secure, Devin gave her a reassuring nod, while the duck effortlessly balanced on one strong shoulder. He was unlike any man she'd ever met. Not many guys would help a pair of sisters honour their father's last wishes? These gestures may seem small to some, but to her they were special. A guy like Devin had to be special for someone — just not her.

Wiping sweat from her brow, her shirt stuck to her skin, desperate for some cooling breeze.

Below her, the road ran in a jagged line like a piece of red string, disappearing over the hazy horizon where the heat waves rose to meet the sun. A flat sea of trees softly undulated like an olive-coloured ocean that spread westward, to meet a fortress wall of limestone ranges lined up like uneven rows of Leggo bricks. In the opposite direction large patches of black soil plains stretched for miles, to meet vibrant green tall gums, a sign of a river, perhaps?

Above her, with its pristine white underbelly exposed,

a lone wide-winged sea eagle glided effortlessly on a thermal, as smaller kites and other flocks of birds shifted over the treetops. It was nothing but pure wilderness, which served up a double dose of loneliness that hit her heavily between her shoulders.

A person could easily get lost out here.

How many got lost on this desolate outback stock route?

She craned her neck to inspect the joints connecting the rotor hub, between the main wind blades of the old water mill, with its rusty tail-vane bearing the words *Southern Cross*. And there it was. A simple metal pipe secured with a set of cable ties to the central down rod that pumped water from underground.

Removing her pocketknife, she stood on tippy-toes to reach with her blade to slice through the plastic cable ties and catch the pipe with ease. Thick duct tape covered the ends. 'I've got it.' She waved at them below. Tucking the pocketknife and pipe back into the pockets of her jeans, she started the climb down.

'*Teà, hold on.*' Worry laced Devin's powerful voice. He pointed down the road where another willy-willy was building steam. Only this monster was as wide as the road.

There was no time to climb down.

'*Tie me off!*' She tightened the rope around her waist, then wedged her legs around the steel structure and braced herself. Did Devin have the strength to keep hold of her lifeline?

Too late now.

Ten metres off the ground she stared straight into the devil's face that roared.

Seven

'Do something, Devin,' cried out Lottie, her hair whipping across her face as she stared at the horror unfolding. Her sister was hanging from the top of a windmill as a dust devil, weaving like a towering tornado, barrelled towards them. She'd never seen a willy-willy this big in her life.

'Take the duck and hide in the car.' Devin forced the duck into her hands, pushing her towards the car while gripping the end of the rope that was whipping in the wind like a kite string tied to Teà, who was clinging to the windmill.

'What are you going to do?'

'Keep this rope secure.' Devin ripped off his hat and sunglasses, shoving them down the back of his jeans and belt.

'But—'

'Teà's tied herself off. I can't let this rope go free or she'll have nothing but that hot metal to grip on to. Her welding gloves may be protecting her from the heat, but holding on to that structure—'

'Has to be burning her chest.' Lottie's heart fell as her eyes widened at that tower, creaking as if it would crumble like a house of cards.

'Get in the car. NOW.'

Lottie struggled to hold the duck and open the front passenger door of the car. The wind was ferocious. She couldn't see anything, just dust and debris whipping around in a frenzy. But the deafening angry roar powered by the wind was terrifying.

From the passenger seat, she held the duck to her chest as stones, twigs, leaves, and bark slammed against the car.

The windmill disappeared from her view in a cloud of dust as the car shuddered violently. She slid to the floor, clinging onto the duck. Its feathers were soft and downy, with its eyes so wide, yet full of trust.

'We'll be okay, Quacker. We'll be okay. We'll survive this and get you to some nice billabong to call home. And our dad's ashes will go where they're supposed to go, and I'll go home to my husband and children. And my sister …' She swallowed hard, gazing up at the furious swirling red fire for a sky, her sister stuck in the middle of it.

When the noise suddenly stopped, leaving them with nothing more than an eerie silence.

Was it over?

She peeked her nose over the dashboard.

The duck squirmed free; its pink webbed feet steady on the seat as she opened the door.

The car was covered in a thick layer of red dirt, leaves and twigs.

But Devin was still standing at the base of the windmill, holding those ropes with Teà climbing down.

'I've got you.' Devin reached for Teà's denim legs, his hands around her waist, and lowered her to the ground like she was nothing more than a feather.

Lottie's husband, Adrian, would never have the strength or the courage to stand and face a storm for anyone. He didn't have to, because Lottie wouldn't be silly enough to climb a windmill in the first place.

'Are you okay?' Devin asked Teà.

'You should have gone and hid in the truck.' Teà scowled at the guy. Fearless, as always.

Devin matched Teà's scowl. 'Like you shouldn't have climbed up there. You know, thank you would've been nice.'

'Thank you.' Teà's whole demeanour changed in the blink of an eye as she reached up and hugged his broad shoulders. 'Thank you.'

Lottie didn't know where to look. She could do with a hug herself. But no, nobody asked if she was okay, now did they? 'Don't mind me.'

'I need something from the truck. Don't move,' he said to Teà.

As if her sister listened to anyone, let alone stay still for a few minutes.

Surprise, surprise, Teà moved, pulling out a small metal pipe from her pocket. 'I got it, Lottie.'

'You did?' She rushed over as Teà used her pocketknife to cut at the thick wads of tape covering the ends of the pipe. It took forever to get it open.

'Here, put this on.' Devin returned with bottles of water and an ice pack he held up to Teà's neck.

'What a champion. Thanks.' Teà gave him an appreciative smile, covered with serious layers of crusty dust clinging to her sweaty shirt.

Lottie was going to insist Teà change before getting back in the car.

Oh, come on! What was it with those two? Always with the deep lingering stares at each other, with Devin plucking leaves out of Teà's hair. *Get a room already.*

Sure, they had a powerful chemistry. It just sucked to have to watch it. Especially when it'd taken Lottie years to accomplish that with Adrian. But with her husband being away all the time, they'd lost that special connection. How come her sister could do that with someone they'd just met?

From the pipe, Teà removed another envelope, encased in a plastic bag. 'Here Lottie, you do the rest. I need a drink.' She took the water bottle from Devin, while holding the icepack against the red line that ran down her chest. The same rust stain carried down the inner thighs of her jeans. Obviously where she'd hugged the windmill's metal frame. How tough was her sister?

Lottie could never compete with that. Teà was always fearless. And perfect.

'Is it bad?' Devin asked Teà, a deep concern worn on his face. It was admirable for a simple truck-driving cowboy. 'I've got some burn cream in the cab.'

'All good. I've had welder flashes worse than that.'

Of course, her sister would say that. Teà was always the tough nut.

'You should've worn your welder's apron,' mumbled Devin, inspecting her wounds, holding out another water bottle for her as he too gulped thirstily.

Where was Lottie's water, huh? *Thanks for the offer, peoples.*

But Devin ignored Lottie, again. He only talked to Teà.

They made the perfect couple. Completely layered in red dust, denim jeans, boots, and gloves. Wearing matching smiles, their white teeth stood out amongst the muck they wore. And the way they looked at each other, it was as if no one else existed around them.

Lottie couldn't remember the last time Adrian had looked at her like that.

But then again, her husband was never home. Leaving her behind to manage the farm, the house, and the dressmaking business. Her days ended with her collapsing into bed exhausted, despising Adrian for running away, like Teà, to live a life elsewhere. Only to return to tell their children of his adventures in the mines, sharing his photos of strange rocks, animals, and insects. Her husband had a life. And it was obvious Teà had an adventurous life, travelling to places she'd never imagined visiting herself.

All while Lottie was stuck at home, only going out for weddings, school runs, and food shopping. For what?

Did her family even miss her as much as her heart pined for their smiles? How her arms ached to hold them, to listen to their wondrous stories of their day.

'What does the letter say, Lottie?' Teà approached with that truck-driving cowboy shadowing her.

Devin mumbled, 'Let's hope the climb was worth it.'

Lottie's home was definitely worth saving.

'It'd be a great place for those wind turbines for power.' Teà pointed to a group of knee-high willy-willys dancing in chaotic patterns in the dust. 'And a solar farm, but maybe the dust would wreck the solar panels.'

'Pfft! How would you know?' Come on, her sister didn't know everything.

'I've just spent the past four months volunteering my time teaching the local indigenous people in the Kalahari to weld the stands for their solar farms.' She wiped her face down with a towel she grabbed from the car, after checking on the duck.

It was Lottie's good plaid towel!

'The Kalahari,' Devin said, 'that's a long way from the sea for a maritime welder.'

'I needed a break from the ocean. And the gig came up. It was great. I was based at the Ranger's Station on the Kalahari Game Reserve in Botswana, helping them build solar stations and wind turbines. In between putting up surveillance cameras, road barriers, and electric fences to stop poachers and control the visitors to the reserve.'

No wonder Teà had a thing for wildlife and ducks.

'Will you go back?' Devin asked Teà.

'No. Job's done. I don't know where I'll head next.' Teà gazed into the wilderness, her expression pensive. 'I was only volunteering—'

'Like a missionary?' Just great! Her sister was a freaking saint of solar stations and a saviour of jaywalking ducks. What next? A future protester on the steps of parliament, complaining about climate change with the rest of the mushroom tea–drinking hippies, just like the ones her father would complain about whenever he saw them on the news.

'No. I was there as a tradesperson. Lots of tradies from

all over the globe do it. Well, are you going to open that letter, Lottie? I did the last one.'

'Okay, sure.' Lottie made quick work on the plastic ziplock bag. A whiz from the countless lunches she'd made for her dad, the shearing teams, now for her children about to join school. She missed her children. Especially those cuddly morning moments where they'd rub the sleep from their eyes and hug her around the waist. Those few precious seconds where she'd hold them tight, smelling their soft hair as it brushed against her cheeks. Did they miss her?

The sooner she finished this hellish road trip, the sooner she could go home, triumphant as the owner of the family farm.

Lottie opened the envelope and unrolled the paper, curled from being in the pipe for a while. 'It's another map.' She spread it over the bonnet, no longer caring about the dust and chips on the car's once pristine polish, now ruined by the dust storm. It should buff out once this outback trek was over.

She unrolled the map that the lawyer had handed her the first time she was called to their office after her father's death. Back then, the map was spotlessly clean. Now it had wrinkles. Its edges were wearing, with spots of dirt splattered in areas, but it was still legible.

Lottie knew the road. She'd been studying this map for weeks, waiting to see if Teà would show up, trying to work out where her father would want his ashes scattered.

Why didn't her father want to be buried with her mother? Or with Teà's mother? Both of his wives were resting in the same cemetery, only metres apart. It's where she'd leave fresh flowers regularly when visiting her mother.

But then, as Adrian had said earlier, her father did like playing games—especially when it came to maps. Sadly, there wasn't anything on the large map resembling this section of hand-drawn scribble.

Her fingertip ran across her father's next set of instructions. *Why are you doing this, Dad?*

'What does it say?' Devin asked Teà.

It wasn't any of that truck-driving cowboy's business.

But Teà read it out for him anyway. *'Head for the Big Dipper's pinch point and follow the creek for the other Gregory Tree.'*

Lottie ran her finger along her colour-coded map, having memorised all the landmarks and roadside tourist destinations. 'The Gregory Tree monument is in Timber Creek. That's six hundred kilometres away.' She'd done her homework.

'Lollie, I think your dad meant the *other* Gregory Tree.'

'It's Lottie!' How rude was this cowboy to forget her name? 'What *other* Gregory Tree? There's only one Gregory Tree monument. That's a boab tree that some explorer graffitied in the 1800s.'

Teà handed the plaid towel to Devin so he could wipe down his dirty face — on Lottie's good towel!

'That guy you're talking about was Augustus Charles Gregory, who discovered this region back in 1856. It's who they named the Gregory National Park after, which is just over yonder.' Devin nodded in the road's direction.

'What is the *other* Gregory Tree, Devin?'

Devin looked at Teà. Always Teà. Only speaking to Teà as if Lottie was completely invisible, forgetting her name. *Rude much, peoples.*

'Only the locals know about it and we like to keep it that way.'

'Why?'

'Tourists clog up the roads and bring rubbish with them.'

'Where is it?' Asked the tourist, Teà.

'It sits on the side of Big Dipper's pinch point. That's a steep turn where road trains and caravans can't get through without risking a serious jack-knifing. I wouldn't risk it.' Devin nodded at his silent truck covered in a layer of dust.

'So why is it called the *other* Gregory Tree?' Teà asked.

Who cares, peoples! A tree was a tree, and Lottie wanted to end this road trip and go home.

'It's the same as the Gregory Tree in Timber Creek, only this one's carved out by the younger Gregory brother. It's a stockman's stop for, um …' He removed his hat to rake fingers through his thick hair.

'What?'

'It's the place where stockmen are buried in shallow graves.'

'A graveyard?' A chill ran up Lottie's spine.

'Boneyard more like it. Herds of cattle died there too. For some, it's a suicide spot. For others, it's a place for a stockman's farewell.'

Teà paused between sips of water. 'That must be where Dad wants his ashes scattered, Lottie.'

'How far is it?' Lottie asked the dust-covered truck driver.

'It's fifty clicks down this road. This track meets the Buntine Highway.'

Lottie's finger trailed over the map. 'I see it. That's the road that leads to Topp Springs Roadhouse.'

'Where I'm headed. I can't go with you on this part.' Devin was already walking towards the truck. 'I've got those choppers to deliver before the weekend arrives. If I leave now, I might be lucky to make it before dark. You two don't need me to be there for your dad's ashes. I told you I'd take you as far as I could; my part of this deal is done.'

'You're leaving us?' A spike of fear crawled up her spine, like spiders trawling through her hair. Lottie turned to Teà. Couldn't her sister drop a button to show her cleavage, flick her hair or smile at the guy? Surely her sister knew how to flirt to get what she wanted? 'Do something, Teà. He'll listen to you.' Because the dumbass couldn't remember her name, or he was being a prick to her on purpose.

'Devin's his own man with a job to do.'

'But you two—'

'Nothing is going on. Nothing will ever happen.' Teà pointed a dirty finger at Lottie, her voice lowered and laced with warning. 'So stop trying to set us up.'

'But you're a single girl and he's—'

'Stop.'

Teà's glare was powerful enough to force Lottie to bite down on her tongue while taking a step back.

Why wasn't Teà taking advantage of her attraction to Devin? They had oodles of annoying chemistry that could be forged into a deep and meaningful relationship. And then her sister could stay out here, leaving Lottie and her family alone on the farm.

Hold the needle and thread, this was Teà. The big sister who'd rather run away from any form of long-lasting relationship, like family. Preferring to disappear for seventeen years. Teà was only here for the money.

And that's what Lottie was hoping for, to buy out her sister and be done with her for good. Or contest the will. Whatever was the cheaper alternative with the quickest result for Teà to take the money and run.

Devin dragged out a chunky container of water and a jerry can of fuel from the truck. 'We'll top up your fuel now. Take this twenty-litre water container, too. You might need it to bathe in later. And I'm suggesting Teà drives.'

Lottie frowned at how quickly Teà went to Devin's aid, snatching the keys out of the Ford's ignition to unlock the fuel cap.

Lottie lifted her nose in the air. 'I've done quite well so far. I can drive.'

'You could drive a little faster, you know.' He lifted the jerry can while Teà held the funnel as they refuelled the car.

'I've got this, Devin. I'd really appreciate it if you could check the air filter after that dust storm.' Teà handed Devin the keys, working like a team.

'Good idea.' He leaned inside the car, popped the bonnet, and patted the duck. 'Teà, you did the Kalahari Desert. You're an adventurer. I bet you've done your share of four-wheel driving. It's why you're so bored you've resorted to making costumes for ducks.' He pushed off the load of dirt resting on the Ford, then raised the car's creaky bonnet to poke around under the hood.

Lottie just stood there in no-man's-land. These two virtual strangers were working on her father's car—which should be her car, if the inheritance deal was in her favour. She could then drive at more weddings, maybe get Adrian involved as a way to keep him home to help her manage the farm. But right now she was helpless, when she should be the one in charge.

'I'm no expert, but I'll admit, four months in the Kalahari Desert helped me brush up my skills. I didn't see an asphalt road for months. But I'm more of a motorcyclist. This country reminds me of the African savannahs, just different.' Teà drained the jerry can, locked the fuel cap back in place, then grabbed a rag from the back of the car. Thank goodness it wasn't another one of Lottie's good plaid towels.

'You really were a bikie chick,' stammered Lottie. And for the first time, the dust-covered duo looked at her like she'd crashed their party! *Hello, peoples, I'm not a ghost.*

'Bike rider, Lottie. I'd graduated from a biker's saddle-warming backpack. Told you that already.' She passed the rag to Devin, dropping the hood of the car.

'Peoples, where are we going? And I'm driving.' She snatched the keys from Devin.

'Follow that small map you've got. It'll take you to the other Gregory Tree.' Devin adjusted his wide-brimmed hat. 'Look for a steep dip in the road, one with a severe left corner in the middle of a floodway. It's dry this time of the year. Leave your car there and follow the creek bed for about a kilometre in a North Westerly direction until you hit the flood plain. Oh, and if there are any waterholes on the flats, check for crocodiles first before you do any skinny-dipping.'

'Crocodiles? This far inland?' Lottie screwed her nose at Devin. He had to be lying.

Devin headed for the truck and rummaged around inside the cab. 'You're heading into the Victoria River District, there's plenty of barramundi and both freshies and saltwater crocodiles in the Judbarra waterways. If you're going to swim, pick a place where you climb into it, the higher the better, coz crocs aren't mountain goats. Rock pools are good. Oh, hey, I've got this tool, Teà. You, being a welder, might find it handy.' He removed a yellow-handled hammer from the truck's cab as Teà walked towards him. That pair were like magnets always drawn together, both wearing matching layers of dust.

'We're not going swimming; we're looking for this tree to scatter our father's ashes.' Then this road trip would be finished, allowing Lottie to find the nearest airport to fly home to her husband and children, sending the Ford back on a truck. Then she could sit back in the comfort of her home to plan the next harvest while sewing bridals gowns for next year's wedding season.

Although, she'd never planned a harvest, or organised a shearing before. Her dad did all of that.

'Well, let's hope you two don't have to stay there, coz they reckon that Gregory Tree is haunted.' Devin held out the hammer. 'This is for you, Teà. It's too small for me, but you and those small gloves …'

'Perfect.'

Lottie winced at Teà, smiling at the silly cowboy, like he'd given her some fancy diamond ring. But it was just a cruddy tool that reminded her of some midget mining pick. 'We don't do ghosts, Devin.' But why was her sister all gooey over some dumb tool?

'I'll take this, thank you very muchly. It's awesome.

Thank you, Devin.' Teà held the tiny hammer as if it was as precious as a miniature sword made of gold. 'Any other suggestions for the road ahead, oh wondrous tour leader?'

The guy looked like he was going to blush. That's right, big man gone to mush.

Seriously, peoples. Did she need to whack their heads together to make them get with the program?

'You'll have over fifty clicks before you hit Big Dipper's bend. After that, you've got another hundred before you hit the Buchanan Highway. This road is what us locals call the Highway to Nowhere.'

Highway to Nowhere … Lottie squirmed at the chill squirreling up her spine to clash with the layers of perspiration.

'This road isn't maintained, so it'll be a tough slog.' Devin pointed to the road that disappeared on the dusty horizon. 'On the other side of the Big Dipper, is the old Knockabout Stockyards. It's a great spot for camping the night. Just be careful lighting fires. The place is a tinderbox for bushfires. You've got swags and enough food to do it.'

Ugh, camping. Lottie scowled over her map. 'I can't find this stockyard.'

'It's not on any map, Lorna.'

'Lottie, doofus. It's Lottie.'

'Yeah, whatever.' Sliding on his sunglasses, he picked up his empty jerry can. 'Camp at Knockabout for the night, then drive straight for the Buntine Highway. Turn right and you'll hit Topp Springs by mid-morning. That's if Teà drives.'

'I'm driving.' Lottie shook the car keys like a bell.

'Well then, we won't be expecting you until sunset in two weeks' time. Be safe, ladies.' He tapped his hat.

Teà blew him a cheeky kiss, holding the dumb tool to her chest as he climbed into the truck.

Lottie jumped at the blast from his ear-piercing air horn that sent birds fleeing from the nearby treetops.

The beastly truck's wheels slowly churned through the

red dust, dragging three trailers loaded with helicopters. It soon picked up speed, heading back to the dirt highway, creating a streaming dust plume to fill the air. The mighty truck engine roared through its gears, then it grew smaller and smaller until there was nothing but the hot, dry breeze.

'Let's go.' Lottie climbed into the driver's seat, keen to prove to the silly truck-driving cowboy she was a perfectly capable motorist. This was her car and her trip to ensure she claimed the inheritance she deserved. Otherwise, all those years of sacrifice were for nothing.

Eight

'I'm not like you, to go rushing off into some outback forest.'

'I think they call it a monsoonal thicket,' Teà said to her sister, struggling behind her on the bendy riverbed trail.

With the tip of her pocketknife, Teà finished scratching her initials, hidden under the thick yellow plastic that covered the metal handle of her new tool. She made a mental note to engrave her initials into it properly the next time she was at a workshop. Folding her pocketknife away, she let the slim hammer swing loose between her fingers, getting a feel for its weight.

Wild bamboo waved like feathers along the clay riverbanks among the scatterings of soft salmon-coloured ghost gums, where vines entwined with leafy shrubs, so thick, they blocked the sun. The depth of shade was a welcome reprieve, within a constantly changing landscape she was eager to see what was around the bend.

'Unless your plan is to lose me on purpose so you can claim the inheritance first, *slow down*.' Lottie leaned against the trunk of a soap tree, its deep green glossy leaves spread among clusters of tiny star-shaped flowers, like jasmine, except loaded with black berries and green ants. Half a dozen orange lacewing butterflies hovered amid various clusters above Lottie's head, while she slapped at a mosquito buzzing at her exposed calves, beneath the hem of her plaid sundress.

'I remember you used to be all about adventure, planning Sunday drives, making your own maps, creating fantasy names of places you were going to visit.' Teà plucked a sturdy branch from the dry rocky waterbed. Thick and light, it was as long as a fishing rod, the driftwood colour washed out. Using the tip of Devin's new tool, Teà smoothed down the sides of the branch.

'I told you to wear boots. Or were you ignoring me because I refused to get changed?' Still filthy in her grungy jeans, Teà was hoping they'd come across a rock pool to bathe in.

'I only own a pair of wet-weather gumboots, my good winter dress boots, and my riding boots. As I haven't ridden a horse in a while, and you said we weren't going on some fashion parade in the outback, I left them at home. I have my sneakers. I just didn't expect to go hiking in a dry river full of rocks.'

'The list of things to take on this road trip included hiking boots.' Along with swags, a gas cooker, food, and other assorted provisions. Teà was looking forward to camping under the stars.

'Your boots aren't hiking boots.'

'I trekked parts of the Appalachian Trail in these. They're the most expensive boots I've ever bought. I've had them re-soled twice. Guy in Turkey does them.'

'Oooh, well aren't you all la-de-dah with your private bootmaker?'

'It costs me a 100 Turkish lira. Guess how much that is in Australian dollars.' Teà sized up the stick to Lottie's height. 'Eight dollars.'

'No way.'

'The freight costs me more, but it's a bargain for this master craftsman, so I always tip him big time. Did you know the Magic Men strippers have their leathers made there? Did you have any male strippers at your hen's night?'

Lottie tightened her ponytail. 'I most certainly did not.'

'Lemme guess, you did the *let's play posh* with some pinkie-raised ladies' brunch with a menu of crustless cucumber sandwiches and pink champagne, watered down with strawberries and mineral water.'

Lottie blinked at her furiously through the beads of sweat. 'You weren't invited.'

'Good. I would've been bored.' How were they even related?

Using her spanking new tool, Teà chiselled off the end of the thick stick to suit Lottie's height. 'Here, this will help you. It's a hiking pole, for balance. Or you can play Gandalf in *Lord of the Rings*. Although you'd be the size of a hobbit —'

'I'm not that small.'

'You were once.' A tiny ten-year-old, the last time Teà saw her baby sister. 'Take it. It will help. Trust me.'

Lottie hesitated before taking the rod.

'Well, don't thank me then.' Teà hoisted her daypack — containing spare clothes, the urn, water, and snacks — over her shoulder, while flipping her new tool in her hand. She turned to continue leading them through the undergrowth.

A rich, sweet honey-like aroma filled the air, its source fat candlesticks of vivid orange grevilleas poking up amongst the pale green holly-like leaves. A black and white honeyeater carefully balanced on a nearby branch to suckle at the flowers' nectar, which also attracted a swarm of tiny native bees.

Higher along the river's banks, a group of muscular wallaroos stood warily between blades of tall grasses. Above them, in the nearby tree branches, two diamond doves shared soft, mournful cooing sounds in the shade of the glossy canopy belonging to the rugged bloodwood trees. 'The duck would've liked it here.'

'Can't believe you left it in the car.'

'Windows are open. Besides, he doesn't want to go anywhere, he's healing.' She gave another easy flip of the tool, the yellow handle landing with a secure thwack in the centre of her palm. Impressed with the balanced weight, and at Devin, who'd thought enough of her to give it to her. It wasn't romantic, but it was so her.

Oh no, Devin wasn't getting the wrong idea, was he?

She was just one of the boys. It was easier that way.

If only she'd stop thinking about the guy like some mopey teenager, staring at her idols on the ceiling of her childhood bedroom. But how could she stop? Especially when that shiver of pleasure would zip through her nerve endings just at the rumbling baritone of his voice, while his heated eyes trapped hers, and that grin softening the hard lines around his mouth only made her thirsty to taste him. Nope, she wasn't going there. 'You should make that duck a coat.'

'I'm not dressing up a duck.' Lottie speared the ground like a wizard. 'What's with you and dressing up that dumb duck?'

Teà stopped and faced her hot and flustered sister. 'To camouflage it. Remember, it's a protected duck I'm trying to keep hidden until it's ready to flock off. Duh!'

Lottie swayed on the spot, to slowly blink as if the clunky mechanics of her thought processes were trying to shift into reverse gear.

Turning her back on her dumbfounded sister, Teà jumped to the centre of the dry bed. The coarse river sand was soft, hopefully making it easier for Lottie still struggling with the river rocks.

What happened to the happy child eager to enjoy each day as if it was a gift? She bore no resemblance to this cranky mother with the roar of a whiny mountain lion suffering from a toothache.

'What's with you and that dumb tool Devin gave you?' The sand shifted under their steps, but Lottie wasn't as short of breath now. 'You look at it like it's some precious jewel when it's just a coal miner's mini pickaxe.'

'Close. It's a chipping hammer.'

'Why is it such a big deal?'

'To finish a pristine welding join, you chip at its excess with a finely balanced chipping hammer. It's like hiding the seam on a dress no one knows is there.' She balanced the small chipping hammer on the back of her hand. 'Look at it, it's the perfect weight and height for my hands.' Devin obviously understood what went into the art of welding, which Teà had turned into a fine craft. 'Besides carting my welding cap and apron in my backpack, I've learned blacksmithing to make tools on jobsites, to suit my hand size. Because the better the tools the—'

'Better the job.'

It was one of their father's repeated mantras. Especially when Victor Voss's second wife, Lauren, would complain about the money he'd spend on tools whenever he'd balk at Lauren buying a new dress.

'So, working for Dad, you somehow turned it into a career that took you all over the world? As a *welder*?'

'I think Dad would've preferred a boy, but he got stuck with me instead.' It was her excuse for being such a tomboy—who didn't mind wearing dresses if the occasion called for it. 'Of course, I needed to get proper qualifications. This welding shop in Port Lincoln hooked me up.' Back then, she was a sixteen-year-old kid who understood the job enough to not waste time asking questions, churning out the work to keep their customers happy. Her first boss was so sad to see her go.

Back then, living off a pitiful first-year apprentice's wage, she was grateful that her boss would drag her to his house on Sundays, where his wife would lavish her with a huge feast. They'd fill her arms with enough containers of food to feed herself for a week, stored in her tiny fridge in the old storeroom where she kept her cot, at the back of the work shed. It's where she'd lay in bed and listen to the sounds of the nearby ocean at night. As the seafood capital of Australia, Port Lincoln was the starting point of a never-ending adventure across the seas.

'So, you got to travel.' Lottie's sweaty scowl was ferocious.

Jealous much? 'I live one big working holiday, hon.' But it wasn't all roses and sunshine smiles, either. 'You?'

'The farm. You know, *my* family's home that we're saving from strangers.'

Lottie never smiled when she spoke about the farm, except to exert an impressive amount of sheer determination to finish this road trip.

But when the dust settled on this inheritance challenge, would it be everything that Lottie had hoped for?

Teà too had high hopes but, sadly, so far Lottie was nothing like the sister she'd remembered, or hoped to encounter.

For almost a kilometre, they trekked under the dense canopy of the hidden oasis, when the foliage fell back to expose a wide-open plain. The blinding sun made them pause as their eyes adjusted.

'I think we're here.'

'I don't like it here.' Lottie's voice was so tiny.

'Yeah, it's not a nice spot for a picnic ... Would Dad want this as his final resting place?'

It was desolate, with large cracks and crevices making up the dried floor of the flood plain.

A few black crows balanced on the ends of horns belonging to sun-bleached cattle skulls, half-buried in the black-sand plain. Entire rib cages belonging to scattered carcasses spread above the soil as if sacrificed to some evil god. The stench of death may be long gone, but the memory still lingered on the breeze of red dust and dry air.

And in the centre stood a large boab tree, with A.C. GREGORY 1856 branded deep into its flesh. Punching through the cracked earth, the bulbous boab with its fibrous pithy bark stood solidly amongst the death and decay. Its swollen trunk had a dimpled effect to its grey bark, along with a creepy bare-branched silhouette that cast an eerie shadow over this forsaken sea of bones.

At the tree, too scared to speak in fear of waking its ghosts, they scratched around the complex tangles of root. Or peered into deep pockets, bored into the trunk, like acne scars haunting a teenager in high school.

'Psst, I found it.' Lottie dragged out an old Army ammunition tin. Unclipping the sturdy iron clasps, she pulled out another envelope safely tucked inside a plastic bag. This time the envelope was only addressed to Lottie.

Didn't Teà deserve a letter too?

Would she want one? Considering it was her father's fault for tearing their family apart. A father who'd abandoned her twice, leaving her to carry a secret for seventeen years.

Lottie's hands trembled, her fingers covered in dirt, her nails broken, as she ripped open the envelope. A separate piece of paper fell out. It was another extension of the map.

More breadcrumbs. Teà sighed heavily, suddenly bone-tired of this silly game. 'You know what this means?' She picked up the piece of a jigsaw puzzle in the form of a map.

'Dad doesn't want his ashes spread here.'

'Would you?'

'No.' Lottie shuddered.

'Good. Let's get out of here. The map says we're to go to Topp Springs, where Devin's probably kicking back having a cold beer after having a decent shower, to grunt out his order for a decent feed.' She could handle plonking her elbows on the bar, to sit right beside him. Except her dad had made them come out here. Why?

'But …' Lottie waved the lengthy letter.

After all these years, her father's spidery handwriting had never changed. 'We can read that when we camp at Knockabout Stockyards.' It had to be better than this spooky place.

'What makes you think I'm going to share this letter with you?' Lottie held the letter to her chest with her chin raised. 'It's addressed to me, and only me. I'm the one in charge here, not you.'

Yes, Lottie truly controlled the purse strings on this trip, their travel budget practically padlocked inside her purse. 'Fine, you can read it while I drive.'

'I'm driving.' Lottie stabbed at the dirt with her hiking pole, heading back to the car.

'Take this water bottle for the hike back.' Lottie wasn't drinking enough.

'I'm not thirsty.'

'You need to keep your fluids up—'

'You're not my mother.' Lottie disappeared into the shadows of the riverbed.

'Fine!' Teà sipped on her water bottle, staring at the empty tin left lying in the dirt, with its lid cast aside. It was an old Army tin, like the one her father used to keep in his shed to store his shotgun shells. He'd told her how the Northern Territory was heavily involved in defending this country.

Is that why this old ammunition tin was out here?

Devin had said this was a place where many old stockmen had died. Did this tin belong to one of them?

She picked up the tin, and something slid across its rusty bottom. She turned it out, expecting a washer or a rusty bolt end to fall into her hand along with the rest of the grit.

Instead, two 1943 copper pennies landed in her open palm. She wiped the dirt off to reveal a crownless male king on one side and a leaping kangaroo on the back.

Could they be the same coins? Her father's lucky pennies that he'd toss in the air in their game of heads or tails, to keep you forever guessing which way it would land.

Could it be the same pair of pennies her dad used to toss from a paddle, in the back sheds? The place where Victor Voss was the masterful ring-keeper managing the square, playing his part as the MC in front of large groups of men holding out wads of cash, shouting *Come in spinner*.

It was all eyes on the spinning pair of pennies until they

landed in the square. If it was two heads of the king, or two tails for the kangaroo, it brought out shouts of, *you-beauty,* or *you little ripper.* Along with thousands of dollars exchanged, lost, or won.

Two-up was the grown-up version of heads and tails. It was illegal to play, except on Anzac Day. Yet her father would say it was just a spot of fun with some mates in the back shed.

He'd also told her the story of how it was a game loved by Aussie soldiers during the World Wars. A game born in the outback goldfields, played among the convicts and settlers during the 1850s. A curious coincidence as she glanced back at the boab tree bearing the date 1856.

She could almost hear those cries of jubilation from the back-slapping, beer-drinking ANZACs, through to the modern-day farmers and stockmen. With smouldering cigarettes dangling from the corners of their mouths, hats pushed to the back of their heads and their shirt's sleeves rolled up high, they'd keep their eyes on the spinner tossing those twin copper pennies in the air.

For as long as she could remember, her job was to walk around the inner perimeter of the coin-tossing square. She had to be the first to find the coins, should they get tossed out of the square.

Every time the back shed lights came on, her father would announce the rules of the game, while she got paid to keep her eyes on those pennies in case of some ruse to rig a simple game with simple rules.

It was the only regular thing she did with her father. It's the only time he'd talk to her and not *at* her as she helped him prepare for the locals to gather at the roofless hunting shack that echoed the shouts, cheers, and jeers of many men's voices.

Did she have the heart to tell Lottie that their dad ran regular, illegal games of two-up on the farm?

What had become of the roofless shack she'd wanted to burn the day her father tore his family apart?

Or was it just another one of her father's many secrets she'd sworn to keep and bury with the ghosts that surrounded her?

Secrets that would surely destroy everything Lottie believed in.

Teà didn't have the heart to tell Lottie. She just couldn't. The squeeze in her heart was enough to know it'd crush Lottie if she dared breathe a word of her father's secret.

Is that what her father wrote in the letter to Lottie? So that Teà didn't have to share that secret.

They may be warring sisters, but Teà wasn't here for the inheritance. She'd only come with some glimmer of hope to reconnect as family. Not for the farm. For family.

Yet, if Lottie kept digging, she'd unearth a secret that would ruin any hope of reconciling as sisters.

Teà wanted this chance to reconnect. She was so sick of being stuck under the rib-gripping, hunchback ache of loneliness. Too scared to strike up new friendships, preferring to stick to what she knew inside her shrinking inner circle, now spread to the corners of the globe. It wasn't her fault; it was fate's fault for placing her under this terrible burden.

So when the local police, from the nearby town of Kang, came and saw her at the Kalahari Ranger's station, it was a wakeup call. She'd been listed as a missing person, along with a message that her father had died, and that her baby sister was demanding she return home. It had ignited a flame of hope inside her. Teà didn't hesitate to book the first flight back to Australia. She wanted to be with her sister.

Yet she'd found Lottie had become some creature Teà normally wouldn't waste her oxygen on, her hopes once again extinguishing under that all too familiar weight of loneliness.

You'd think she'd be used to the loneliness. After all, you died alone, leaving behind those you loved to live their days loaded with loneliness where it hurt to raise your head in the mornings.

She held out the dirty pennies in her open palm.

She could carve out a paddle. Perhaps find a chunk of driftwood on her way back to the car. It'd keep her mind occupied because her little sister was avoiding the deep conversations Teà had yearned for.

Teà dug around in her daypack and pulled out her change purse, emptying all the notes and coins into the old ammunition tin. She closed the lid, pushed down the heavy-duty clips sealing the contents airtight, then hid it back under the boab tree. 'Have a beer on me, boys.'

And with a nod at the boab, she turned away, flipping the pennies in her hand. 'Find a penny, pick it up, and all day long you'll have good luck …'

Nine

'You seriously don't expect us to camp out here, do you?' Lottie's hands ached from gripping the steering wheel all day, dealing with the stress of driving along the notorious stock route, the Murranji Track.

As they'd headed further west, thick scrublands crowded the sides of the dirt road, before it had opened up to a flat valley void of any shrubbery.

Highlighted by the setting sun, a collection of sun-faded wooden railings made up the dilapidated stockyards. The Knockabout Stockyards wasn't much to look at.

'I'm not risking our necks with you driving in the dark.' Teà was furious. Slamming car doors, kicking at rocks. 'Not when you nearly *killed us!*'

'I did not. I was well within the limits.'

'It's only because you were driving so bloody slow that we're not wrapped around that gum tree.'

'It's not my fault those little kangaroos—'

'Wallabies.'

'—jumped out in front of us.'

'They do that at sunset. But as we don't have a set of spotlights on the car and no bull bar, we're staying HERE.' Teà stamped her boot and a puff of red dust rose and fell around her filthy jeans ingrained with red dust, like her shirt. Teà hadn't changed after the windmill, preferring to stay in her mucky clothes, whittling wood on the passenger side, with the duck balancing on the back of the bench seat beside her.

Until Lottie nearly hit a group of wallabies.

The Ford had swerved to slide in the dust. The duck flapped its feathers in her face, and Teà was forced to kiss the bark of a ginormous tree trunk through the open passenger window. That's when Teà's mouth exploded with an astounding string of f-bombs as she clambered over the back seat, kicking out at Lottie's luggage on her way through to the driver's side—just to get out of the car.

Leaving Lottie to tremble, with her sweaty grip slipping on the steering wheel of her father's stalled Ford.

'I didn't want to mess up Dad's car.' In all fairness, Lottie had nearly totalled the car.

Teà's glare was positively evil. It made Lottie gulp from behind the steering wheel. 'Fine, we'll camp the night. I hate camping.'

'You used to love it.' Teà whipped open the driver's door and snatched the keys from the ignition. Juggling them in her hand, she stalked around to the boot of the car. 'You were always badgering Dad to take us camping and fishing.'

'Dad stopped all of that when *you left*!' Lottie jumped out of the car to stab at the air between her and her smug older sister, who was tossing their swags into the dirt. 'You left and everything stopped.'

'That's not true.'

'It is.' Why lie when the truth hurt more?

Lottie dragged her cumbersome swag to the far corner behind the timber railings. 'What are you doing? Don't you dare think you can camp near me. You can go waaaay over there.'

'Fine with me. I don't mind exploring. And you snore.'

'Do not. Adrian would've told me so.'

'Adrian's too scared to tell you anything. He doesn't want to incur the wrath of Little Lottie.' Teà dumped her swag on the other side of the yards, partially concealed behind the rails. 'Is this far enough, *princess?*'

'I. Don't. Care.' Lottie was over it. 'All I want to do is have dinner and read this letter.'

'Fine. I'll sort out the meals while you sit back and play the pampered princess, enjoying her bedtime reading. And no complaints about my cooking, either.'

'Can you cook?' Because Lottie did the cooking in her household.

Teà rummaged around in the esky and pulled out a beer, cracking open the lid. 'More than Mac and cheese, cupcake. Christ, I need a dozen of these after playing the passenger who barely lived to *tell the tale!* I could have stabbed myself.'

'It's not my fault you decided to whittle wood in the car. I want all those shavings out of there, by the way.'

'The car is full of dust, Lottie. Why bother cleaning it when we're not even halfway to wherever the hell Dad is sending us?' Teà dragged out the small gas cooker and set it up near a group of rocks on the far side of the car. 'He's torturing me, right? This is payback. It has to be.' Her complaints continued in between mouthfuls of beer while she rummaged through the assorted bags for food.

As Teà slammed pots and pans, Lottie found a shady patch hidden well away from the car. She unrolled her swag and plonked onto the bed.

She then stared at the envelope bearing her name: *Loretta Louise Voss-Nolan.*

The only time she saw her full name on an envelope was for bad news and bills.

How come she scored a personal letter from their father, and Teà didn't?

She squinted back at the car. Is that what was upsetting Teà? That their dad had left her out?

Maybe it would've been better if her father didn't write her this letter, struggling to find the courage to open it.

'Are you going to read that letter, or stare at it all night?' Teà put a plate covered in foil onto Lottie's swag, then turned on a small lantern. 'I was going to light a fire, but then I remembered Devin said the Knockabout Stockyard was a tinderbox. He's not wrong.' The dry ground was brittle and crunchy under her boots.

'What is this?' Her nose twitched at the plate, not daring to pull back the foil.

'My famous Campfire nachos without the campfire. It goes well with the beer. Here, have one.' Teà dumped the can beside Lottie's leg.

'I, um …' Lottie was also dirty. She had a sock tan from a thick dusting of dirt that ended above her white ankles. Her new sneakers were no longer white, but a dirty ochre colour.

'The beer is perfect for washing down the dust we've been swallowing all day. It's not like it's the first time you've drunk beer.' Teà grinned, opening another can, to then swig deeply. She sat on a nearby rock to peel back the foil on her dinner plate. 'I remember you used to steal sips from Dad's beer when he wasn't looking.'

'Did not.'

'You used to rush up to him, just to be the first to pour him a glass of beer whenever he came inside for dinner. Then you'd secretly take a sip straight from the long neck while hiding inside the fridge.'

The memory tugged at the corner of Lottie's mind like a moth-eaten velvet curtain being pulled back inside a gigantic theatre, complete with rows of empty seats, where the movie premiering was called *The Life of Little Lottie.*

'Remember when your mother busted you?'

The memory curtain flapped a little wider to reveal the lecture she'd copped from her mother. Soon followed by her father fake-scolding her, while giving her a shiny coin telling her to spend it on girlie drinks at the school tuckshop instead of drinking his beer. She'd never touched beer after that.

Until today, cracking open her beer can.

'Eat up before the campfire nachos get soggy.' Teà

dangled a cheesy triangular corn chip into her mouth, then washed it down with a hearty chug of her beer. Her sister looked right at home, dressed in dusty jeans, drinking beer like a bloke in the bush.

Teà looked like their father. Remembering all those camping trips they shared as children, beside pretty streams and warm campfires. Never once had she been scared, because she had her father and her big sister to protect her.

Peeling back the foil, Lottie inhaled the aroma of coriander and other spices. Her stomach grumbled and her mouth watered as she bit into her nachos. The crunchy corn chips and the soft bean combination were far more flavoursome than expected. Eating with filthy hands, yet so ravenous she didn't care that she was drinking beer and devouring the best plate of nachos in her life.

But she couldn't say that to Teà.

'You cooked this quickly.' As quick as it was for Lottie to eat and drink her beer can dry.

'You were busy staring at that envelope.' Teà took the plates and empty beer cans, swapping them for another can.

Two cans of beer, in one day. *Look out peoples, it's a party.* 'I hope you're packing up everything.'

'Don't worry, Little Lottie,' Teà said with a deep bow, 'I'll do the dishes and return all cooking goods back to the car for our quick getaway in the morning. I'll leave you to lock up.'

'Where's the duck?'

'Over there. He's foraging for something. But I'll tuck him into the car for the night.'

As the sun lowered and the stars started to shine, Lottie sipped on her beer. 'I can't remember ever doing this. Drinking beer and eating junk food.'

Pots and pan clattered, bags rustled as Teà repacked the car. 'It's not junk food, there's only tinned vegies and beans in that dish. It should make for an interesting drive tomorrow. Good thing the Ford isn't air-conditioned.'

'You're so crude.'

'Lighten up, Lottie. It's just us and the stars.'

'You're so casual about everything.' It was irritating.

'Because in my job planes get delayed, ships switch courses, and the wrong tools and equipment gets delivered, or there are none on job sites. I let go of the little things and stopped losing sleep over it. You should learn to do it too.'

Lottie frowned at her sister, rustling around in the car boot. 'Like you let go of us, your family, by leaving without saying *goodbye*?'

'I couldn't say goodbye. You were asleep.'

'But to just leave so quickly?'

Teà shrugged, tossing a towel over her shoulder, then grabbed some soap, a small washtub and Devin's chunky water container. 'I was made an offer I couldn't refuse, so I took it.'

Was Teà going to have a bath? In the dust?

'But you never contacted us again.' Lottie wasn't moving. Her belly was full, with her shoulders and arms suddenly heavy from driving all day. She was exhausted. But the more beer she drank, the nicer it tasted, now onto can three. Or was this can number four?

'Some places I worked made it impossible to contact anyone—'

'I'm sure they had a postal service in the Sahara Desert where you volunteered all your spare time.' Spare time was a luxury in Lottie's world.

'It was the Kalahari Desert.' Teà pointed to the darkening stockyards. 'Look at where we are now. Can you send a telegram, or a Christmas card, from the Knockabout Stockyards?'

'So, it's not all glamour in the jet-setting scene, is it?' Lottie grinned evilly behind her beer can. Through the rail's gaps that made up the deserted stockyards, the last hint of the sunset slowly dropped behind the silent valley.

'Manning the oil rigs with a bunch of sea-hardened roughnecks, you leave the princess parade at home. Especially with my job.'

'So you buried all femininity to be one of the boys as a *wel-duh!*'

'Lottie, you may sew pieces of material together and create gorgeous wedding gowns. Me, I weld two massive sheets of metal together that become ships or stands for solar farms to provide power to a remote village in Africa. It's like sewing on a different scale.'

Was there a compliment in that rant? 'Do you do anything crafty with your welding?'

Teà's voice rose from the other side of the car where she was having her sponge bath, with the duck quacking and splashing in the tub beside her. 'When I have nothing better to do, I weld up the scrap. What happened to those sculptures I'd made at the farm?'

'Gone.' Lottie shrugged, staring at her name on the envelope. 'Everything that belonged to you is all gone.'

'That was to be expected.' Teà towelled herself off behind the car. Then she pulled out her toothbrush.

'What do you mean?' Wiping her tongue across her own teeth, Lottie didn't have the energy to find her own toothbrush. *Bah*, it could wait until morning.

Lottie giggled behind her beer can. If only her children could see her now, they wouldn't recognise her.

Teà spat out toothpaste, then gargled some water. 'I was invisible in that household, Lottie.'

'No, you weren't.'

'You didn't see it. After all, the world was all about Dad's little mate Lottie. Do you remember your birthdays, those big parties, the enormous cakes you had for your birthdays?'

'Of course, I do.' Lottie loved her birthdays. With her mother they'd plan months in advance, deciding on what to make, build, bake and who to invite.

'Do you remember what they ever did for my

birthday?'

Lottie blinked at the letter in her lap. Again, the moth-eaten velvety curtain, hiding her childhood memories, shifted.

'What about Christmas? You got the toys, the big dollhouse, the new bicycles, and that pony ...'

Lottie shrugged. She'd loved Christmas, decorating the house with her family from top to bottom. Even though her father complained about it, it was one of those rare times she ignored Victor Voss.

'Do you remember what I got for Christmas?'

Lottie blinked in the darkness again, as Teà brushed her hair, then applied her assorted lotions.

'Nothing.' Dressed in fresh jeans and a clean shirt, Teà stood on the edge of the camp light. 'One of my reasons for leaving was I'd become invisible. I was being ignored as a daughter. Instead, I was being treated like some unpaid lackey on the property. Feeding the animals before school, fixing fences after school, cleaning troughs. I believe you're doing all that now.'

'It's what farm kids do. I have my children collect the eggs.'

'You're a grown-up, Lottie. A mother. Did you want to grow up and be a farmer's daughter forever?'

'Hey—you're one, too.'

'No, I'm a maritime welder. An adventurer. I'm my own woman. I don't let my job define who I am. Do you?'

'What do you want from me? *Why are you here, when you don't care about the farm*?'

'I'm here to find answers. Like you.' Teà pointed at the letter. 'It's why Dad dragged our sorry arses out here into the middle of nowhere. He knew we'd have to camp well away from any outside influences, without any chances of phoning anyone being so far from the nearest cell-phone tower. We're just lucky Devin stuck around for as long as he did.'

'You like Devin.'

'Nothing's going to happen. So stop your matchmaking, right there.'

Wow, she'd forgotten to call her family. Not that she could now. Did Adrian contact the lawyer to contest the will? Did he remember to take their daughter to her weekly piano lesson? Should she enrol Sophie into a pony club?

Did her dear Pip's tooth fall out? It'd been wriggling for ages. Would Adrian remember about the tooth fairy? Would he bother to look up from his phone to take a moment and enjoy the wonder in their son's eyes after finding a gold coin under his pillow?

Teà tenderly tucked the duck into the back of the car, slinging her daypack over her shoulder she closed the driver's door. 'I've tossed the car keys next to the urn, on the front seat of the car, so you can have a bath and lock up. Or do you want me to lock it up now?'

The car was so far away. 'I'll do it in a minute.'

'Fine. Drink some water before you go to sleep. You don't want to dehydrate, or you'll be no good to drive.' Teà dropped a box of tissues and a bottle of water beside Lottie's swag. 'Happy reading.'

The brittle ground crunched under Teà's boots, following her torchlight that led to the far side of the railings. There was a bit more rustling around, sorting out her swag. Then the torchlight was doused.

Finally, Lottie had her privacy.

She sat cross-legged, pulling her small lantern closer. With shaky fingers, she opened the envelope and unfolded the pages, now smudged with red dirt.

To my little mate, Lottie.

Congratulations on making it to the halfway point. Well done, kid, for making it this far. Knew you could do it, and I know you'll finish this trip too.

Heck, you should see me sitting here with a smile, looking at the old photos on my desk in the office. You with that bright gappy-smile as a fair-haired bub, to the fine mother you are today. I've never been prouder.

I know, mate, I flamin' should've said something sooner. But it's hard for a bloke like me to say things like this.

Your mother used to snap at me, complaining she had no idea what went on inside of my noggin. Heck, half the time I don't know either.

But kid, I know exactly why I made you and your sister, Teà, take this journey together.

Not that I don't trust your husband, Adrian, to go with you on this journey, I wanted my girls to be together. Not the son-in-law—who's a bit soft for my taste—but he's perfect for you. You've got to admire that lad's loyalty to family. Adrian never once complained about not being involved with the farm, coz I wasn't going to let him either. And he was smart enough to make his own money, to provide for his family the way a man should. I respected him for that.

Besides, a man's gotta earn his own way, especially when he's got a family to provide for. So I will rest peacefully in the knowledge that Adrian is the type of man to always put you and his family first.

I wished I'd learned that lesson sooner.

As for the car …

No doubt you'd be tightening your ponytail wondering why I made you take the Ford to my old stomping grounds in the Northern Territory outback.

The Ford was always the family car. I brought you home for the first time in that car, with your mother complaining about not having your baby basket secure enough. I didn't care that it wasn't good enough for those ever-changing newfangled road rules, it worked, didn't it. I got to drive you home. Heck, I made sure my daughters got their first trip home from the hospital in that car. You even let me bring my grandbabies home in that car, with you and Adrian in the back seat. Remember?

Kid, you loved the old Ford as much as I did.

I used to chuckle, watching you play inside it when you didn't think anyone was watching. Parked in the shed, you'd sit on a stack of cushions to get high behind that steering wheel. Your little legs swinging far from the foot pedals, imagining you were going on some long road trip. You were so young then.

You'd tell me many times you wanted to take the old Ford right through the centre of Australia.

Well, guess what, kid?

I may not have been the best father, but today, I hope I made your wish come true.

I know the burdens you were carrying, and I know I'd never made it easy for you and Adrian when you were newlyweds — especially after your mother was gone. But you stuck by me, kid. Sharing your life, watching my grandbabies grow, was the greatest gift a man my age could ever hope for.

And it's because of those burdens you carried, I never told you I was sick.

You see, about a year ago I went and saw the docs about my headaches. I never told you this, but that fancy specialist found brain tumours. Three of the buggers.

On the long drive back in the old Ford from Adelaide, after hearing those results, that's when I started planning this entire trip for you and your sister. At first, those quacks only gave me six months. Bah. Didn't I beat them bastards!

Heck, no, I wasn't having any of that flamin' chemo or them operations that came with more warning labels than a nuclear reactor. And I certainly didn't want to live on a diet of pills that made me sicker than a dog dying of dingo-bait.

Now don't get mad at me, kid, for not telling you I was crook. You may think you'd want to look after someone you cared about who was sick, but I just couldn't do that to my little mate, Lottie.

If you're reading this, and if Teà came with you, ask her. Teà would understand my reasons for choosing to die the way I did. She'd know better than anyone.

Just don't kill her. Because Teà's sacrificed a lot for you, far more than you've ever known, kid.

Heck, it's one of the many reasons why I've made it a condition in the will to include Teà on this Sister Trip.

Your older sister is a strong woman. She's resourceful

enough to not only help you, but she's also thoughtful enough to let you run the show. Teà will listen to you and, if you let her, she'll help you make sense of this situation. Just don't hate me for the things you may hear about me. Just remember I love you, kid.

But don't think for one second you can put one over your sister. Teà would be one of the few who'd stand up against the wrath of Little Lottie.

Heck, I used to chuckle watching your own family scatter to the back sheds when you blew your stack over something silly. Like the time you yelled at the kids for stealing your green thread—which was me, by the way. I used it to string up the tomatoes.

Look, kid, I want you to have a conversation with your sister as you drive the old Ford that is my gift to you. It's yours. I may not have driven it much in the end, but I saw how much you cared for it. Polishing it up for weddings, letting it become a part of many other families' stories on their special days.

Just remember that it's okay to let others help you to steer down that long road of life. You don't always need to be in charge. And it's okay to share the burden with others, like your husband.

So what if it's not perfect? Nothing in life ever is. It took me a long time to learn that lesson, so don't waste your time today on things that won't matter tomorrow.

Take care of you, your family, and your sister, because you have always known the true value of family, sacrificing yourself for everyone around you, which included me.

Enjoy your road trip, kid. Sing a song, crack a beer or two, get dirty and let your ponytail fly, because I know you never got your honeymoon. You never took a holiday. So this is me making you take one, letting you know that it's okay to live your dreams. Life's too short not to.

All my love,

Dad.

PS: I've always been proud of my little mate, Lottie. Be good, kid, and please find it in your heart to forgive me for my secrets—

I wasn't perfect as a man, or as a father, but I will always love my daughters.

The tears welled up in her eyes. She dragged tissue after tissue free from the box, as tears splattered onto the page. Her throat ached as her limbs turned into heavyweights. Lottie lay on her swag, curling her body into a ball, clutching her letter to her chest, to stare at the sea of stars. She was a little girl all over again, the daughter who truly missed her father, the fragile female who cried herself to sleep.

Ten

An engine started. A door slammed. Tyres crunched on stones as dust flew from a car roaring down the road.

Teà sat up, still tucked inside her swag bed.

Did her sister just drive off without her?

She slid on her boots. '*Lottie*?'

She ran through the stockyards to find Lottie curled up in her own swag, empty beer cans scattered around her, with a line of drool trickling from the corner of her mouth. 'LOTTIE. WAKE UP!'

'Can't I have five more minutes, Mum?'

'The car is gone.' Teà raced to the empty car park where Devin's 25 litre water drum stood by the rocks. It's where she'd left it while bathing, as the duck paddled in the small tub.

The duck!

'Oh no, no, no.' She sprinted to the middle of the road hoping to see the car, but all she saw was a trail of dust, heading further inland.

Doubled over, hands on her knees, she tried to push down the panic and fear, not only for herself but for the duck in that car. 'You didn't lock up the car last night, did you?'

'What?' Lottie sat up with her hair everywhere.

'Tell me you took the keys from the car last night.'

Lottie wiped the sleep away from her eyes. 'I drank too much beer last night.' She picked up her water bottle.

'No, you didn't drink enough water yesterday. I told you—' What did it matter now? 'Get up, Lottie, we've got to go.'

'Why? We've only got a two-hour drive to Topp Springs. Ugh, I could do with a shower.'

'How are we going to drive when we HAVE NO CAR!' Teà's voice echoed through the empty stockyards, as she pointed down the deserted road.

'Dad is in that car!' Lottie gripped her hair with the panic shining brightly in the whites of her eyes. 'If we lose Dad's ashes, I lose everything.'

'Roll your swag up and let's go.'

Lottie stumbled from the swag to stagger over the gravel. 'Why does my tongue feel like I licked the dust all night?'

'You're hungover or dehydrated from the day before.' Where was the strait-laced soccer mum now?

'What do we do?' The fear quivered in Lottie's voice.

'We walk.' Teà rolled her swag up, hoping, no—dammit—praying the duck was okay. 'We're not in phone range, so we can't call anyone. All we can do is hope we'll spot some traveller heading to Topp Springs.' The old Ford would stand out in this land of four-wheel drives, utes, and trucks. That's if it didn't get dumped in some back country.

'I'm not lugging this bulky swag around. I need my toothbrush.'

'Bloody princess,' Teà muttered, lifting the large water container onto the flat rocks to use as a table. She unscrewed the top lid to allow gravity to push on the water as she pulled on the bottom lever to fill all the water bottles she carried in her small daypack. 'Fill up any and every bottle lying around. We're going to need it.'

'Let's leave the swags.'

'We may need them to camp tonight if we don't get to Topp Springs; it's a hundred kilometres away. A man walks an average of five Ks per hour, which means it'll probably take us over twenty-four hours to walk, non-stop.'

'But …'

'I'll roll it tight. Anything that isn't necessary we'll leave here to collect later.'

'I'm not coming back. Once I'm done scattering Dad's ashes—'

'That are in the front seat of our stolen car, being babysat by an injured duck!'

'You're more worried about the duck?'

That was true. 'I like that duck.' A whole lot more than she liked her little sister right now.

Teà flicked the dirt off the plush plaid sheet Lottie kept in her swag, dumping the pillows and extra bedding to make the canvas camp bed as light as possible. A few white pages floated on the breeze.

It was the letter to Lottie that they'd retrieved yesterday.

'Oh, no!' Lottie gave chase, stomping on the pages tumbling on the breeze. 'Look at what you did! *You ruined my last letter from my father.*'

Teà bit on her tongue, struggling not to say something snarky. How was a piece of paper going to provide food, water, and shelter?

Hadn't Lottie grasped the seriousness of their situation?

Or was the silly woman in denial?

With both swags reduced to the barest minimum, the rest of the linen was left folded by the stock rails. Teà went through her small daypack, which held essentials such as her passport and other forms of ID. Her linen shawl, mobile phone, torch, some light snacks left over from yesterday's hike, her gloves, and the pocketknife she never went anywhere without. Her otherwise empty purse held the two copper pennies and the two-up paddle she'd been making. Some sunscreen, gum, and another small water bottle. At least they had about ten litres of water. Even if it was going to be a bugger to carry Devin's bulky water container, she'd do it.

'Oh, no.' Lottie squealed. 'I got my shoes wet.'

Teà's face fell in horror at the water container spilling out their most precious resource. '*Pick it up.*' She raced over to pluck it from the soil.

'Not my fault. You put it on the rock.'

'It was on a stable foundation to make it easier for us to fill our water bottles.' There was less than half a litre left.

'Not my fault.'

'Yes. IT IS.' Teà's lips flattened, tasting the salty sweat. Her hands shook into fists, grinding her teeth. 'It's about time you take some responsibility for your actions. You left the keys in the car.'

'No. *You* left them there.'

'Because you said you'd lock it up. How can you be such a colossal cock-up!? How are we related?' She threw her hands in the air in defeat. 'That's it, I'm done. I'm done pandering to your control-freak fetishes. And I'm done biting my tongue.'

Lottie crossed her arms over her chest as the sarcasm dripped from her words. 'Puhleese, don't hold back now. Let it all out, why don't you?'

'Fine! You are nothing but an egotistical, narcissistic, ponytail swinging prima donna, who thinks the world owes you. Well, guess what, Lottie? It's time to put away your pre-schooler's princess crown and join the world of grown-ups.'

Wrestling with her anger, Teà emptied the last of the water from the big jug. It didn't even fill up Lottie's bottle. That left them with less than two litres of water to survive a two-day hike in the outback.

'How dare you tell me to grow up, when I'm a mother!' With her dainty nose pointed high in the air, Lottie tugged on her ponytail that pulled her face tight.

Teà had to look away, never more tempted to smoosh Devin's empty water container into her sister's snooty face.

Instead, she left it beside the discarded pile of folded linen and picked up the two swags. They were so much lighter now, but she knew they'd be heavy in a few hours.

'You're a kid who never left home.' Her baby sister was a spoiled brat, in her old-school-styled dressmaker's wardrobe. 'Go on, admit it. This is the furthest you've ever travelled in your life.' And they had a long way to go, especially without a car.

'I had things to take care of. I had responsibilities that even Dad recognised and thanked me for. I sacrificed a lot for Dad, to look after him and help out with the farm. And where were you? Getting some suntan in the Sahara.'

'Kalahari.'

'Whatever! At least I have a home, unlike you.'

'Everyone has a different interpretation of home. It's more than four walls and a roof, you know.' Teà adjusted her swag's straps to hoist it higher over her shoulders, then her small daypack. She didn't do handbags, having witnessed many travellers get their handbags snatched or pickpocketed over the years. And here she was without her trusty black backpack, which contained all her credit cards and was currently sitting in the boot of the stolen car, because Lottie took the back seat for her plaid luggage. All of it gone. *Idiot!*

'Carry your own crap. I'm done babysitting you.' She tossed the half-empty water bottle at Lottie's mud splattered sneakers and headed down the dirt road.

'Where are you going?' Lottie cried out. 'You can't leave me here.'

'Watch me.' She was done. Completely and totally done dealing with that dumb damsel living her life in constant distress. How the hell did Lottie cope in the real world? Was it because Lottie hardly ever left the farm?

Well, Teà was done pampering to the needs of the wannabe-posh princess. She didn't care about the farm or her father's final wishes. None of it mattered now. Not when their survival was at risk.

They could die out here.

She blinked at the revelation, and at her own heart's incredibly strong beats, along with the tightening of her belly, which straightened her spine, unearthing her deepest desire to survive.

It surprised her.

When not that long ago, there had been some crazy moments in the darkest depths of her loneliness, where grief had ravaged an endless pit of sorrow that drowned all joy in her soul. It had been a dark period when she'd been left with nothing but the endless suffering, flooding her empty bed with tears. How many times had she'd wished to hear the black wings of the angel of death, to hear the grim reaper's scythe slice at the wind to help her get free from the weight of grief and loneliness.

But right now, fighting her fear made her hands shake, the breath rattled in her lungs, raising her chin to face her greatest challenge on the unknown road ahead. She wanted to live.

'I did not come here to die with the ghosts of the Murranji Track.' Like hell that was going to happen. And she started, one foot after the other, determinedly leaving all her excess baggage behind.

'I'm sorry.' Lottie staggered in the dirt, sniffling tears. 'Teà, I'm sorry, okay.'

But Teà ignored her sister and kept on walking. Her eyes remained on the colossal salmon pink sky, with its cool breeze barely a whisper across the land where the sun had yet to peak over the ranges. As the first of the birds' morning songs serenaded her, she steadily followed the car's tyre tracks along the trail.

'Please, Teà …'

Teà gritted her jaw and kept on walking, ignoring Lottie's childish tears.

Last night, she'd heard her sister's true tears after reading their father's letter. She'd recognised the mournful tears of grief and understood how hard it was to raise your head above them.

With nowhere to hide, no chores to finish, or family responsibilities to tend to, Lottie had finally surrendered to the strain of grief. She was a daughter who'd lost her father, and she needed to grieve.

You could never run from grief. Hell, no. Teà had tried. Crossing continents even, to flee the suffocating power of grief. It was a painful lesson to know that distance didn't matter when it came to grief. Denial was only putting off the inevitable because you could never fully escape that unbearable loss for daring to let someone into your soul.

'Teà? … Please …'

Nope. Not giving in. She kept her focus steady on the distant horizon, following the car tracks through the scrub.

Another stumble, a shift in the sand, and Lottie got a little closer behind Teà.

'Stop, Teà, please? I'm sorry.'

'Shut up and keep walking, Lottie. I'm not carrying you. I'm done being your servant. Why not go find some boab tree and etch today's date into its trunk. That should keep you occupied until you get rescued. I'll send help in a few days—if I survive.' Nope, she was doing this. *Hell, yeah.*

'You'd leave me out here? Alone?' Lottie's voice rose in horror. 'You'd desert me, *again*?'

That cut deep, forcing Teà's step to falter. Even livid at Lottie, she couldn't share that secret. It was Teà who'd been the daughter their father had abandoned. Twice.

'Walk, princess. Shut up and walk.'

'I can't. I don't understand what's happening.' Lottie crumbled to the ground, a miserable whiny wretch.

Teà stopped.

Did she dare pamper the woman, or should she do what she really wanted and slap Lottie over the head?

Or did she turn her back on her family for good?

A solitary wallaroo stood on the verge, where the track met the mulga scrub filled with deep thickets of

Lancewood and Bullwaddy trees. Its fawn coat was soft, the stocky shoulders square, with its black-tipped ears twitching.

Lottie's echoing whimpers were truly pitiful.

Teà spun around in her boots, barely containing her anger. '*Get up.*' She roughly dragged her sister to her feet. 'Put your swag over your shoulder. Slather on this sunscreen.' Teà slapped the sunscreen into her sister's palm.

'Can I trust you with the water, or do you want me to keep it? Because only our survival matters now. Not the car, or the farm. This is all about *us. Surviving*.' Teà pointed back to the deserted track that ran past the Knockabout Stockyard.

Aw, wrack off! They hadn't even made fifty metres! At this rate they were never going to make it.

'Do you want to end up like those cattle carcasses surrounding the other Gregory Tree? Remember, this is the dry stretch Devin warned us about. It's the Highway to Nowhere.' Those last words made her swallow hard.

Lottie's voice was weak, the terror alive in the whites of her eyes. 'How long will it take us?'

'As long as it takes. Let's go. One foot after the other. Move.' Again, Teà started her steady stride along the track. They only had two choices: they could walk, or they could lay down and die.

Eleven

Teà's pace was impossible, Lottie struggled to keep up. They'd been walking for hours. Her feet hurt, she had blisters from her shoes that just sucked. It was hopeless.

'Was the duck really in the car?'

Teà's scowl was ferocious.

Obviously a taboo subject, but Lottie had to say something. To know that they were the only two human beings walking along a deserted stock route was mortifying. The panic churned so hard, she swallowed bile, suffering heartburn while too scared to sip on what little water they had.

'You're right. This is my fault.'

'Damned straight it is.' But Teà kept walking.

'I said I'm sorry.'

'What are you sorry for, Lottie? Losing the car? Wasting our water? Or for being such a control freak throughout this entire journey? You do realise all our money is in that car.'

'You had money. I saw it in your purse when we were at the roadhouse.'

'I emptied everything I had in my change-purse into the tin under the other Gregory Tree. The rest of it is tucked away in my backpack, sitting in the boot of the car.'

'Why did you give your money to a tree?'

Teà shrugged. 'It felt like the right thing to do. I found the pennies there, so I exchanged it.'

'Why?' She didn't get it. 'That money could've come in handy.'

'Hey, what I do with my money is my business. You were the one in charge of the budget, the one in charge of the car, so you were the one who stuffed up.'

'But—' Her big sister, Saint Teà was right. Again.

'I'm sorry.' Lottie had never said the word sorry so many times to anyone. Normally, she'd get away with it. 'I'm sorry. I'm not used to any of this.' Lottie waved her arm at the silver-leaf shrubs, under a pale blue sky. The only sound was the scuffing crunch of their shoes over the red gravel.

'No one is. We all enjoy the convenience of motor transport to take us to far distances, so we don't have to worry about bothering with, as our Ford-loving father used to call it, the old-fashioned foot-falcon.' Teà kept her boot stride sure and steady.

'I should've bought hiking boots when I had the chance.' Feeling the dirt sifting between her socks, filling her sneakers.

'It was on the list.'

'Fine, another thing for me to be sorry for.'

'No, you're not.' Teà's eyes were fiery beneath her scowl. 'You wear these invisible earmuffs, filtering out anything you don't want to hear, ignoring people who are trying to tell you something important. You're like this perverted version of the Japanese proverb of the three wise monkeys where they hear no evil, see no evil, speak no evil. Where you ignore all sound advice, while blind to any warning signs staring you in the face, doing only what Lottie wants.'

'I listen to brides about their gowns.' Her shaky voice was lost to the nothingness.

'You'd have to because they're paying you. But I bet you convince them on what to wear so they don't look like out-of-shape mouldy marshmallows.'

Lottie tightened her ponytail. 'I do have a reputation to

keep.'

'As the only dressmaker in your small town. The competition must be tough, huh? Do you even like dressmaking?'

'It pays the bills.'

'Not an answer, Lottie. We have all this time, so you'd better tell the truth.' Teà then jabbed her finger at Lottie. 'Not just to me, but to yourself. Hey, who knows, this could be our last conversation.'

'Stop it. You're scaring me.' Her heart pounded in her chest, her throat dry and scratchy like sandpaper.

'Good. You need to be scared.' Teà stabbed at the air between them. 'You need to get out of that comfort zone and break down that crusty cranky shell of a miserable woman I don't even like. What happened to the Lottie I knew? She has to be in there somewhere. Or is this wretched melodramatic excuse of a woman who you are now? Lemme guess, you have some perverted desire to play the part of suburbia's mythological Karen meme, with that I-demand-to-speak-to-the-manager ponytail of yours. I'm surprised someone hasn't shared one of your pathetically petty rants on TikTok, to entertain millions of people all over the globe. You'd have your own hashtag — *Karen in the wild!*' Teà's laughter was bitter on the breeze, now warming as the sun rose higher.

'There is no such thing.'

'You live in a bubble.'

'NO, you do! Volunteering to play Saint Teà in far-off countries. What were you doing out there anyhow?'

'Searching for something.'

'What?'

Teà shrugged. 'What was in Dad's letter?'

Lottie stumbled in the dirt.

'I've gotcha.' Teà's grip was firm around her arm, helping Lottie to correct her stance. 'Where's that hiking pole I made you?'

'In the back of the car.'

'With the duck.' Teà grimaced as she let go. 'Christ, I hope they're kind to that duck. We'll take a five-minute break.'

Under the dappled shade of the tree, Lottie dumped her heavy swag in the middle of the road. The swag was soft to sit on, giving her sweaty back and shoulders a reprieve.

Teà scrounged around the base of a large gum tree. Its grey bark was peeling in large butter curls around the bottom of its trunk, to reveal pristine white bark towards its crown. It had a wide canopy, with vibrant clusters of orange and scarlet fire balls of colour dangling like Christmas fairy lights among the draping olive-grey leaves. Among the thick limbs, black-winged cockatoos feasted on the nuts and flowers.

A small spiky-headed lizard scampered across the road as Teà pulled out a large stick tangled among the cream grasses bent over from the winds. 'This'll do.'

'What did you find?'

'For you.' Teà pulled Lottie to her feet.

Lottie could've stayed there all day lying on her swag, watching the birds and lizards. A stark contrast for a woman who never had time to sit back at home.

Teà sized up the branch. 'It's not as good as the one I made back in that dry riverbed, but it'll do.'

The pole was coarse in her hand, rough, yet round. 'I'm going to get splinters. Can I borrow —'

'No. You are not borrowing my gloves.' Teà dug around in her pack and pulled out the knife that she was always playing with. Etching the yellow handle of some silly tool Devin had given her, or whittling wood to make a dumb two-up paddle. No one played two-up anymore, except for Anzac Day.

'What are you doing with my swag?' Lottie wanted to cuddle her pillow, but Teà had dumped it in the dirt along with the rest of Lottie's fine linen, back at Knockabout Stockyards.

Teà unrolled Lottie's swag, removing the plaid sheet and began cutting the luxurious material into strips.

Lottie gasped at the horror unfolding before her. Every slice of Teà's pocketknife through the fabric scraped down her spine. 'What are you doing? That's Egyptian cotton. Those plaid sheets are—'

Teà's scowl silenced any further protests. She then wrapped a wide strip of plaid around the top end of the hiking stick's coarse wood, bandaging up a handle of sorts.

The realisation of what her sister had done for her brought on another set of fresh tears to sting Lottie's eyes.

'Pick up your swag.'

'But—?' What was Teà planning to do with the rest of the sheet? And how come she only cut up Lottie's swag and not her own, that she was busily plaiting into rope?

But then Teà wrapped the plaid rope around Lottie's swag to secure it against her upper back.

'Comfortable?'

'Not really …' Quickly responding to her sister's scowl. 'But it's much better.' Lottie couldn't lie. No matter how dire the situation. 'What do you want me to do with the rest of this sheet?' That lay limp in her hand.

'Didn't you say it was Egyptian cotton? Well, make a turban out of it. You're the dressmaker, make up something to cover your skin.' Teà dragged a lightweight linen scarf from her bag. In a well-practiced move, she threw it over her head, then around her neck like a hijab, covering her hair, neck, and face. 'We'll fry if we don't cover up.' She rolled down the sleeves of her shirt way past the knuckles. She scooped up her swag, adjusted her day pack, took a sip of her water, and started walking.

Again, Lottie struggled to keep up.

It took ages for her to work out the turban, because it kept slipping. But she finally managed to fashion something that protected her skin from the sun.

Her sweaty hand securely gripped the pole wrapped in cloth. After a few hours she'd finally found her hand-pole combination.

'Are you slowing down for me?' Pride and hope filled her chest that they could do this.

'Are you going to tell me what's in that letter?' Teà's steps were steady, her boot tracks firm in the shifting soil beneath their soles.

Lottie didn't want to think about her father's letter. Folded over so many times, it scratched against her skin, hidden inside her sweaty bra.

She pulled it out, the ink spreading from the sweat, the outside dirty. She wasn't leaving it behind and shoved it deep into the middle of her swag.

Readjusting her swag over her shoulder, she re-tied her headscarf and faced the road disappearing into the never-ending outback.

It really was the highway to nowhere!

Fear slammed into her throat, which was so dry. Licking her lips, all she could taste was salt and sunscreen, it was a putrid combination. But she didn't dare take a sip of water; Teà had them on water restrictions. She had to talk about something to get her mind off how dire their situation was. 'Dad left me the car.'

'Well, you drove it like you owned it.'

'You're not upset?'

'No. It's just a car to me.'

Lottie's eyes flared in surprise.

'It obviously means something to you.'

'Um, yeah.' She strained to force down the gritty lump in her raw throat. What she'd give for a glistening tall glass of water accompanied with a jug of iced tea. And a towering tub of ice cream.

'Go on …'

'I used to sit in the car and imagine going on road trips after you left.'

'I see.' A lopsided grin crept across Teà's face. 'That's why Dad had us drive it.'

'Dad remembered I always wanted to take it through

the centre of the country.'

'Which you can honestly say you did.'

They walked in silence for a while. The car was nowhere to be seen.

Hold the needle and thread. Was this trip a gift from her father? His way of saying goodbye to Lottie?

Duh, her father did say that in the letter!

Lottie winced, lifting a hand to shield her from the sun. Was her brain broiling, to not realise that sooner?

Her father had also been right about Teà.

Even though she hated Teà for dragging her arse out of bed this morning, to frogmarch her across this lonesome outback track, Lottie had to admit that without Teà she would never have left home. Or worse, she would've curled up in her swag to wait for someone to rescue her from the Knockabout Stockyards.

But not Teà. No way, buddy. Her big sister laced up her boots, and determinedly got them moving. Teà wasn't waiting to be rescued. No sir, that girl was rescuing herself, and Lottie was just being dragged along for the ride.

It brought on another glimmer of hope.

She tied the ends of her scarf under her chin, just like Queen Elizabeth did. The same way Teà dressed up the duck.

Oh, how marvellous …

Lottie's scarf captured the wind like a kite, cooling her skin.

She re-gripped her pole and followed her sister, refusing to think of dying alone like the many stockmen on this stock route. 'Did you know Dad was dying? It wasn't a sudden death.'

'I thought it was a stroke?'

'Brain tumours. Diagnosed a year ago, but Dad refused treatment.'

Teà barely nodded as a sign of recognition.

'Dad said you'd understand why he'd refused treatment.' It hurt that her father didn't want her help.

'I'd do the same.'

Lottie gasped, the dust shifting as she stopped walking. 'Why? Dad had so much to live for.'

Teà didn't stop, keeping that same steady pace. 'Dad spared you the unnecessary pain. Not only to you, but to your children. Believe me, that's a good thing. There's nothing worse than watching someone you love waste away in a hospital bed, waiting for them to take their last dying breath. Dad did you a favour.' Teà dug around in her daypack and produced a muesli bar.

Lottie's stomach clawed with hunger as her parched mouth salivated, rushing to catch up as Teà cracked the bar in half.

They ate in silence, sparing a few sips of water to wash down the crumbly oats as they kept plodding along.

'What happened to your mother?' Lottie asked. 'I know she passed away, but no one said much except she got sick.'

'Ovarian cancer.'

'When?'

'When they discovered she was pregnant with me.'

'Really?'

'My mother refused to undertake treatment until I was born.'

'How do you know?'

'Whenever Dad binged on the rum, which was usually the anniversary of her passing, he'd tell me.'

'Dad wouldn't blame you for your mother—'

'You bet he did. You could see it every time he looked at me.' Teà slammed her boot into a large stone like it was a football. It arched high above the pale pink wildflowers to land with a thud in the gravelly soil and dead grey grasses. 'I know he did. He used to tell me I looked like my mother, making us both feel guilty that she'd kept me instead of choosing to live.'

Their father couldn't be that bitter, could he? 'How old were you when she, um, passed?'

'Seven on my way to seventy.' Teà sighed, her eyes squinting at the horizon, each step steady. 'By that stage, we'd been through years of constant trips to the hospital for chemo treatments. Having our hopes rise over some latest operation that hacked away at my mother from the outside, while this disease was eating away at her from the inside. And the pain she was in …'

'You remember it?'

'It's impossible to forget.' Teà shook her head but kept on walking. 'After school I'd collect the newspaper for Dad at the newsagent, then pop in next door to the pharmacy where Ruth Oxford would give me my mother's medications.' Teà scowled. Her heavy step more pronounced, as if stalking to kick another rock. 'I did my homework beside Mum's hospital bed. Played hopscotch in the corridor or slid down the bannisters in the loading docks. I was on a first-name basis with the staff, because we spent so much time trapped inside those wishy-washy walls. It might sound like a horrible thing to say, but we all put our lives on hold.'

'How?'

'We were living like you. Never venturing too far from the farm or from Mum's hospital bed.'

Again, Lottie stopped, gasping at the dry air. She did not live like that. Did she?

'Don't get me wrong, my mother was truly a wonderful woman.' Teà's tone softened, even sharing a wispy smile. 'I loved my mother. Dad completely loved her. He was so heartbroken when my mother passed that he took off, leaving me in the care of my grandparents.'

Lottie's eyebrows rose. Their father abandoned Teà? It couldn't be true. 'How come I'd never heard about this?'

Teà sneered.

'I was ten when *you* left Me! Our father wouldn't do that, desert us. So you take that back.'

'You were a baby, so how would you know. And I'm sure Dad wouldn't want to talk about it, or that you'd be bothered to listen to my sob story.' Teà's scowl was ferocious. Head down, her pace quickened.

They strolled in silence with the curiosity gnawing at her. Lottie had to ask. 'Where did Dad go?'

Teà shrugged. 'He wasn't gone long. My grandparents died in a car accident, and he came back with a new wife and baby.' Teà narrowed her cold eyes at Lottie. It wasn't jealousy or rage; it was something unreadable.

Lottie had to look away. 'I thought your mother died on the farm.'

'Mum wanted to. My grandparents and Dad begged the doctors to let Mum come home. But we couldn't afford a full-time nurse to care for her. They could barely afford the medicine as it was. Dad wasn't working, what with looking after Mum. We struggled for a while.'

'What happened?'

'Mum finally passed away.' Teà faced the road, heaving a deep breath. It sounded more like a sigh of relief. 'Mum is buried with her parents, in the graveyard beside the church where you were baptised. I remember you as this tiny baby, wearing this big dress that was made from your mother's wedding gown. Do you still have that christening gown? I remember Lauren wrapping it up in special tissue paper.'

'I do.' Lottie raised her head, her heart warm at the memory. 'I used it for both my children. It's an heirloom I'm hoping they'll use for their children.'

Teà's hard eyes softened as her stride slowed a fraction. 'That's nice. Lauren would've liked that. I'm sorry I wasn't there for Lauren's funeral … and for Dad's.'

'How come you weren't?'

Teà's brow creased into a frown as she brushed at the dust along her nose. 'Would you have wanted me there?'

'I kind of hoped you'd show up. When my mother passed, Dad was sad. But only on the day she died. Then it was business as usual.' Lottie scrunched up her sweaty forehead, swallowing the hot air, gripping her pole tighter.

'Dad ticked me off, making me believe he didn't care that my mother was gone. He didn't react at all. Nothing. Not compared to your mother —'

Teà spun around and stood mere inches from Lottie's face. 'If my mother had terminated me and got treatment for her cancer, she would have survived. Instead, she chose me! And my father never forgave me for that. Don't you get it? Our father had to carry the burden of asking *was today the day the love of his life was going to die? A* question he was forced to ask for over seven freaking years!' Teà's hurt was loud and clear in words that tore a gaping wound in the silent world.

Lottie floundered for some offering of a condolence, but she was completely speechless.

And yet it explained so much about her father, the way he'd reacted to her own mother's passing. Tea was right, people did grieve in different ways.

It also made sense why Teà didn't get close to people. A single woman at Teà's age was what her mother would have called an old maid.

'Can you believe Dad never let my husband help on the farm?' Lottie asked after some time.

'When did this start?'

'Adrian only mentioned it to me back at the roadhouse, and Dad mentioned it in his letter.'

'And you never noticed it? Not once. The entire time you two were married.' Again, Teà sneered at her.

The flames of shame licked at Lottie's cheeks from another relentless lesson slamming her in the face. Sheepishly, she dropped her head. How oblivious had she become to not notice sooner?

'Dad said in the letter, it-it was a good thing,' Lottie stuttered, desperate to save face. 'Dad wrote he was proud of Adrian, providing for me and our family. Making his own money.'

'I bet Dad did that to Adrian because it happened to him.'

'Excuse me?'

'Dad used to bitch about his masculinity and his pride as the breadwinner being slapped around for looking after my mother, living off my grandparents who were busy working the farm. Dad was trapped in this situation; did he go to work or stay by his wife's bedside?'

'I feel like I don't know the man.' The father she'd shared the same roof with all her life.

'You saw the good side of Victor Voss, Lottie.' Teà tenderly touched her upper arm.

'Dad did thank me for letting him be a big part of our lives, watching his grandchildren grow.'

Teà's hand fell, her head lifting to the wind as she resumed her stride. 'Dad was a proud man. He enjoyed standing on his own two feet. Victor Voss didn't like anyone else being the boss of him, either. Maybe he was sending a message to Adrian to not become some freeloader on the farm.'

'Adrian's not like that. He works hard on the mines.'

'Adrian got to escape.' Teà's grin grew as her stride picked up. 'Running away for two weeks, then home for a week to just sit back with his feet up. That's a sweet deal.'

'My husband—not that you'd know how to be with a husband—does not sit back and rest at home.' Okay, he did, irritating Lottie to no end. Not that she'd share that with Teà. 'Adrian runs errands for me when he takes the kids to school. He takes them on excursions after school and on weekends so I can work in peace.'

'So, Adrian gets to be the fun dad, while you stay behind to play the cranky mummy.' Teà's teasing tone was irritating. Even worse when she practically skipped along the trail.

'In Dad's letter he said he respected Adrian for putting his family first.' With her nose in the air, she tugged her ponytail tighter. 'Adrian loves me.'

'If he didn't, Adrian would've divorced your cranky, controlling ass a long time ago. Not only did he put up with Dad's old-fashioned macho ways, but you!' The sound of Teà's laugh was bittersweet.

A laugh so unexpected, Lottie almost forgot their situation. 'You're right.' She should've frowned. She should've bit back or something. Instead, the most extraordinary thing happened …

Lottie laughed, too.

Her laughter echoed around her, magically lightening the weight across her shoulders, allowing her to stand taller and open her chest, so she could breathe easier.

Her father, her husband, even her sister had been right. Lottie needed to take a good look around. She needed to let go.

Her step quickened to a spritely stroll, keeping up with her sister as they reached a small rise in the road.

'Oh no.' Teà stopped, as her jaw dropped.

Lottie followed the direction Teà was facing, where the red road disappeared on the horizon. There was nothing out there. No buildings. No houses. No traffic to stir up the dust to let them know there was a car coming. Nothing but the desolate outback.

It wasn't just the highway to nowhere—it was the highway to hell!

'We're going to die out here, aren't we?'

Twelve

Devin sat leaning his back against the wall, his elbow resting on the bar of the Topp Spring's Roadhouse. On the far side of the room, a wide-screen TV replayed last night's footy match. The jukebox played some random tune.

By the windows, a few stockmen played a game of cards, while more cradled their beers at the wooden bar, sharing tall stories of the last muster. All of them sun hardened, with red dirt ingrained in their sweat-stained Akubra's. It was in their clothes, their calloused hands, and even in the creases around their eyes.

Pearl, the owner, pushed chairs under tables, wiping over their laminated tops. Giving a satisfied nod, she headed back to the bar. 'Another beer, Devin?'

'Ta.' He put his empty glass on the bar mat and went back to staring at the view of the road through the glass doors.

'Are you waiting for someone?'

'Could be.'

'Me too.' Pearl checked her watch. 'We're expecting a lot of visitors this weekend. Are you racing in the Pussyfoot Cup?'

'Nope.'

'What about barrel racing with the girls, luv?'

He grinned over the fresh beer. Pearl sure knew how to pour the perfect beer, unlike some backpacking barmaids. 'Where's Patrick at?'

'There …' She glanced at the middle-aged man coming through the side door. 'Got 'em all sorted, luv?'

'Campgrounds gonna be chokkas. Got a few more caravans than expected. The rooms are full.' Patrick pulled out his ledger from behind the bar. 'G'day, Devin. You still here?'

'For another night.'

'Good to see you're getting out and about. I like your new helicopter. Jezza and the lads are stoked with theirs. They've got muster bookings, and even a couple of tour flights this weekend. Can you see yourself doing the tourist thing?'

'Hmph.' Devin had done his bit, playing tour guide to a couple of sisters.

Again, he looked at the door, and then at his watch. 'You haven't had a couple of sisters by the name of Voss show up, yet?' He may have missed them while he was offloading trailers.

'Not yet, luv,' said Pearl. 'We saved them the best rooms in the house. We're not givin' 'em up for no one. Promised Vossy I did.'

Devin squinted his eyes at the publican. 'Did you know Victor Voss?'

'Too right, I did.' Pearl gave a short sharp nod, plonking a hand on her bony hip. 'He was a proper scallywag, that Victor Voss. But I owed him one, and I always keep my promises …' She paused to straighten the bar mats that decorated the countertop. 'I wonder what Vossy's daughters are like?' Pearl narrowed her grey eyes at the front doors that faced the intersection where the Buchanan and Barclay Highways met, both roads made of dirt. 'You've got that letter ready, luv?'

Patrick flicked through the thick ledger kept behind the counter. '*For the Voss Sisters*,' he read from the envelope's white face. 'All tucked up in here for when they arrive, luv.'

Devin shuffled in his seat. 'When are you expecting

them?'

'Lawyer rang and told us they were coming,' replied Pearl. 'He told us they'd show up today if they kept to the schedule. How do you know them, luv? Especially since you don't talk to strangers?'

'I met them at Rusty's Roadhouse, where Rusty delivered a letter, sending them down the Murranji Track. Do you know where the Voss sisters are headed?'

'Nope. Just instructions to pass on this letter. Along with a wad of dosh to pay for their meals and accommodation for a few days. We've been holding on to Vossy's letter for months.' Pearl paused. 'May God rest his scallywag soul.' She remained silent for a moment, her husband tenderly rubbing her wiry shoulders.

Pearl then adjusted the other side of the bar mat, to create a perfect join in the pattern advertising some beer brand. 'When did you see the Voss sisters?'

'Yesterday. Left them at Bore 13. They were heading to the other Gregory Tree.'

Pearl shuddered. 'Hate that place.'

'Told them to camp at the Knockabout Stockyards last night.' If he didn't have the trailers on, he may have followed them down that track.

Patrick tapped his watch face. 'If the Voss Sisters camped at Knockabout last night, they should've shown up long before lunchtime.'

'Not with Lottie's driving.' Devin shook his head, his thumb wiping down the cool condensation on his beer glass. 'A drunken steer could walk faster than that woman's driving.' Lottie was a shocker of a driver. Teà must have the patience of an unnamed saint to put up with that. If Devin was in Teà's position, he would've demanded he take over after ten minutes. If that. *Can you spell d-r-i-v-e to the speed limit, son?*

'Which one's Lottie, luv?' Pearl asked.

'The younger Voss sister. Short, blonde hair. A royal whiny pain in the arse.' Not once did that Little Miss

Uppity thank him for helping them out. 'They don't even look like sisters.' He shouldn't even be thinking about them, wasting his time watching for that old blue Ford. He should've gone home at daybreak, as planned.

'What is the other sister like, luv?'

'Teà.' He sighed, wiping off the fine sheen of dust across his face. 'Tall, black hair, dark eyes. Smart. And tough.' His lips curled into a soft smile. 'You should've seen her shimmy up that windmill to get the note from their father, and how she held on during a nasty willy-willy too.'

'That gully's a nightmare for those willy-willys. They nearly pushed me off the road in the ute a coupla times,' said Patrick.

'Teà held on. Covered in dust.' He'd never been more relieved, wiping the dust from his eyes, with his whole heart in his throat, to discover Teà hadn't let go of the rope. And neither had he. Devin had to admire that about her. 'Teà's got grit.' G-r-i-t. By the bucket loads.

Devin swung around to face the bar, keeping his back to the door, cradling his beer. Teà could handle anything. He didn't need to worry about her. She'd worked on oil rigs, in deserts and oceans.

Yet he was still here, hoping to share another beer with her. Perhaps another sunset together, to watch the last rays of the sun, and the way it reflected off her hair like black water.

Hell, if he was honest, he wanted to share the same breathing space with the female who was all feline grace, with her long, steady, silent stares that would evaluate him as a man. Not for who he was or what he had, just the man in the moment.

He wanted to rummage through the truck's toolbox to find more gifts for Teà, to see her smile again. That woman didn't smile enough. But when she did, dammit — the earth tilted off its freaking axis.

No one looked at a simple ten-dollar tool the way Teà

did. When he'd handed her his chipping hammer, the appreciation in her eyes was more than just gratitude. It was a moment when the world had truly slipped away in slow motion to leave just the sound of his hammering heart.

He'd only bought that hammer at some southern roadside tool shop when loading up the trailers. It was small enough to get into the space beneath the handle of the ratchet strap and the base of the helicopter. It had been lying on the floor of the truck ever since. He didn't know why he gave it to her, he just did.

But the way Teà gripped that chipping hammer, and how she'd smiled up at him, it was as if he'd given her the entire universe. Wearing the best form of make-up he'd ever seen on a woman—a thick layer of red dust—sharing a smile that wasn't half-hearted, but a full, wide, raw and revealing smile. Yet it was so much more than a smile, especially the way her mouth curved; it somehow magically repaired the frowns he was so used to hiding behind, making him want to smile with her.

Even now he was wiping at the smile daring to form on the corners of his mouth that normally didn't bother to smile. All because of a woman named Teà Voss. *Can you spell b-e-a-u-t-i-f-u-l, son?*

Behind him the door opened suddenly, followed by a large commotion. Chairs scraped across the concrete floor. Glasses fell, playing cards scattered, as people shouted, and feathers flew.

'What the hell is going on?' Pearl wore the pants in this pub and everyone knew it.

'It's this duck, Pearl.' A ringer in a crusty hat, with a missing front tooth, held up a squawking duck. 'It's wearing checks like someone's dressed it up like a doll.'

'Nah, that's tartan, ya drongo,' said another bloke.

'It's the same as me flannel shirt, but fancier,' said another stockman. 'Who'd dress up a bloody Burdekin duck for? They're protected.'

'What did you say?' Devin shoved past the men to the centre of the room where they stood around the ringer holding a white-headed, web-footed Burdekin duck. 'Where did you find that duck?'

'It was staggering all over the road, near your truck, boss.'

The duck flapped and carried on; the ringer struggled to hold on.

Devin recognised the plaid bandage on its sore leg.

'Let it go.' Devin's voice was strong. Used to being in charge.

The duck quacked and hissed, trying to flap its wings, as it limped heavily across the table, only to leap into Devin's arms.

'What are you doing here, duck?' It had grease on its bill, but there was blood splattered on its white chest feathers and on the plaid scarf that had fallen around its shoulders. 'Is this your blood?' He asked the ringer, looking on with concern.

The ringer held up his hands like he was under arrest. 'Nah, I swear boss, he was like that. Squawkin' and carrying on like it was hurt.'

'Do you know that duck, Devin?' Pearl asked.

'It's Teà's duck ....' His stomach knotted, as the hair on the back of his neck pricked under an icy chill that ran deep into the marrow of his bones. 'Something's happened to the Voss sisters.'

Thirteen

The heavy hostile air danced around them as it sucked the moisture from the soil, their skin, and from their souls.

Sunburn chapped Teà's lips as the wind churned the dust to swirl around her boots, filtering grit into her eyes, as she mind numbingly put one foot in front of the other, step after step after step.

'Can't we stop for a minute?' Lottie pressed her dirty palms together as if in prayer. Her plaid sheet was tossed over her head and shoulders like an Arabian hijab, without the colour and pizazz of a belly dancer. But the plaid material highlighted the blue in her eyes. Sadly, it also pronounced her sister's cracked lips and burnt cheeks.

Teà didn't enjoy playing the bad guy, but she was afraid if they stopped, they wouldn't start again. She peeked at her watch, hidden in her pocket. 'We rested half an hour ago. We've got to keep going. Here, put more of this on.' She held out the sunscreen.

'It's not working.' Lottie pushed her hand away and shunted along with heavy steps, the soles barely hanging on to the body of her shoes. 'It's melting off faster than I apply it. Or it's like adding oil to the frying pan accelerating the cooking process that was once pristine skin.' Lottie exposed the pink skin on her arms. 'I'm ageing a hundred days every minute. My skin is like a plucked chicken sitting in an oven's roasting pan with tight skin about to crack, or it's wrinkles upon wrinkles to create crevices of dirt.' She grimaced, wiping at the sweaty dirt and grime gathered in the crack of her inner elbows. 'I know how damaging the Australian sun is. I always make sure my children wear sunscreen every single day. Yet, here I am, literally blistering and broiling alive.' Lottie paused in her prattle that had been nothing more than a continuous stream of gibberish for hours.

But it stopped Lottie from panicking.

'I wonder if Adrian remembered to put sunscreen on our children. Do you think he did?'

'I'm sure Adrian did. Here, Lottie, drink some of this.' Teà held out the water bottle.

'But that's your water.'

Even if they were going through it so fast, her little sister needed it. 'It's this or you'll start sucking on some green ant bums.'

'Ugh.'

'I hear it tastes like lemon.'

'Fine, this'll do.' Lottie took a tiny sip, barely enough to wet her lips.

'You can have a big mouthful.' Besides her baby sister's ramble of utter nonsense, Lottie was dehydrated, suffering from a slight hangover from the few beers last night.

Teà remembered her first bout of dehydration, the dizziness, the body cramps, and the crippling headaches that went with it. And she was a hell of a lot more accustomed to the extreme heat than her sister.

Again, Lottie staggered with a crab-walking sidestep, forcing Teà to hook her arm through her sister's to keep them on the straight and narrow. They needed to keep moving.

Food they could go without. Squinting at the unfamiliar scenery, Teà tried to remember her father's camping lessons on bush tucker. She could never remember if it was okay to eat the black berries or the red ones that teased her from nearby shrubs. Did she dare lick at the nectar dripping from the flowering grevilleas like the birds did for energy?

'There's another one of your Cousin It trees.' Lottie barely raised her arm to point.

It had been a joke, miles back when they first spotted them rising from red desert sands. A tall skinny shrub reminding them of a fluffy green *Cousin It* from *The Addams Family*. But on closer inspection, the fluffy foliage was green strings of tiny cactus spikes, worse than rose thorns.

Following the Ford's tyre tracks, she searched for signs of water among the cream tufts of dried grass lining the sides of the red road, that sometimes went blue under shadows.

Time dragged as they trudged through scalding sand, so thick in pockets it had bogged the car, evident from the tyre tracks. And the genius makeshift gathering of twigs and barks used to help the Ford get past the quagmire. There were two vehicles, the Ford was following another set of sturdy four-wheel drive tyres.

They followed those same tyre tracks where the road blended into pockets of buttery cream, before turning into a compact black soil, between the generous stretches of crushed ochre crunching beneath her boots.

But it was always the same shimmery watery road that disappeared on the curve of the horizon, and where those heartbreaking limestone ridges got no closer. Once they'd stood like soft custard-coloured curvy ranges, shifting to shades of a dirty rugged red, now going purple as that glowing sphere of gas and fire sent its piercing rays of light to burn their skin.

Then Lottie stopped. Her eyes squinting into the distance. 'Do you hear that?'

A few birds squawked, cooed, and laughed. No doubt sharing the news on the outback telegraph of two silly white girls staggering along the Murranji Track.

They'd been walking this track since sunrise and hadn't seen a soul all day. Not one car.

A few hours ago, hope had flared sky high when they'd found an airstrip alongside the road, complete with a windsock and brightly painted stones to outline the smooth dirt runway. But they'd wasted precious time and energy searching for a tap, a water tank, something. Who'd build an airstrip in the middle of nowhere like that?

They'd spotted cows, a dingo, wallabies, brumbies, and goannas. They'd screamed as they danced on their toes around a long, fat snake. But they'd paused to smile at a camel weaving amongst the low bush with her baby in tow.

And they saw lots and lots of birds, who were getting the best seat in the house anticipating their demise, following their journey like they were part of some televised drama of *Survivor*, outback style.

Lottie cocked her head, a spark in her once sunken eyes. She gripped Teà's hand. 'Listen.'

Teà dropped her head to listen.

It was too soon for Lottie to completely lose the plot, imagining sounds. Next, it'd be visions of some mirage being born under this sweltering forty-plus-degree heat. Which would work out to be well over a hundred degrees in Fahrenheit.

'What am I meant to be hearing?' Behind her was nothing but the long red track. Up ahead, the same. But in the distance, a flock of birds scattered along the tree line. 'It's the birds, that's all. Something must have frightened them.'

'Just like the time Devin tooted his truck's horn.'

'Air horn. They're fun. Fog horns on ships are better. I had one strapped to my bike and used it to wake up misbehaving drivers who couldn't see me when I was lane splitting through traffic.' Now who was rambling?

'What's lane splitting?'

'It is when you ride your motorbike between the rows of cars lined up at traffic lights.'

'They scare me when they ride like that, I worry some

biker is going to knock off my side mirrors.'

'Never touched them. But I've seen some riders punch at them when a car gets too close. People don't look for motorbikes, all cocooned in their cage on wheels, with the AC blowing and some music blaring, yakking on their phones. Do you do that?'

'Do what?'

'Play music?'

'Mostly the radio. I imagine you'd have a special playlist.'

'I do.' Funny thing was, Teà couldn't remember a single song. Should she turn on her phone, and scroll for some happy singalong tunes? Or did she save the battery?

Lottie cupped her hand behind her ear. 'Can't you hear that?'

Teà held her breath and listened hard as more birds fled to the skies.

Honk. Hooooonk!

She wiped the sweat from around her eyes as if to eavesdrop on the outback's secrets carried by the hostile heat that barely created a breeze.

Honk. Hooooonk!

'Is someone coming?' *Please be real. Please be real.* Another group of white galahs bounded high from the treetops to head northwards.

'There! Look, Teà.' Lottie pointed to the road's end where a watery haze rose from the sunburnt soil. It hurt her eyes.

Was it possible she'd fried her eyeballs?

The haze shifted, playing tricks on her, making it hard to focus, but it looked like something big was moving behind the glassy waves of heat.

Again, she rubbed at her gritty eyes and focused harder. *No. It can't be.*

'Is that Devin?' She croaked hoarsely, her throat like sandpaper.

It *was* Devin. Seated high in the driver's seat of his

truck, sharing another round of horn blasts. *Honk. Hooooonk!*

Suddenly Lottie had all the energy in the world. Dumping her swag and pole to wave her torn sheet high in the air like a plaid flag, as Devin shifted down through the truck's gears.

Teà could only stand and watch. This wasn't real.

'Look. It's Devin.' With a wide smile, Lottie skipped ahead to meet the truck. She was that little girl all over again, merrily greeting their father on his return to the farm in his old truck.

But it was a modern beast of a semi-trailer, void of any trailers. It pulled up with a hiss, and it was as if the entire world of hostile heat sighed.

The door opened and just like the first time she'd spotted him on the lone highway, Devin jumped effortlessly from the truck. Only this time, with his sexy cowboy swagger and that wide hat brim shading his eyes, he completely and absolutely took her breath away.

'Are you girls okay?'

This time, she didn't mind him calling her a girl. She didn't care what he called them.

Lottie hugged Devin, who gave her a cold bottle of water that she quickly poured over her feverish head as she drank from another.

Maybe this little hike had done Lottie some good. It certainly made time for conversation, and a lot of crap got aired.

But not everything.

'Teà? Are you okay?' Devin rushed toward her, carrying a humongous water bottle, as tears welled in her eyes.

'You're here?' Or was this some cruel mirage of her most perfect fantasy, floating on some happy cloud of dust?

'I am.' His hand rested on her shoulder.

He was real! 'H-how—what are you doing here? Why?'

Her fingers, feeling his cool shirt, the skin on his arms, the strength in his shoulders, the shine in his eyes. He was really here.

'I got worried about you. Are you okay?'

A single tear trickled down her cheek as the smile widened across her face. She just couldn't stop smiling. Struggling to catch her breath, she couldn't stop staring at those captivating caramel coffee eyes that were deliciously better than just brown. 'I am now.'

Bugger her inner rules that only loaded her up with layers of loneliness, she needed to feel. And now. Throwing her arms around his broad shoulders, gripping him tightly to just breathe him in. 'I know I stink, and I'm sweaty and gross, but I need this right now.' Like her lungs demanded air, her mind, body and soul craved to hold him tighter, in a hug that was worth more than a thousand words and more than money could buy.

'You're not gross. Not at all,' he said close to her ear, holding her just as tight.

'Thank you, thank you, thank you.' She clung to him as all the negativity in her world disappeared. She held him, or he was holding her. She didn't care that it was longer than a hug should last. Only better.

Feeling that pull in her chest as the strength in his hug eased, she'd expected him to let her go, instead he just held her, tenderly stroking her hair, while her tears of joy dampened his shirt.

'Are you sure you're okay?' He wiped at her tears. Even though he was trying to be gentle, his fingers felt like sandpaper on her oversensitive sunburnt skin.

'I'm okay. A bit thirsty.' Her trembling hands struggled to unscrew the lid on the water bottle.

Devin opened it, even helping her lift it. 'A bit?'

'I'd wrestle a crocodile for a spot in his river, kind of thirst.' She spoke between gulps of refreshing water, letting it trickle down her shirt, to cool her skin. 'I thought you were out delivering helicopters.' She pointed to the truck free from any trailers where Lottie was busily guzzling more water. 'Please tell me that truck has air conditioning?'

'It does. Come on, let's get you out of the sun.' His fingers laced through hers to lead her to the truck. 'The owners at Topp Springs have your rooms ready.'

'I could do with a shower. Do they have a pool? I'd settle for a muddy puddle if they had one.'

His smile was glorious, and his laugh infectious. She leaned into his side for support. She didn't care if she was breaching boundaries; she needed to lean on someone. Who better than her freaking hero?

'Someone wants to say hello.' He opened the truck's passenger door, and she craned her neck up to wince at a face full of feathers.

'Quacker?' Happiness flooded her so much her legs weakened. She thought she'd die from pure joy. 'Where? How?' She checked over the duck, making a fuss. Or was that her babbling?

'A ringer found him on the road. That's how I knew something was wrong.'

There was no stopping the well of happy tears now. Not only did she hold the snuggling duck, she also couldn't stop hugging Devin. 'I'm sorry, I'm not normally this emotional.'

'It's okay, you've been through an ordeal.' His touch was so gentle and surprisingly intimate.

'It was Teà who kept us going.' Lottie, with bright eyes, had miraculously recovered, straightening out her ponytail. 'Teà said we'd be okay.'

Devin handed out cold rags dripping with deliciously cold water. He wrapped one around Teà's hot neck. 'How long have you been walking?'

'Teà hid her watch and wouldn't tell me. It's been a while. We started before the sun got up.' Lottie talked in between mouthfuls of water, while wiping down her face.

'Teà?' His eyes locked on hers. 'How long?'

'Eleven-and-a-half hours. We're okay, thanks to you.' She patted his muscular chest. 'We're okay, aren't we, Quacker? I'm so glad you're okay.' Hugging the cooing bird, it snuggled into the crook of her neck. She never got this attached to an animal. It never happened. Let alone a wild bird.

'Come on, let's go to Topp Springs.' Devin helped Lottie climb up first. 'There's another letter waiting for you both.'

That killed the joyous reunion. 'We lost.' Her chest ached with the responsibility landing heavily over her shoulders.

'What do you mean?'

'Whoever stole the car, stole Dad's ashes. If we can't deliver Dad's ashes to his final resting place, the inheritance deal is over ...' Only now did she allow herself to think of the loss, considering all the effort they'd put into this. They'd lost.

Even Lottie knew it, defeatedly sinking into her seat inside the truck.

Devin gave Teà's shoulder a tender squeeze. 'Hey, we'll sort something out. Don't give up.'

'Normally, I don't give up that easily.' But ...

'I noticed. Look at what you've just done.'

A small smile spread at the realisation, as did the inner courage inside in her chest. She was still here. Still standing. Damn, they'd made it. The pleasure prickles rushed over her scalp. They'd made it.

She gently cupped his cheek, so tempted to kiss his lips. Instead, her lips barely brushed his strong jawline, peppered with a sexy dark shadow. 'Thank you. For just being here.'

'I'm glad to be here for you.'

She didn't have the energy to fight her emotions that

were free and wildly full of life. She was alive. And all she could do was lean into him as if to feed off his energy.

'Can we go? I'm starving,' whined Lottie.

Devin rolled his eyes, but the shine matched his smile. 'Did you teach your sister any manners on your walk?'

'We've made a start.'

'Good. Come on.' He held out his hand to her like a gentleman. 'I believe it's your shout for a beer?'

'Um … We lost our cash and our bankcards in that car. All I can shout is gallons of water.'

'Hey, don't worry about that. I'll take care of you and your sister.' He gave her hand another encouraging squeeze. She didn't want to let go. 'Right now, let's get you to the roadhouse so Pearl can spoil you both. She knew your father.'

Devin helped her climb into the cab and settle into the middle seat, the duck in her lap. With her sister on one side, and Devin on the other, Teà was glad to see the last of the Murranji Track.

Pity it was game over. They'd lost the car, her father's ashes, and the inheritance challenge for the farm …

But with Lottie reaching for her hand and giving it a squeeze, the fragile bonds of sisterhood had truly begun to heal. Somehow that made it all worth it.

Fourteen

Teà rested her bare feet on the neighbouring barstool, her back leaning against the wall, giving her a magnificent view of the Topp Springs roadhouse.

According to Pearl the double P in Topp stood for the owners, Patrick and Pearl. The amazing middle-aged couple who had greeted the Voss sisters like long-lost daughters from the moment they'd arrived in Devin's truck last night.

While Lottie was being fed and hydrated, practically falling asleep in the bar, Teà sat on the phone reporting the car stolen with the police. But Lottie had lost more than just cash and her bag, she'd lost her pride over the car and the farm, too. Failure was a tough lesson for Lottie.

The soft morning sunshine highlighted the duck's pristine white feathers, where it waddled around the base of her bar stool, playing with one of her boot's laces.

Further along, Patrick was busily putting down chairs and sorting out tables, getting ready for a big day. While Pearl laid out bar mats, stacked glasses and checked the kegs from behind the long bar.

Teà plucked up a penny she'd been soaking in a dish of cola, rubbing at its copper surface with a polishing cloth. She'd been wracking her brain trying to find a way to salvage their situation. The car was gone, the urn gone, and this silly game their father had them on was over before they could finish it. Yet they were so close.

She dropped the penny back into the dish to soak some more. Took a sip of her coffee—she'd drunk more than enough water for a while—then removed the other large penny and started polishing it up. The copper was starting to shine.

The side door to the rooms pushed opened and in strolled Devin. His boot stride sure and steady, in well-worn jeans that hugged a set of sturdy thighs only highlighting the roll of his hips in a swagger that just exuded raw sex appeal. Fantasy be damned, he was hot. And her hero.

Devin made himself a coffee at the urn steaming at the far end of the bar.

She couldn't wipe the smile off her face—even though she tried, it wouldn't stop. And that rushing swell in her chest made her sit straighter with that ooze of warmth spreading all over. 'Of all the gin joints, you had to walk into mine …'

'You stole my seat.' Devin lifted her legs, putting her bare feet in his lap.

Whoa! She may have been a vulnerable mess yesterday, but today, she was back in control. Lottie, however, was still recovering—or sulking. 'What are you doing?' She pushed the hem down on her borrowed dress.

'Being nice. What are you doing?' His thumbs pushed into her bare feet, rubbing them, tenderly pressing on her pressure points.

'Polishing pennies …' Her back arched, her eyes fluttered shut, as goosebumps washed over her head and down her spine. 'Aww, that is so good.' She could purr.

But she couldn't afford to fall under his spell.

Okay, five minutes.

Maybe ten …

'Who taught you to do this?' She was in heaven. Right here. Right now.

'Mum. She used to pay me and my brother to rub her feet. I was going to offer last night, but you and Lottie were curled up like sleeping babies. Where is your sister?'

That sobered her up enough to find her strength to sit upright. 'Still in bed.' She braced herself, sliding into her socks, then her boots. 'Yikes.' Thank the heavens for Pearl and her pills. And for a decent bootmaker.

'Let me help.' Devin squatted down to help her lace up her boots. No man ever did that.

'Thank you.' Was this how Cinderella felt? Except her glass slippers were a pair of boots, and the prince was a truck-driving helicopter pilot.

Devin gently stroked the duck's head, and it leaned into his leg. If it was a cat it'd purr, too.

'Is your sister okay?'

'Lottie's upset we lost Dad's urn.' Besides, Lottie deserved some time out to relax, and to sleep for as long as she needed it. It didn't sound like Lottie took any time out for herself. 'I'm as much to blame for not locking up the car.'

Devin playfully nudged her arm as they faced the bar. 'Hey, have some faith. People around here are quite superstitious. I bet as soon as those car thieves find that urn they'll pull over and leave it there.'

'But where?' She wanted it here.

'The lad's right, luv.' Pearl joined them, straightening up the bar mats that lay beneath the polished pennies. 'Word's out about the Ford being stolen, and how you girls were bringing an old stockman home to rest. A lot of blokes round here respect that. You bet they'll be keeping an eye out for it.'

'Our last day is tomorrow. The lawyer was very specific about us scattering Dad's ashes somewhere by four o'clock tomorrow afternoon.' She tapped on the standard business sized envelope—another breadcrumb from her father when she'd been hoping for answers.

There had to be a reason for this trip, other than a gift for Lottie to realise her childhood dream of driving the Ford through central Australia. There was something else brewing—especially with her father's specific time to finish this trek. Another secret, perhaps?

She knew her father was big on secrets. Ones she never wanted to reveal to Lottie, not when they'd just started to become friends.

But it was also a stark reminder to not get involved with Devin. She couldn't. Even though it was a struggle to put the lid back on her feelings for the guy, it couldn't go anywhere. Devin was a smart guy, he understood that. After tomorrow who knows where she'd end up. She had no plans, except to be with Lottie—not Devin.

And she still needed to figure out what to do with the duck waddling across the shiny floor of the roadhouse. A strip of bandage around its leg, his limp barely visible, and the bent feathers on its wing were almost fully aligned. She needed to find that duck a billabong, to at least give someone a happy ending to this road trip.

'What did this letter say?' Devin asked.

She unfolded the envelope and read: *'Welcome to Topp Springs, and to my favourite friend Pearl's place. Sit a spell at her bar, as you gather all the pieces of the maps and work on the puzzle from x to x to show my final resting place.'*

She sighed, folding up the letter. 'All the pieces of the map are in the car, rolled up next to the urn on the front seat beside Lottie's handbag, which is carrying our entire travel budget. That car thief scored well.' She pulled out the pennies soaking in the glass, to furiously dry them with a polishing cloth.

'I told you I'd help you and your sister out,' said Devin.

She patted his arm. 'You've done so much already; I can't thank you enough. I don't want to bother you anymore.' She was used to taking care of business for herself.

'No bother.'

'Besides, luv, you and your sister are welcome to stay till you work something out.' Pearl pointed to the pennies on the bar. 'You did a good job on them.'

The pennies looked new. Teà put them on the paddle she'd made, giving them a slight flick to watch them flip and land back where they'd started. She'd been practising it on their walk yesterday; they'd kept her occupied for hours.

Playing spinner was child's play, but there was an art to it too.

'Your father loved his two-up.' Pearl plucked a bottle of rum off the shelf and poured herself a nip. 'Any takers?'

Devin shook his head, sipping on his coffee.

'Thanks, but I don't do rum,' said Teà. 'I know Dad did.'

'Well, a pub's open somewhere, eh?' Pearl chuckled at the private joke, then tossed down her nip. 'As Victor Voss's daughter, I bet you know all about the game of two-up.'

'I might.'

Pearl leaned closer, putting her hand over Teà's. 'Look at me, girlie.'

Teà kept her poker face steady.

'I reckon you and me can solve your little cash problem.'

'How?'

'I should offer you the same deal I did with your dad.'

'What's that?'

'You'd give me ten per cent of the house winnings or a hundred cash, whatever's greater. But in this case, I'll skip the house rules on this one.'

'Did my dad play two-up, out here?'

'Girlie, it's because of your dad running his regular game of two-up, I got bloody customers.'

'No way.'

'This place was just a shed with a fuel pump out front, bore out back, a generator and a long drop. Nothing more. But I've built her up over the years. And your dad and his two-up games brought the stockmen to this place on pay weeks. And I owed Vossy. Even if he was a rolling stone with his pennies and the ladies, he always ran a clean game.'

'Where was this, Pearl?' asked Devin.

'Out the back. Patrick, my love? Come 'ere a second.' Pearl waved at her husband to join them before she spoke with Teà. 'You reckon you can run a coupla clean games like your old man? Coz I'll spread the word.'

Teà barely nodded. 'Who'd play?' There was no one else around the deserted roadhouse that sat beside an outback crossroad of dirt.

'You know that it's illegal to play two-up except on Anzac Day, Pearl.' Devin gave a coy grin from behind his coffee mug.

'What happens out the back of me pub has nothing to do with me.' Pearl plonked her hand on her bony hip and shared a schemer's wink. 'Get ready to skip in them boots, girlie, coz there's a mob of cashed-up stockmen comin' in for the Pussyfoot Cup.'

Fifteen

Surrounded by sunburnt stockmen stood a woman in a simple black summer dress and lace-up boots, effortlessly spinning two pennies in the air.

She was stunning to watch.

Devin shook his head, amused at Teà's mischievous eyes, as she easily captivated those around her. A single woman who looked like Teà was a rarity, especially in a place like Topp Springs. But a woman tossing pennies proposing a game of two-up had got them even more curious, especially when stockmen would bet on anything, from racing frogs, to donkeys, cards, dice, now this. There weren't too many places to spend their fists full of dollars.

Courtesy of Patrick, Teà set up an area using a large piece of carpet. All she did was toss a few coins and one bloke wandered over, then another, then another. Pretty soon, she had a mob.

From the centre of the square, Teà effortlessly commanded the crowd. While fascinating him with her feline grace, her shapely lean legs, and her long hair trailing down her spine.

Teà was a woman used to moving through the world with more bravado than most men. It might be intimidating to some men, yet he found it incredibly attractive.

Normally he was the boss, but not today, and he liked it. Teà never sucked up to him, never toyed with him or talked down to him. She treated him like an equal as he helped her set up the two-up area to raise money.

He'd even offered her money, but her independence wouldn't allow it—agreeing to only borrow cash. And even then, he practically had to push a hundred into her hand. He wanted to give her more, hell he could afford to spoil her. And yet she refused to take his money, making his respect for her skyrocket, as his admiration for her only deepened.

No one did that in his world—especially when they found out who he was.

How long would it take for someone to whisper in her ear? Especially with this crowd of locals gathering to play a game of two-up.

The world only saw him one way, and very few knew him. Because he was a guy who hid his defects very well. Did he dare tell Teà?

Can you spell d-i-s-o-r-d-e-r, son?

Had he finally found a female strong enough to treat him the same, after he'd confessed everything?

Dammit, he was never meant to get involved. Yet, the urge rose like fire in his chest, with an overwhelming desire to come clean and tell her everything, before it was too late.

But when?

Not when she stood tall and unwavering, before the gathered group of men, sharing a quick grin. A smirk. Playing with boys, like one of the boys. But she wasn't— not in that dress.

Sadly, Teà's last day was tomorrow. A reminder of why she wanted nothing from him.

Yesterday he'd seen her raw and wounded, with tears staining her cheeks, in her unbridled gratitude towards him. Her small hand in his, trembling and frail as he drove them back to the roadhouse.

Tender one moment with her care towards an injured duck. Patient and protective over her younger sibling. Feminine and soft as she hugged him before she curled up beside her sister. There was such an incredible depth and warmth between Teà's layers. He wanted to explore everything about her.

The moments she'd tuck her hair behind her ear and smile at him. The front bar, the truck, on an outback track, by a windmill, now in front of a group of men. She only shared that smile with him. And he'd been watching her enough to know.

It was the same smile when she stood on the crest of the deserted Murranji Track where he'd found her, standing there with a smile so pure and unguarded. That smile, with that damned wide curve of her plump lips and the shine in her eyes, made him feel like a freaking king. A smile that practically cracked open his bones to spread sweet honey into his soul.

But they were running out of time.

Right now, her attention returned to the crowd.

'We'll make these rules simple, fellas ...' Teà held up the two pennies as the men's voices reduced to a murmur. Teà was the ringmaster about to dazzle these outback circus clowns jostling for ringside seats. He couldn't stop watching her.

'Welcome to the grown-ups' game of heads and tails,' she said. 'As we're all working class here who work hard for our dosh, all cash denominations are allowed. Those wanting to put a bet on double heads, wave the cash you're spending above your head.' Teà gave a quick demonstration by waving the hundred-dollar bill she'd borrowed from Devin to play. 'Those going for tails taps his bum with cash in hand.' A few low whistles murmured as she playfully patted her rump, but she was no fool, Teà was the one in charge of this crowd, this game, and his pulse!

'You're all accountable for your side bets,' she said, walking around the inner circle. 'So loud voices, boys. You don't want to miss out. And for those gentlemen with an eye on a lady among you, consider this as the perfect way to strike up a conversation and a side-bet.'

Some of the stockwomen grinned, some dropping their heads to hide rosy cheeks and smiles, all holding cash in one hand, and a beer in the other.

'Before we can play, is there anyone willing to be the spinner? They'll get the chance to double their bets. So don't be shy, all you have to do to play Spinner is drop a bill in the centre before the side bets can begin.' She pointed to Devin with a cheeky grin. 'Devin is the bank, who the spinner will be betting against, if you dare to play...'

'Now, those new to the game of two-up, to play the spinner, you use this paddle known as the kip. You toss it above your head and let the pennies spin.' She threw the coins that spun with expert precision in the air to land at her lace-up boots. 'I'll allow you a free spin if you muck it up. Only one. If the pennies don't spin, you lose. If you throw the pennies out of the circle, you lose. The spinner needs to throw double heads or tails three times to win and double their money. If the spinner spins five odds in a row, they lose their bet. Clear as mud?' Teà stood in the centre holding the kip with the shiny copper pennies catching the sunlight. 'So, who wants to play spinner first?'

With a lick of his thin lips, and a nod of his large grey hat, an old stockman tossed a hundred-dollar bill into the centre square. 'I'll have a go, miss.'

Teà scooped up the hundred, passing it to Devin with a wink, before handing the kip and coins to the new spinner.

'I remember your old man playing out here.' The stockman removed his large grey hat, and held it to his chest. 'I'm sorry for your loss. Victor Voss was a good bloke.'

Everyone stopped, hats removed, and there was a moment of silence.

Devin had never been prouder of this place and of those around him.

Teà's head dropped; her eyes were glassy from the public display of mourning surrounding her.

She may seem strong and like one of the boys, but she was a woman who'd been through hell. He'd seen her vulnerability, and that only drew him in deeper to drown in these uncharted feelings he had for her. He'd seen behind her mask to hold her gaze long enough for him to pick out the stars barely concealed within her dark eyes, treating him to a glimpse of the glorious galaxy working inside her.

Teà was so different from any woman he'd known. Stronger. Smarter. With something driving her. He couldn't help but want to touch her, be near her, to understand her. He wanted to dig past that shell to find those soft spots he'd seen in her darkest hours, or in those moments when she thought no one was watching.

But he was. He couldn't stop watching, like she'd become his obsession.

It was like he was in hell, licking his lips, thirsting for a taste of heaven by daring to kiss her. To inhale her essence as he imprinted his mouth on her lips and claimed her. But this was not the place, and time was running out, and he'd only do so if she allowed it. Teà had to give permission first.

Can you spell m-o-r-a-l-s, son?

Teà wasn't going to give him the green light; she'd said no from the start—and he shouldn't be holding his breath with what little time they had left.

Teà was in charge. Not him. And she was the only person he'd let be the boss of him too.

Her chest rose as she inhaled deeply, putting on her mischievous poker face to whirl around to face the crowd. 'Ready to head 'em up, boys? Place your bets.'

The roar was deafening.

People tapped their heads with assorted cash, crossing the square to bet with another mate. While others tapped their tails hollering, 'Tenner on tails'.

Some shouting, 'Fiver on heads.'

'Gotta lobster here, fellas,' said the guy, tapping a twenty-dollar bill against his hat.

'Anyone gonna match me for a pineapple?' Another player waved a fifty-dollar note behind his bum, like he'd farted.

In the middle of it all stood Teà, right at home controlling the game, as she placed her bets.

And in less than twenty minutes, Teà slipped the *tonner* she'd borrowed from him into his top pocket, with an extra fifty as a thank-you tip.

Hundreds, if not thousands, changed hands, amid excited shouts and choruses of laughter, as beer spilled, and backs were patted among the dusty air alive with a jovial energy.

'Game on,' called out Teà, holding the twin copper pennies in the air, before handing them to the new spinner. All those around them paused. Their heads craning back as the spinner tossed that pair of copper pennies into the cloudless outback sky, hoping to double their bets.

'*COPPAS!*'

In a flash, the men dispersed. Teà gave the hundred back to the spinner before sliding her coins and paddle into her daypack, that looked a lot fuller since the first round of two-up.

'What's going on here?'

Devin rolled his eyes, recognising the whiny know-it-all-motherly tone. It was Teà's sister, escorted by a fresh-faced constable and the local sergeant.

'You're a long way from town, Sergeant.' He shook hands with the officer, while ignoring the large wad of freshly accrued cash in his back pocket. Every time Teà gave him the nod, he'd place a bet. And win. He'd never had so much fun watching coins fall from the sky.

'G'day, Devin. You in for the cup, too?' The sergeant poked up the brim of the trucker's cap that was part of their uniform, tucking his notebook into the pocket of his cargo pants.

'Helping out a friend.' He wanted to be more than just her friend. Sliding his arm territorially around Teà's shoulders, to openly glare at a few lingering stockmen fluffing up their rooster feathers, thinking they'd had a shot at the prize she was.

But it was comfortable, his arm over her shoulders. Just like yesterday, helping her walk back to his truck on Murranji, walking her into Pearl's, walking her to her room. It felt so natural, and not once did she shrug him off, but ever so slightly leaned on him like he'd become her safe space amid her greatest adventure.

'Are you Teà Voss?' the Sergeant asked.

She nodded, completely expressionless, yet surprisingly calm. Considering what they were doing was illegal.

'We spoke last night on the phone. I've taken your sister's statement to get the details on the stolen car and send out an APB. There aren't that many main roads out here, so with luck, someone may spot it. An old car like that will stand out.' From his expression, the police sergeant wasn't holding out much hope.

And neither was Devin. The endless landscape that surrounded them contained lots of dirt roads, firebreaks, cattle trails, and well-worn wallaby tracks that ran in all directions. Finding that car would be like finding a gold nugget in a crater full of concrete.

'Thank you.' Teà nodded politely, but he could tell she wasn't holding out much hope either, as they watched the police walk away. 'You okay, Lottie?'

'Tired.' Lottie had her ponytail in place, but she had bags under her eyes, and wasn't wearing some plaid schoolteacher's dress. She was also sunburnt, big time. Standing in a pair of oversized thongs, her white feet shone brightly below her sock tan. 'What were you doing?'

'Making some cash.' Teà's eyebrows bobbed up and down as she opened her daypack and started piling cash into Lottie's arms. 'Here, put this somewhere safe. It's for our travel expenses.'

'Where did you get this money?' Lottie crushed the cash against her chest.

Devin rubbed the back of his neck as a surprised chuckle escaped him. He'd never realised Teà had accumulated that much money, considering she'd borrowed cash from him to play.

Can you spell h-u-s-t-l-e-r, son?

'Hey Lottie, do me a favour and give this cash to Pearl.' Teà held out a few hundred-dollar bills to her sister. 'Tell her it's her commission. You can manage the rest.'

'But I have no bag, no purse. Nothing.' Both sisters were wearing borrowed clothes. 'You hold on to it.'

'Are you sure, Lottie? You know how to budget,' Teà asked.

Lottie shook her head. 'No, you hold the cash. I'm not in charge anymore.'

You could've bowled him over with an emu feather as Little Miss Uppity, the pompous dictator, who'd incessantly ranted about their travel budget, the fuel prices, demanding she drive, pushed the cash back into Teà's bag and zipped it up.

What the hell happened out there? Devin scratched the back of his neck as Teà shrugged at him with surprise.

'I'll give this cash to Pearl on my way back to bed.' Lottie limped back to the roadhouse, using the money to shade her from the sun.

Devin gave Teà's shoulders a squeeze. 'Your sister will be okay.'

'She's lost everything, Devin. The farm was her home. It's going to kill her to go back to her family.'

'I can help you. I'm here to help.' Guilt thickened his throat, pressing like a hot rod across his shoulders.

She gazed up at him with that same steady level of measurement that came without any judgement, but also a soft smile across those lips. 'You've been nothing but a huge help from the second we met. I already owe you so much, I won't use you. I'm not like that. Here, take this for the fuel.' She dug around in her bag and pulled out a handful of cash.

His heart damned near melted all over his dusty boots to recycle liquid warmth through his bloodstream. He closed his hand over hers and held it in place. 'You owe me nothing.'

'But—' She gazed up, to then look past him. Her smile fell as her eyes narrowed into a scowl. 'I don't believe it!' She bolted towards the car park.

'Where are you going?'

With her skirt flicking up, hair flying, Teà raced towards the corridor of parked trucks. 'It's your tool, Devin. The chipping hammer you gave me. I'd left it in the car!'

Devin's eyes zeroed in on the small, yellow-handled chipping hammer swinging loosely in the fingers of a cattleman.

Was it the same tool?

Sixteen

'Excuse me, sir?' Teà rushed up to the middle-aged man in a cowboy hat. 'May I see that tool, please?'

He looked at her like she was crazy.

'I had one just like it.'

'Yeah, sure, miss.' He handed it to her with a shrug. 'G'day, Devin.'

'Blue.'

'In for the cup with your folks?'

'They're in Sydney. Mason's having another baby.'

'Struth, how many is that now?'

'Three.'

'Fair dinkum.'

While the two men casually chatted, Teà's hands trembled with hope, she struggled to roll down the yellow plastic covering the hammer's handle. *Was this the right one?*

'What were you going to do with that chipping hammer, Blue?' Devin was so calm.

'I was just returning it. Had to give the flamin' second fuel tank's tap a knock, some rock on the road flicked up and crimped it. That hammer was small enough to get into that prick of a spot under the truck's back tray to fix it. Smallest chipping hammer I'd ever seen.'

'It's the same one, Devin.' She held out the metal handle displaying the initials T-V. 'I scratched my initials in the handle while Lottie drove us to the other Gregory

Tree on the Murranji Track.'

Taking a step back, Blue adjusted his wide-brimmed hat. 'Hey, you're not one of the Voss sisters?'

'I am.'

Blue's face fell to show nothing but pure remorse. 'I'm sorry about what happened to you girls. That's a bugger about your car getting stolen. You're bloody lucky Devin found you like he did.'

'I know.' The guy was her freaking hero.

'Blue, where'd you get this tool from?' Devin asked.

Blue tossed his thumb over his shoulder. 'Moppet's mate, Snowy. In for the cup.'

'You don't mind if we give it back to Snowy, for you.'

'Nah, all good.' Blue nodded with a finger tap salute on his hat brim. 'Say g'day to your folks for me.'

'But …' She wanted to ask the guy more questions.

'Blue didn't pinch it. He's not that type of bloke.'

She trusted Devin, ever since she'd opened her eyes after that dusty willy-willy had passed, still clinging to the rope on top of a windmill. Debris and dust covered the Ford, but Devin still stood strong. He never let go of the rope that was her lifeline. And then when he showed up yesterday on the Murranji Track … She trusted him.

But it didn't mean she had to trust anyone else. 'Do you trust him?'

'Yeah, Blue's all right. Why did you scratch your initials into that tool?'

'Because I like it. I was going to engrave my initials into it properly once I got to a workshop.' She flipped it over in her hand, letting it slap squarely into her palm for that perfect balance. 'I mark all my tools, especially when working with other tradesmen.'

'You really like that tool?'

She shrugged with her shoulders high, feeling every bit the dork, she was. 'I know it's weird, but I do. It's the right size and weight for my hands. But you know what this means? We have a lead.' The excitement coursed through her veins. Just maybe they had a shot at finding the car. 'Where do we find this Snowy?'

'At the back of the racetrack. This way.'

Devin led her through the gathered crowd of all ages. Children's laughter mingled as they raced among the adults eager to catch up with friends. Groups of older men stood in a circle with their hat brims lowered, deep in conversation. While others leaned their arms over the rails, sharing a beer, watching horses in an arena. All wearing denim jeans, boots, and either trucker caps or assorted Akubras.

'Where did these people come from?'

'Around. They're in for the campdraft and the Pussyfoot Cup.'

'A camp what?'

'Campdraft. It's where stockmen and women show off their skills as riders while working with cattle.'

'Like a rodeo?' There were stacks of horse floats sitting behind beefy four-wheel drive utes, and trucks. They were a home base for saddles, stirrups, bridles, halters, reins, and harnesses being prepared on freshly brushed horses that were lean, powerful animals.

'It's a bit more technical than that. It's more about the horse and rider working as a team. Rodeoing is all about keeping their butts in a saddle for eight seconds. What these guys do takes skill. It's worth a watch.'

'Maybe I will.' The combination of horses and their sun-hardened riders, slinging stock whips over their saddles, were impressive to watch. Her father would've loved this. 'So what is the cup for?'

'The last race of the day.' Devin pointed to the gap, well past the stables and assorted horse floats, to the gathering of gum trees that shaded a large truck. Tethered to its side were over a dozen camels in various stages of being saddled.

'It's a camel race?!'

He nodded. 'Snowy runs the camels for the cup, for

those crazy enough to want to ride a spitting desert donkey.'

She grinned at the guy, playfully nudging his side. 'This coming from the man who stops to look after a duck.'

His lips barely curled, but he was smiling. She could tell. He was a guy who had lots of tells, but he'd understood her enough to read her signals for betting over a game of two-up. They made quite the team.

'Come on, let's talk to Snowy. But watch yourself, this guy's a bit of a carnie. You two might get along, with you being a two-up hustler.' Devin led her past the camels, calmly chewing on their hay, to the back of the truck to find an enormous white-haired man, working on some odd-looking saddles.

'Snowy, gotta second?'

'Woo-wee, what do we have here? If it isn't *the* Mr Devin Asher gracing me with his presence.' Snowy even bowed. 'Your highness.'

'Huh?' She'd heard the men call Devin *boss* during the two-up game, but this was different.

Devin's expression hardened, just like it had done back at Rusty's Roadhouse. 'Snowy, this is Teà. Blue said you loaned him that chipping hammer, and we want to know where you got it from.'

'No idea what you're talkin' about.'

'This one.' Teà held out the yellow-handled tool.

'Found it.'

'Where?'

'Stuff falls off the back of trucks all the time, see? Corrugations are especially rough this time of the year. You know how it goes, some jackeroo not tying down his load properly, the missus taking her hubbie's ute for a spin to town, the truckie forgettin' to close the lid on his toolbox.'

Devin crossed his arms over his chest. 'How about a navy blue, 1970, XY Ford Falcon 500, carrying the ashes of a dead father, being driven by his two daughters?'

'Now hang on a second there, mate.' Snowy was tall, but Devin matched his height. 'I had nothing to do with that, see?'

'Who did?'

'Who wants to know?' Snowy raised his double chins high, crossing arms over his barrel chest.

'Me! It was *my* sister's car carrying *my* father's ashes.'

Snowy stepped back from Devin, to rub thoughtfully at his ruddy chins. 'Tell you what, let's do a trade. You want information, and I need a jockey, see.'

'Come again?' This outback race meet didn't look like there was a satin-wearing jockey anywhere among this crowd of cowboys.

'I'm short a camel jockey. I didn't bring out all my camels for only a few people to ride, see. And it seems that those who were going to pay for the privilege spent all their hard-earned dollars on a little backyard game of two-up.' Snowy looked straight at Teà. 'Know anything about that.'

'Not my problem.'

'But it's my problem, see? I feed these darlings, water them, and train them like they're family.'

Teà wasn't buying it. 'I'm doing this for my family, too.'

'But you see, I'm part of a tradition passed down from my Afghan great-grandfather, way back when he ran the camel trains from here to Alice Springs. Those camels worked hard helping to build the train line, carting in supplies to many outback regions, like this place. Why do you think they called it the Ghan?'

'Spare us the history lesson, Snowy,' warned Devin.

'All I'm saying is that there's very little need for these gentle, hoofed mammals these days. And being a cameleer is a dying trade, you see. So, to bring these beauty's here, I've gotta get some form of compensation. You understand, don't you?'

Teà also understood what he wasn't saying, loud and

clear. 'How much?'

'Enough to buy a saddle and a bum to ride it. Can you ride a camel?'

'How about just the cash?' Lottie might get angry at Teà bartering their cash away, but they had a lead to chase down the car.

Snowy dabbed at the sweat on his brow with the towel draped over his shoulder. 'I need all my camels racing, see. Otherwise, it's not a fair race. Which means if it's not a fair race, the punters won't care who wins the cup, then they'll lose interest and not show up next year, which means I'm out of a job, left struggling to feed these beauties.'

'Fine. We'll take a camel.' She shrugged at Devin, shaking his head. 'I've never bought a camel before.'

Snowy's white teeth were a stark contrast to this snake-oil salesman's tanned complexion. 'It just so happens, little lady, you're in luck, see. If you care to follow me, I'll introduce you to a fine Arabian camel, also known as the strapping *Camelus dromedarius*.' Snowy walked and talked like a second-hand car dealer, leading them past the other camels to the last camel tucked in at the very end. 'There's your winning ride.'

She screwed up her nose. 'It's small.' Not that she knew anything about long-legged camels, but it was tiny compared to the other gigantic sandy-coloured beasts that towered over them.

'And young,' said Devin. 'Is it broken in properly?'

'Absolutely. Pearl would have my head if I let the ringers run a green one.' For a big man, Snowy tenderly stroked the neck of the camel. 'This is Buttercup. A descendant of the mighty camel team that won the Great Australian Camel race in 1988. Isn't she pretty?' The camel lazily chewed like a cow, with long lashes shading its gentle doe eyes. 'Do you need a crash course on how to be a camel jockey?'

'Me, no. But I do know of a pony club princess who might need one.' She rummaged through her bag for the cash, eager to get this over and done with. They had just over twenty-four hours to finish this inheritance challenge. They might still have a shot.

But Devin placed his hand protectively over hers. 'Just hold on a second, Teà … '

She blinked up at him. Surely Devin wasn't going to interfere now? Not when he'd been helping her without hesitation. She was desperate to find that car and he knew it.

Devin squarely faced the white-haired cameleer. 'Snowy, is this information going to help the Voss sisters find their stolen car?'

Hot. Damn. Devin was a no-nonsense, boardroom-negotiating, businessman in a cowboy hat! Paired with that stern dead-eye stare and deep tone, it was sexy as hell.

'Will it be worth their while?'

Snowy gave the wide, toothy smile of the Cheshire Cat. 'Yeah, it'll be bloody worth it.'

Seventeen

Lottie stared at her new phone. Her finger hovering over the screen displaying the only phone number she knew. She only ever rang one person. But she just couldn't bring herself to press dial.

Dumping the mobile onto the mattress, she flopped back onto the bed, defeated.

In the bathroom, the duck splashed around in the tub having a fat time. The clunky air conditioner whirled in the background as she gazed at the slow-moving ceiling fan.

She'd failed. The car was gone. Along with her dad's ashes and all their money. She'd miserably, totally, completely, and utterly failed.

Oh, how was she ever going to tell her family that they no longer had a home?

Ugh! Dragging her hand down her face, she sat up, just hearing Teà's voice, *time to grow up, princess*, and hit dial before she chickened out again. 'Hi, Adrian. It's me.' Because she didn't even know what her new phone number was.

'Hey, I was getting worried something had happened,' said Adrian on the other end of the phone. 'You were meant to call yesterday.'

'Um, the car got stolen …' She quickly relayed the terror of yesterday.

'Please tell me you're okay?' His fear and genuine care made her ache to have him hold her. She missed her man.

'I am. Sunburnt today. Yesterday I was a bit

dehydrated. They had a bush nurse check us over last night, in the bar.' Lottie didn't care it wasn't some fancy hospital. Given never-ending glasses of cold water, in between bowls of ice cream. To then wallow in a tub with ice cubes before bed, where she held her big sister's hand until she fell asleep. 'I didn't call last night because I was exhausted and slept an entire fifteen hours straight. I've never done that.'

'Sounds like you needed it. I wish you'd sleep in more. It's why I take the kids out on weekends.'

'But I had too much work to do. And Dad didn't like me lazing around.'

'There's nothing wrong with resting now and again. Most people call it self-care.'

'You'll be happy to know I am resting now. I have my feet up on a bed, watching some random show on TV.' This never happened in her world.

'Good for you.'

'Oh, Adrian, we lost.' The words tumbled over her lips, making her heart fall, with her heavy head resting in her hand. 'We've lost the farm.'

'But—'

'Dad's urn was on the front seat of the car, resting beside Dad's hand-drawn maps. We need those breadcrumb pieces to sort out a puzzle for the final destination to scatter Dad's ashes, and we only have until tomorrow. Four o'clock.' What an odd hour for a Sunday.

'Do you want me to call up the lawyer? Which reminds me to chase up about contesting the will.'

'You can do that tomorrow.' Then it was truly over.

'Is that why you're hiding in that hotel room?'

'What can I do? I don't know where to look, and I have no car to go anywhere. The police said they'd do whatever it is they do.'

'What's Teà up to?'

'Gambling.' She frowned.

'Excuse me?'

'I couldn't believe it.' She tossed her arm in the air. 'Leave that girl alone for half a day and I find her out the back of the pub playing two-up.'

'Sounds like your sister has fully recovered.' Adrian chuckled. 'Why did she do that?'

Lottie sighed, sitting back. 'My bag got stolen. All the travel allowance is gone. We needed cash.' Saint Teà to the rescue, again.

'How much did you lose?'

'Nine-and-a-half thousand.' Although, it looked like Teà had won more than that.

'The lawyer gave you ten. Didn't you spend anything on fuel and accommodations?'

She winced, confessing her stingy rein on that cash. 'I'd been trying to budget, hoping we'd have some left over to spend on something we may need at home.' A home they no longer owned. 'Oh, what do we do, Adrian? I'm scared.'

'We'll get through this, Lottie. We can go anywhere. We don't have to stay here. I can work anywhere, you can too.' Her husband sounded excited.

'What about the children? Their friends.'

'Sophie's about to start grade one. Do you remember your friends in grade one?'

'No.'

'Me neither. But that doesn't matter to me, not when I live with my best mate, who is the most amazing mother to our children.'

'Aww.' She practically melted in her seat.

'Lottie, I was going to suggest we sell our share of the farm.'

'To who?' When she'd been planning to buy Teà out.

'Mick Hamilton.'

'The guy leasing the back paddock. Did he collect the keys?'

'He did. That's when he told me he'd like first crack if we were going to sell. Mick's already got plans for the shearing sheds and everything. He can afford to buy us out. The land's gotta be worth something decent, although the appraiser said little when he came through.'

Lottie sat up, blinking at the deserted room. 'What appraiser?'

'The lawyer sent one. It's to be expected as part of the conditions of your father's will. At least we'll find out how much it's worth and if we sell the farm—'

'And do what? Live where?' She clutched a hand to her strained heart. Her entire world was that farm. It's all she knew.

'Put the money away, go on a road trip around Australia. We could homeschool the kids on the road until we found a place we wanted to live.'

'Where did this come from?' Because it sounded like a well-rehearsed speech.

'Guy at work is doing the same with his family. His brother just did the trip with his kids, rented out their house for a year, and said his family has never been closer. We could do that, Lottie.'

'How long have you been thinking about this?'

'Since your father passed away. I'm not a sheep farmer. All I ever did was help drive the harvesters occasionally. Victor knew when and what crops to plant, where to shift the sheep, and who to organise for shearing. Do you?'

All she did was pay the bills while doing the bookwork. 'Dad did all of that.'

'What about Teà? Is she a farmer?'

'Did you know that Saint Teà's a maritime welder who worked on rigs and stuff?'

'I did.'

'Since when?' Because it took her three days on the road to find that out.

'We chatted while you were sorting out stuff for your road trip.'

Lottie stopped her frown, remembering both Teà and Adrian had offered to help. But she kept saying *I've got this*, believing they'd muck up her system while going through her checklists, busily filling up a car that was gone. None of it mattered now. 'I'm not sure what Teà knows about sheep, but she doesn't mind learning. She did a lot of research on that duck we found.' The duck doing laps of the bathtub. If that duck hadn't found Devin, how long would they have been stranded on the Murranji Track?

She shuddered to think.

'Did Teà ever tell you what she planned to do with her share of the inheritance?' Adrian asked.

'No. Nothing. I only just found out she was a welder and can run a two-up game. But it doesn't matter, Adrian, we lost.'

'I don't see it that way.'

'How do you see it?' Because Lottie was lost. Miserable. And lost. Forever destined to bear the shame of losing their home. She'd never be able to look at her children's faces without feeling guilty.

'Don't you get it? We'll finally be free of the burden this farm is. You don't have to watch out for your father anymore and do what he says. It'll just be you, me and the kids. Our family. You'll be free to do something wonderful with your life, to do what you want.'

There was a knock on the door. 'Lottie, I need your help.'

The duck quacked, flapping its feathers excitedly in the tub.

It was just too much! Leave her home? Did she have any choice? 'I've gotta go. Teà's at the door.'

'Please think about what I said and find out what Teà wants to do.'

'I will. Love to you and the kids.'

'Hey, Loretta?' Adrian's voice softened.

She paused, hearing her full name.

'Thanks for the conversation. I love you, too.'

She stared at the phone, truly missing him.

It was also the first decent conversation they'd had in a long time, without her demanding her husband write down a list of chores to complete. It was a conversation about a future that she was unsure of. All she knew was the farm.

This was not the reaction she'd expected from her husband.

'You in there, Lottie?' Teà knocked again.

'Coming.' Lottie unlocked the door.

'I need you to put on these jeans and boots.' Teà dumped the clothes on the bed on her way to the bathroom. 'Hey, Quacker, I've got some more watermelon and pawpaw for you.'

'Why do I have to put these on? Pearl said our clothes will be ready soon.' Her legs were sunburnt, her feet hurt to slide into shoes, and her whole body ached from having walked a gazillion miles through the outback.

'You need them for the cup.'

'The what?'

'You'll never believe it, but Devin and I found a lead about the car. We found my yellow-handled chipping hammer.' She flipped it over in her hands like flipping a coin.

'No way? Is it the same one?'

Teà pulled down the handle's yellow plastic cover to show the childish scrawl for the letters T-V. 'Got my name written all over it.'

To think she'd told Teà off for being silly about graffitiing that dumb tool. 'Where did you get it?'

'Well, now comes the tricky part.' Teà leaned against the laminated sign requesting motel doors be kept closed at all times because of snakes who liked to hide under beds. *Ick.*

Lottie pressed against their door, ensuring it was shut tight.

Then Teà held both of Lottie's hands, the excitement shining in her eyes. 'Lottie, we've got a shot at finding Dad's car, to then work out the puzzle, and scatter his ashes tomorrow in time to win your inheritance.'

Lottie's eyes widened. 'Really?' Did she dare to dream?

'But I need your help.'

'What can I do?'

'Get dressed. I want you to come and meet Buttercup. You're going to love her.'

Lottie quickly dressed, only for Teà to drag her out of the hotel room, leaving the duck to wallow in the tub.

The sun bit at her sore skin as fine dust swirled in the air to give the world a smoky red haze.

'Where did these people come from?' There were utes, trucks, horse trailers and a sea of cowboy hats everywhere.

'They're here for the campdraft. You can ask Devin about the technicalities.' Teà led Lottie through the crowds, ducked under a rope and crossed a dirt track to where Devin was waiting.

Devin held out a riding cap. 'Got you this. Teà said you can ride?'

That would have to be the first time he'd spoken to her face, instead of always talking to Teà. 'I haven't ridden in a while.'

'Lottie's a proper pony club princess with a stack of ribbons back at her house to prove it,' said Teà.

'Only for dressage and show jumping. These look like working horses.' They were incredible animals with complex muscles shifting effortlessly beneath their riders, seated on saddles that held ropes and stock whips. 'So, what am I riding? A donkey?'

'Close. A camel.' Devin nodded at a lone camel tied to a roped rail.

'A what?' Her face dropped.

'I'll let Teà explain while I fetch your oversized desert donkey, shall I.' His chuckle irritated her, along with that cocky swagger of his. Nodding at other passing riders, right at home with this crowd, leading the camel towards them.

Was this really happening?

'Teà? What is Devin talking about?'

Teà checked the straps on Lottie's helmet. 'For us to get the information we need about the car, you need to race on Buttercup. We need you to play jockey, like a seat filler at dinner parties. Oh, look, isn't Buttercup just adorable?'

'Pfft.' Devin grumbled under the brim of his hat. 'They're a feral pest.'

'Hush you, don't upset Buttercup.' Teà gently stroked the camel's neck. 'Just ignore the cute cowboy, and meet your jockey, Lottie, who is going to help you win.'

'Why?' Lottie craned her neck all the way back at the sheer size of the thing. And that hump.

'We don't have time to explain the details. The race is about to begin.' Teà held out an odd-looking vest. 'Apparently, you need to put on this chest pad. Snowy said so.'

'Who's Snowy?' The chest pad looked like something a motocross rider would wear. But she didn't spot a bike anywhere. 'This isn't what a rodeo rider wears, is it?' *Hello, peoples.* There were cowboys everywhere.

'You could say that.' Devin gave a cocky grin as he tapped the front of the camel's chest. '*Hut-hut.*' Buttercup groaned like it was in agony, lowering itself to the ground, tucking its legs almost daintily beneath its body. 'Your Arabian chariot awaits.'

'I'm not getting on that thing.' Lottie started walking backwards.

But Teà tightened the vest's strap around Lottie's ribcage. 'You are so. I can't ride.'

'You ride motorbikes.'

'Things with engines, not animals. I'm sure riding a camel is the same as a horse, except for the hump in the front.'

Then a large man with white hair joined them. 'You lot didn't tell me you had a ring-in?'

'A what? Teà?' Lottie was so lost. In a hot helmet and vest.

'All the other camels have got big men on them. You've

got yourselves a proper camel jockey, see.'

'Snowy, you said you wanted a rider, so we got you one,' said Teà. 'We're paying for the privilege of Lottie putting her bum in that seat.'

Lottie turned to her sister. 'You didn't? All that cash.'

Teà winced. 'I like to think of it as an investment in *you*. Now get on.'

'I don't know what I'm doing.' But she had no choice, and ever so gingerly mounted the animal, to slide into the funny saddle behind the hump. All while it contentedly chewed with a bored expression on its face.

'Don't look down, Lottie, just lean back and hold on,' said Devin.

Hey, Devin said her name correctly! Finally.

But then Snowy was grabbing her hands to grip the strange pole at the front of her saddle. Checking her helmet and telling her the ways of camels. He could've been speaking another language for all she knew. It was so surreal.

'Up you get, Buttercup. Hut-hut.' Snowy patted the camel's rump, and it groaned louder than a crowd of hundred-year-old men full of rickety joints.

Then, in a frightening whiplash motion, it flung Lottie back in her saddle, before flicking her forwards, to almost slam into Buttercup's mighty neck as it rose from the sand.

It rattled her brains.

She gripped the saddle's front handle, desperate to remain on the back of this beast with its odd, jerky side-to-side gait.

'This is nothing like a horse.' There was no bridle, just a halter, as if walking a big-hoofed dog. *'I don't know what I'm doing. I can't do this.'*

'You can,' said Teà from her safe place on the ground.

Devin led the camel, with its soft padded toes that were soundless in the sand. At the starting line they stood among a group of camels that were huge. They really were ships of the desert.

'Devin? Got any tips for Lottie?' Teà nodded up at Lottie with a look that read, *you can do this*.

Easy for Teà to have so much faith, when it was Lottie being made to straddle this strange saddle.

'You can't control them,' said Devin.

'Well, what am I doing up here?' For a woman who was a control freak, this was terrifying. She could feel the panic attack clawing its way around her lungs.

'All I'm saying is the more you push them, the more they'll balk.' Devin nodded his enormous cowboy hat at the camel beside them that suddenly plonked itself onto the ground, facing the wrong way to race. It gave a deep baritone gurgling groan, as Snowy and the others tried to convince the big bull to get up, but it refused to move.

Buttercup seemed oblivious to the raucous crowd, affectionately nudging at Teà, who was scratching its long neck and chin.

'Camels are intelligent but highly emotional creatures that can be as stubborn as hell,' explained Devin. 'Just remember to stay calm.'

'Easy for you to say.' Devin stood safely beside Teà, forcing Lottie to ride. Why didn't Devin ride if he knew all about them, huh?

'These camels only have one thing on their mind: food and water. All you do is hold on while they race back to Snowy, who'll be holding up some treat for them.' Devin pointed back to the camel truck that was a thousand-million-trillion kilometres away.

'Like a donkey with a carrot?' Teà stroked Buttercup's neck. It sniffed at her hair, then wrapped its long neck around Teà like a python in a hug. 'I've never been hugged by a camel. How cool is this.'

Devin protectively stood by Teà, his large hands on the camel's head and chin in case it did squeeze Teà's head like a boa constrictor. 'Don't try to steer it, and let it have its head,' he said. 'All you do is just keep your butt in that saddle and cross that finishing line. If you can ride a horse, you'll get used to its gait in no time.'

'What are my chances?' *Of surviving!*

Devin grinned.

It was a devilish grin. The kind that said, no good would come from this.

Where was a ladder when she needed one?

'You've got an eighty per cent chance of it actually racing,' he said. 'Or it'll just walk the track, leaving you with a sore tail bone, because they're not that comfortable to race.'

She glowered at the couple below her. The panic rising, she struggled to breathe under the armoured chest plate that was way too tight. 'I want off. Now!'

'Listen to me, little sis. Just think of what you'll win.' Teà put her hand on Lottie's leg, nodding at her with encouragement.

It did little to soothe her panic.

'Focus, you've got this. We'll get the car back, Dad's ashes, and the maps. You're racing for your home, Lottie.'

Didn't that force her to swallow her fear.

'I've got to find a bookie to put a bet on. I'll be betting on you, Lottie.' Teà gave a thumbs up, then tugged on Devin's hand. 'Come on Devin, I want you to use your phone to tape the race. We'll send it back to Adrian and the kids. Just don't fall off, Lottie.'

Comforting. Not.

Lottie hung on tighter to the saddle of the lanky-legged camel, which was a gazillion times bigger than a horse. Its sheer height offered a panoramic view of the stockyards, surrounded by various horse floats and trucks.

On the other side of the racetrack, a jovial crowd had gathered, all wearing denim jeans, wide-brimmed hats, and long-sleeved shirts.

Small children played in groups across the lawns. Toddlers danced under a sprinkler, while other children wore face paint, eating simple sausage sangers, wearing tomato sauce as part of their smiles. Her children would love this, and so would Adrian.

She nodded to herself, gripping the saddle's front rail, and the rope for reins. 'I can do this for my home. This is for my family.' And prepared herself for the biggest race of her life.

Eighteen

Perched behind the hump of the camel called Buttercup, Lottie waited for the race to begin. She wanted to puke! To run and hide from the sun stinging her skin.

With only a handle and rope to grip, boots in stirrups, and her thighs gripping the awkward saddle, she waited for the siren to start the race in a strange world surrounded by even stranger people. Which might be a good thing — she'd hate for anyone back home to see her like this, she'd never be able to walk through her hometown again, if she pulled a stunt like this.

Looking an absolute fright, wearing a stranger's clothes, sitting on a camel, in the dust, while suffering the biggest personal crisis of her life.

But she couldn't escape if she tried. This was for her home.

All she had to do was stay in the saddle. Right? Teà never said anything about winning.

Come on, there was no hope in Hades she'd win, not against the field of men who looked like they were born in the saddle. She was out of her league, in a world of red dust and cowboys.

Lottie had only ever done the polite pony club shows. Where mother's ran alongside their child, saddled to teeny-tiny ponies in neat uniforms, polished boots, and horses with plaited manes. Not camels that sat in the dirt.

What was Teà thinking! Lottie couldn't do this.

An annoying fly buzzed around her face, as sweat streamed from beneath the hot hardhat and chest plate. Her mount, a small camel, sat in the sand, along with fourteen others resting in a staggered line. She'd never been in a race like it. It was literally a sitting start.

The camel jockeys tried to contain their mounts. A big bull got up and wandered towards the spectators, stretching its long neck over the crowd to lick at a child's ice cream cone.

Teà waved from the sidelines with Devin beside her, both with phones in hand taping her as the countdown began. Oh no, she'd just die if this race got posted to Facebook.

'Five … Four … Three …' Shouted the spectators.

The children were the loudest.

'Two …'

'One.'

A siren blared.

Once again it was a case of near whiplash in the saddle. Lottie held on for dear life as if riding a mechanical bull, as the camel launched to its soft feet, and they were racing.

The speed of the beast surprised her. Suddenly she was going at about sixty kilometres with no way of steering the damned thing.

Camel jockey butts slapped saddles; others fell off. She'd never realised how hard it was to stay in her seat.

Surprisingly, she soon found her rhythm, matching the gait of the animal as they thundered along in an awkward gallop.

She was the smallest rider out there, on the skinniest camel on spindly legs, but Buttercup ran with her heart, as the long-legged beauty lumbered along the track. 'Go, Buttercup, go.'

Over a dozen camels raced in a chaotic order, weaving along the track, some turning to run the other way. Their hoofs shovelling arcs of sand behind them as they raced down the straight.

Many cheered on their riders as they passed the halfway mark and the pack of racing camels spread out.

Two big camels vying for the front position blocked the lead. They forced Lottie and her smaller knobbly kneed camel towards the rails. She was helpless to do anything.

She was going to die!

'Look out, Buttercup.' She wrapped her arms around the hump and squeezed her eyes shut tight. Her stomach plummeted as the camel ducked, then bobbed and weaved to scoot through a gap between the big bulls and their riders.

They were through!

No way!

'Go, Buttercup.' Lottie leaned forward in the saddle, like a proper jockey. Hope and adrenaline flooding her veins. She could win this, for the farm, for her family.

But where was the finish line?

Unable to steer the thing, she just held on as Buttercup ran towards Snowy, his white hair almost glowing like a halo in the sun.

Then the mass of cowboys roared, waving their hats in the air.

She spotted Teà in the crowd. 'Did we win?'

Teà nodded at her, giving her a double thumbs up.

'We won!' Arms in the air, she rose from her saddle, riding the greatest high in her life.

'Well done, Buttercup. Who knew you had it in ya, my darling?' Snowy held out a carrot to the camel, stroking her long neck.

'We won, Snowy.' She couldn't stop smiling.

'Me too. I put a lot of money on you, what with you bein' camel-jockey size, see ... Down you get, Buttercup. Take a load off, my lovely.' Snowy instructed the camel to sit, where Lottie clumsily staggered off the saddle. 'How ya feeling?'

Lottie spontaneously hugged the camel's neck. 'Thank you, Buttercup.'

The rest was a blur. People came from all over to shake her hand, or pat her back, as they led her to a small podium. She may have been the shortest among those cattlemen, but she stood tall. Holding the Pussyfoot Cup in front of everyone, it fuelled her smile that came from her heart. She didn't think she could smile any wider, hoisting the trophy above her head.

Lottie had never won anything of this magnitude. She wanted to happy dance like a loon, under the showering rain of uncorked champagne that she happily lapped up with her tongue. Her hair was sticky and flat from the sweet champagne and sweat from the helmet. Sweat saturated her shirt as she eagerly removed the cumbersome chest plate. She was a mess, wearing a smile, with her fingers glued to the cup.

She squealed with delight as two men carried her on their shoulders all the way to the pub. She waved to the crowd as if she'd won the Melbourne Cup and spotted Teà waving at her, giving her another thumbs up.

If only her family could see her now.

Nineteen

'Where is my father's car?' With Devin beside her, Teà fronted Snowy, who was removing a saddle from one of his camels. 'Deal's a deal, Snowy. We paid for a seat, got you a jockey to race, so where is the car?'

'I have no idea, see.'

The anger flared inside her. 'You said you did.'

'I said I'd tell you where I got that tool from.' Snowy rummaged around in his truck, scribbled on some paper and handed it to Teà. 'It's a mud map, see. Devin will know the place.'

'What place?'

'Finn's Camp. I broke down nearby and Sheila's mob helped me. That's where I got that yellow hammer. I just forgot to give it back.'

She glanced at another hand-drawn map. *More breadcrumbs.* This time to Finn's Camp. Was it a holiday camp for tourists?

Even though she wanted to celebrate with Lottie, she was determined to find the car. Then she'd celebrate. 'How do we get there?' She had no car.

'We'll take my truck.' Devin led the way as they weaved through the crowds.

It was another world, seated high in the cab of Devin's

truck. It dominated the dirt road filled with corrugations and potholes, that never bothered this mechanical beast of metal and muscle. Driven effortlessly by a dreamy cowboy in denim.

Devin slowed down by a property of broken fences. A roly-poly tumbleweed, the only other traveller, lurching along the road.

'Snowy conned us, didn't he?'

'That's what Snowy does. But he gave us a lead. I wish I'd thought of this place sooner.'

'Should we call the cops?'

'They'll be back in Katherine by now. And if that Ford is at Finn's Camp, we'll need to be quick before it's gone for good.' Devin pulled out his shotgun and placed it on the dash for all to see. 'Do you know how to use a gun?'

'Shooting ranges.' She gulped at the lethal weapon.

'Don't worry, this is more for show. Finn's known to get testy when on the homebrew. Pearl's banned him from Topp Springs bar because of his rum-fuelled behaviour.' He steered the beast down the dirt lane where cars lay like sunburnt relics of a long-gone era.

'What is this place?'

'Finn's Camp. Otherwise known as LandCruiser Dreaming.'

'Huh?'

'It's the nickname the locals give a place where cars go to die. Especially out here.'

The place was nothing but an ocean of assorted vehicles. Mostly LandCruiser utes and troop carriers. Bent and twisted, rusty and tyre-less. Some had broken windshields, bonnets missing, or were matted with weeds. The further they followed the track inland, the older and rustier the vehicles got.

'Dad's Ford isn't here?'

'Let's hope not. I should've thought of it sooner.'

She tenderly squeezed his muscular shoulder. 'Hey, we've been busy. Have you been here before?' A group of motley dogs barked, straining on their chains.

'Not if I can help it. Watch their dogs, don't pat them. They're not pets.'

Teà didn't want to get out of the truck.

A large shed stood to one side, surrounded by a group of old caravans. A tin roof covered the raised deck that had an assortment of chairs scattered around a large table, facing a wide-screen TV. The rest was a maze of car wrecks resting among the tumbleweeds.

The truck stopped with a hiss of the air brakes.

'That's Sheila.'

A dark-skinned woman with curly hair squinted up at the truck, her plump apple-like cheeks prominent as she grinned, exposing two missing teeth. 'What you doin' here, eh, Devin?'

'Sheila, we're looking for a 1970 XY Ford Falcon 500. It went missing from Knockabout Stockyards yesterday morning.'

Sheila screwed up her nose, swatting at a fly. 'Nah, I know nothin' bout that, eh?'

'That car is carrying the ashes of a dead man on the front seat.'

Sheila's face when positively white as she started walking backwards. 'What did you say?'

Devin climbed down, helping Teà to the ground.

'There's an urn on the front seat of that car, containing my father's ashes,' Teà said.

'What ya carryin' a dead fella in a car for, eh?'

'We're out here to scatter his ashes. It's what my father wanted.'

'No-no-no.' With her plump lips pursed tight, Sheila vigorously shook her head. 'That's not right, eh? That's bad business that. Ghosts are no good.'

'I had no choice. It's my father's wishes.'

'Why'd he do that for, eh? Why not bury 'im where he died? Then smoke the place.'

Teà shrugged. 'My father used to work out here.'

'Who dat?'

'Victor Voss.'

Sheila narrowed her eyes at Teà as she thought for a moment. 'Not that fella who ran the two-up out back of Pearl's place, eh?'

'That's him.'

'Didn't he chase some woman down south?'

'My mother.'

'Huh? He had it bad, eh.' Sheila grinned, her white teeth on either side of the gap stood out against her dark skin. 'I guess love will do that to ya. Unpredictable it is, eh? Look at where I ended up, coz of love.' She waved her hand at the junkyard.

Yeah, Teà knew all about the dangers of love. She wasn't going near it again. Not even for the dreamy cowboy playing the part of her hero. She had a job to finish first, for Lottie's sake.

'Do you have the car, Sheila?'

'Honest to god, Devin, I know nothin'.'

'Didn't you see Snowy this morning?' Devin asked.

'Nah, yesterday he was 'ere. His trailer broke down right out front of the place, loaded with all his camels, eh. Gave us a carton of beer for our troubles, and a couple litres of camel milk. I'm making cheese just like I'd seen on the idiot box the other week.'

'Snowy said you gave him this tool.' Teà held out her yellow handled chipping hammer.

'Me, no. I don't touch tools. I was havin' a cuppa with Snowy, watching over his mob of camels. Finn and my boys fixed Snowy's truck. Hold the phone.' With two fingers to her lips, she whistled long and loud as the dogs started barking. '*Wombat?* Where you at, eh?'

'Where is your husband?' Devin looked around warily.

'Finn's in Katherine. Took my other boy, Digger, to the hospital.'

'Is everything okay?'

'Yeah.' Sheila swatted at a fly. 'Cut himself, got these

scratches all over him. Reckons he fell in some barbed wire. He hadn't had a tetanus shot in a while, probably needs a coupla stitches. He'll be back later with a load of shopping. Where the bloody hell is this boy at, eh?' Sheila started stalking towards the sheds. 'Wombat!'

'What did I do now, Ma? I'm busy. Dad's left me with a list of stuff to do.' From behind a shed door, strolled a guy, about seventeen, with skin the colour blend of dark cinnamon and rich maple syrup.

'Devin and his missus are wantin' to know where you got that yellow-handled hammer from.' Sheila pointed at the tool in Teà's hand. 'Don't you lie to me, Wombat. You'd better not be stealin' again, eh?'

Wombat brushed oil-stained fingers through his black curly hair. 'I wasn't stealing. Swear it.'

'So where did you get this tool from, eh? Tell me now, boy.'

'From this old Ford.'

'What did you say?' Teà was about to say more, but Devin snagged her wrist, shaking his head. Even without saying a word, she understood he didn't want her to interfere with the mother and son. Just like he never interfered with her sibling-bickering with Lottie.

'What Ford you talkin' about, eh? We got nothing but Toyotas out 'ere.' Sheila waved her hand at the car wrecks.

'Nah, a proper vintage Ford, Ma. Me and Digger were cruising the Murranji and there it was, just sitting there at Knockabout Stockyard. No one was around, like the car had been deserted.'

'What did you two boys do, eh? The truth, Wombat.'

Wombat held his palms up as if surrendering to his mother. 'Me and Digger weren't gonna touch it at first. We reckoned the owner offed himself, coz there was notes and a map next to this funny-looking cookie jar.'

'It's an urn. You didn't open it, did you?' Teà had to ask.

'Nah. Who are you?'

'She's the owner of that car you and your brother stole from Knockabout, eh.'

'We stole nothin', Ma. I swear on the life of my Xbox, we didn't nick it. Me and Digger checked around and everything.'

'How far did you search?' Devin asked.

Wombat squinted an eye, while scratching the back of his head. 'We didn't wanna look too close in case the fella did knock himself off. We didn't want to wake the dead, if you know what I mean.' Wombat's skinny shoulders shuddered. 'The car was covered in dust, inside and out. There was no campfire, no campfire smoke. Just this wild duck. It scratched the hell outta Digger before it flew outta the car.'

Sheila wagged her finger up at her much taller son. 'Was that before or after your brother claimed to have cut his arm on some steel fixin' Snowy's truck, eh?'

Wombat sheepishly shrugged.

'I'd better get on the dog and bone to your father. We'd better have them quacks check Digger's got no rabies or somethin'.'

'Why didn't you report finding the car to the police?' Teà asked.

Wombat screwed his face up.

Sheila cocked an eyebrow at her. 'Eh?'

'Finders keepers,' explained Devin. 'It's what this place is built on.' He nodded at the enormous mass of discarded cars. There were even a few boats and broken caravans in the rear.

'You found these cars?'

'We find all sorts on the side of the road,' said Wombat, sharing an easy grin. 'Then sell it on eBay.'

'The Ford wasn't on the side of the road. It was parked inside the Knockabout Stockyards.' Teà's anger was flaring. 'My sister and I were sleeping in swags by the rails. And we didn't light a campfire because Devin warned us that place was a tinderbox. We were only staying there for the night.'

Devin dropped his hand on her shoulder, before stepping in front of Wombat. 'Did you know you stranded two women at Knockabout, with no food or water, by taking their car?'

'Wombat!' Sheila fairly whacked her son over the head. 'That car had better be in one piece, eh? Or I'll have Devin drag you and your brother behind his truck to the nearest police station, or back out to Knockabout and let you pair bloody walk back. So where is the car?'

'We haven't touched it, Ma. Swear it. Not since that duck attacked Digger and he had to go to the hospital. We only found that yellow tool on the Ford's front seat and used it on Snowy's truck to help knock open the bolts to the back door to unload his camels. That was before we fetched Dad and the ute with the rest of the tools to fix his axle. Dad hasn't even seen the car to tell us what to do with it.' Wombat pushed the shed door wider and led them past vehicles in various stages of being chopped apart.

Teà's heart hammered, looking fearfully to Devin.

They weaved through more cars, then past a hanging tarp to a clearing. There, standing under the shade of a simple lean-to, stood the dark blue Ford Falcon 500.

The relief was enormous. She nearly fell to her knees.

'Please let it be here.' She rushed to the car, to find the keys still in the ignition. She lifted the urn off the front seat and checked its seal was unbroken.

'What's that, Miss?' Wombat asked.

'My father.'

Wombat held his stomach as if he was going to be sick, scurrying to hide behind his mother.

Sheila clutched her throat, taking a step back. 'Bloody hell. We're gonna have to do a proper smokin' of the place now, eh?'

'What about the rest of the stuff?' Devin leaned into the car. 'Where are the maps?'

Twenty

The last of the sunset's colours disappeared across the outback as Teà raced the blue Ford down the dirt road, driving five times faster than Lottie ever did. Her fingers dancing on the breeze from the open driver's window. And the car just purred.

Up ahead, the roadhouse shone brightly beneath the dark sky blanketed with stars. The carpark numbers had dwindled to leave only the revellers settling in for the night.

She parked near the pub's front doors, spotting Lottie inside. She tooted the car's horn.

Lottie staggered outside, still wearing her borrowed jeans and racing shirt, now filthy. 'Where did you get it?'

'Devin helped me find it.' Teà waved at Devin, parking his truck by the helicopter still resting on the single trailer.

'Lottie, we've got the maps. The cash, everything.'

'Ssssaint Teà does it again.' Lottie hugged Teà, who copped a face full of sticky hair. The normally prissily dressed Lottie was a train wreck, stinking of camel, sweat, and beer, but she'd never looked happier.

'Looks like your sister's had a few,' said Devin, coming up beside her.

More than a few, the way Lottie was leaning against the car to hold herself up. 'How much have you had to drink?'

'I dunno.' Lottie shrugged with a swagger. 'People just kept giving me beer, wine, champagne. But I think I have found my love of beer.' Beer sloshed in her glass as she took another swig. 'Augh …' She wiped the back of her mouth with hand. 'I now get why they drink it.'

'I think we need to find you some water.' Because Lottie wasn't a regular drinker.

Pearl stood at the open doors of her pub. 'Did you get Vossy's ashes, luv?'

Teà dragged the urn from the front seat. 'Sure did.'

'You got it.' Lottie snatched the urn from Teà and hugged it. 'Hi, Dad. We can s-s-save the farm now. Oh, I must call my husband and tell him we got Dad back.' Lottie held up her phone, she squinted at the keypad while swaying on the spot. 'What's my number again? You know, the only number I have on this phone.'

'Lottie, we have your phone here in the car.' Teà passed Lottie her handbag.

'You'd better save that urn from your sister,' said Devin, opening the Ford's back door. 'I'll deliver your bags to your room while you take care of the cheap drunk. What's with all the plaid luggage?'

'They're not mine. I only have the backpack in the boot.' But he was right, Lottie was a mess.

'They're my suitcases. I got them for the honeymoon holiday I never had.' Lottie held the phone inches from her face. 'I shhink I need glasses. I can't read my phone screen.'

'Why not bring your sister and that urn inside, luv,' called out Pearl, holding the door open for Devin carrying a handful of plaid cases. 'There's a mob of us who'd love to give Victor Voss a proper wake, Territory style. The scallywag deserves it.'

While Devin got their luggage inside, Victor Voss's urn sat beside the Pussyfoot Cup on the front bar, where beer was drunk, and tall stories were shared.

Teà needed to work on the maps, to figure out where they were going next, as the four o'clock deadline was closing in. But it was impossible. The excitement was infectious, and she really wanted to party with her sister.

'Shh-saint Teà needs another beer …' Lottie waved at Patrick. 'Did you know my son's name is Patrick, too? We call him Pip.'

'I know, luv, you told me already.' Patrick plonked a bottle of water on the counter. 'Sorry, but I'm puttin' you off tap.'

'Agreed.' Teà had never seen Lottie this bad. Even though she wanted to hear the stories from those who knew her father, her sister was a drunken mess.

With the help of Devin, she dragged Lottie to their room. In the bathroom, the duck was curled up on a nest of towels, with its head tucked under its wing.

Lottie lay spread-eagled across the bed, snoring like she was cutting wood. Lottie's plaid luggage filled the corner and tables, leaving them with no room to swing a duck.

'Think she'll be hungover tomorrow?' Devin asked. 'Or she'll get a headache when she looks at all that plaid luggage in the morning.'

It was a lot of luggage, with her black backpack leaning against the wall. Teà was contemplating having a shower, when her eyes landed on the roll of maps. She'd never have gotten them without Devin's help, they wouldn't have made it this far without him. 'Did I say thank you for your help?'

'Not necessary …' He dropped his head, rubbing the tip of his nose as if to hide his blush.

Teà grabbed the maps and closed the door, leaving sleeping beauty to snore the roof off.

'What are you going to do now?'

'I'm going to find a quiet corner to try to work on this puzzle. We only have until tomorrow to finish this inheritance deal.' She knew how much it meant to Lottie.

'By what time?'

'The lawyer said by four. Late afternoon.'

'That's very specific.'

'I know. Don't ask me why, I haven't got a clue. But I'm

sure it'll all make sense once we get there.' Wherever that was.

From the bar, someone dropped a glass. A chorus of male voices shouted, 'Taxi!' The jukebox was still blaring in full party mode.

Not that it was late, but she didn't feel like going back to the bar either. 'How big is your room?'

'Why?'

'Is it big enough to roll out this map? You've seen the challenge for space in my room, and with that noise …' She pointed to the bar as men bellowed out some song. Was that a football anthem? She couldn't quite work it out.

'Don't you want to talk your fans into another game of two-up?'

'I'm not doing that again.'

Devin grinned before leading them down the hallway and unlocked his door. 'Why not? You looked right at home.'

'Only because we needed the cash. I'm normally not like that.'

'I'm not judging. I understand why you did it. You're incredibly resourceful.' Inside his room, he removed some paperwork from the small table, shoving them on top of his duffel bag, dumping it on the floor beside the bed.

'I have to be. I've been on my own for a long time.' At least this week she hadn't felt the burden of loneliness, not since she'd received news that her sister was searching for her. Hope still simmered of a family connection with Lottie, that was still in a fragile state. If they solved the puzzle and beat the deadline, it should cement their bond as sisters. She had to do this for Lottie.

'Is that by choice? Being on your own?' Devin's manly spice was divine. She struggled to concentrate, rolling out Lottie's colour-coded map.

Yet, his question deserved an answer.

She sighed as she gazed deeply into a rich world of coffee and caramel, those eyes that saw past the shields she'd been living with for so long. 'No.' It was never her choice. 'It's just what it is …'

He gently stroked her hair, his finger tenderly tracing down her jawline, ending with his thumb barely brushing her bottom lip. 'Loneliness is a heavy burden, isn't it?'

Loneliness was an all-too-familiar companion. But being with someone was scarier. She stepped away, his hand falling in the space between them that suddenly felt like a canyon.

'We bury ourselves in our work, so we don't feel that loneliness, until …' He sighed heavily with his confession, the emotion drenching his every word. '… It's at its worst at night when the lights are low, and the place is at its quietest. That's when loneliness is at its loudest.'

How did he know?

His voice deepened. 'Let's not be lonely, together …' Again, he dusted his thumb over her bottom lip. Goosebumps scattered up her spine from a look that should be illegal in some countries. Hell, anywhere within this hemisphere.

'Just one night.'

Her fingers twitched from her pulse pumping too high for her to handle. She struggled to breathe.

His eyes dropped to her mouth as she licked her lower lip.

Why was she resisting?

She had no reason to. It's not like she could get attached to anyone—not again.

Dammit, her brain just wouldn't work right. Because this heavenly man, her hero on more than one occasion, was willing to appease her loneliness. Offering her a commitment-free, one-night-only deal.

Come in spinner.

She leaned forward to collide with his lips. Crashing against his mouth, as he wrapped his body around her as if to shield from all the bad, and she needed something hot. Muscular. And oh, so good.

He leaned into their kiss, his tongue darting to swipe at her lips with a taste of heavenly temptation and glorious male.

It took her a while to realise the raspy groan was her own, as his hot palms bent her frame to his will. Chest to chest, she melted against him like hot butter as he tasted her lips, her skin, his teasing warm breath against her ear.

The fingers of a god loosened her tense shoulders to wrap around her hair as his mouth possessed her like the devil. There was no stopping him now. All she could do was surrender to this hot-mouthed, hard-bodied male.

She had no control over her needs. And no smooth moves. Especially when he pushed her against the wall, pulling her hair to one side, to bend and nibble at her neck. Sliding his hands down her arms, to mould her hips, then up to her chest, turning her into a trembling hot mess, as another stifled moan of sheer pleasure escaped her.

Her groans brought his attention back to her mouth, where he stopped and stared at her.

Heartbeats hammered as he continued to stare.

It made her falter. Now was not the time. For any of this.

Was she ready to do this? To have him kiss her with a mouth that could easily take possession of her just on the taste of desire.

Yet the way he looked at her, she felt it on all levels. It was more than just lips, or hands fisting her hair, or the hard press of his chest against hers. It was everything in this one overwhelming embrace.

He closed his eyes and kissed her. It tasted of both desire and respect—two things she'd never known a man like this could give her. His tongue orchestrated a slow kiss that didn't stay slow for long before it became manic.

So focused on connecting, they'd gone beyond kissing to just breathing against each other's mouths as the layers of clothing were quickly shed. It led to more explosive kisses laced with dynamite, demolishing all her inner shields, to leave her as naked and exposed as her body, lying on the bed.

'Teà.' His voice rumbled, the arousal in his voice and in his touch matched hers.

She'd felt nothing like this before; it was almost too intense, too overwhelming. The panic made her shift her hips back, away from the sheer power of his beautifully chiselled body. He twisted his fist into her hair and pulled, elongating her neck, his tongue tasting her, bending her to his will, tilting her head against the mattress.

She had no choice but to wrap her arms around his neck, to pull him closer, and allow him to claim her.

He made a deliciously deep noise of triumph, falling to his knees, his body hard like warm granite, thick and luxuriously long.

'Teà, you can say stop.' His voice rumbled deep, yet shaky, barely hanging on like she was. Their eyes locked as if there was a war raging between them, and she dragged in a ragged breath.

She wasn't going to deny this for either of them, not when she was already drunk and dizzy on their lust.

She rolled her hips, opening herself for him as his hand slid over her thighs. Thick fingers kneading her flesh, to stroke her strong and deep, swiftly bringing her to the edge. His strong thighs between her legs, with his thick hard length pressing against her. His hand angling her hips, he tucked her in closer.

She gasped at the sheer size filling her, the delicious friction as her body tightened around him to ride his rhythm. His thrusts quickening, to allow them both to freefall over the edge. His deep groans fuelled the fire zipping through her nerve endings, filled with lust and passion like a conduit of the most intense pleasure. Nothing held them back until she melted, froze, floated, and exploded in waves of breathless ecstasy.

They both shuddered until their breathing returned to normal. He rolled off her, tucking her into him, with limbs entangled in a whole new level of intimacy. 'Stay ...' He whispered, his arm tenderly around her, cradling her gently as his heart rate slowed down against her back. 'I want you to stay.'

It felt right. He felt like home. And that's what scared her more.

Twenty-one

The early morning sun was barely peeking over the alien landscape that stretched forever in all directions. Soft grey and salmon pinks filled the sky that softened the wilderness into an outback wonderland. From her table, Teà had the best view from the front bar of the Topp Springs roadhouse.

As Patrick mopped the floors, Teà spread out Lottie's colour-coded map. On top of it were the six individual maps they'd collected from this seven-day road trip. The maps themselves were simple drawings, all drawn by their father, with instructions scrawled on the top.

The first map they'd received from the lawyer. Along with their travel allowance, the list of items to take, with instructions to travel to Port Augusta as part of the first official day of their trek. The second map was waiting for them in their hotel, advising them to drive to Coober Pedy.

Day two, it was a trek to Coober's underground hotel that had been a blast in a land that looked like they'd landed on the moon. There they'd received the next map with the brief instructions to drive to Rusty's Roadhouse near the Devil's Marbles.

Day three had been the longest stretch of the journey. With the train line running alongside, they were pretty much confined to the car for twelve hours, on a mission to finish this seven-day journey.

The breadcrumbs were nothing but simple hand-drawn maps, featuring jagged singular lines that ran across the page from top to bottom with an X at one end, and another simple X at the other. There were other markings, main points for certain areas, but they were rather simple compared to Lottie's detailed map of many colours.

At the end of day three, they'd received another map from Rusty at his roadhouse. This time an L-shaped jagged line led them from Rusty's, to turn off the main highway to head to Bore 13.

Who knew day four was only a taste of the many challenges to come? Travelling to Bore 13, along the Murranji Track, they'd found the map at the windmill. From there, they followed the simple broken line to the Big Dipper's pinch point pronounced in a circle on the page. The map's lines, dots and squiggles would never have prepared them for what they'd found at the other Gregory Tree.

The map they'd found there, tucked in Lottie's letter, informed them to go to Topp Springs. It seemed like a simple enough request at the time.

But it was the most challenging, walking the Murranji Track, stranded, until Devin found them. Taking them to Topp Springs for the next breadcrumb, this time no map but just a set of instructions to rest and work out the puzzle.

But the maps were nothing but squiggles, lines, dots, and crosses. She couldn't work it out.

Surely her father wouldn't make it too hard for them.

The Ford's car door closed, making her look up from the maps. It was Lottie, putting her plaid suitcases away.

'What are you doing?' Freshly showered, back in her plaid dress, with her blonde ponytail in place, Lottie made herself a coffee from the urn at the bar.

'Trying to work this out.' Teà leaned back, running her fingers through her damp hair. She'd showered in her own room, leaving Devin sleeping. It was hard to walk away, him naked and beautiful, tempting her to stay. But what she was feeling for him was wrong on so many levels.

How was it possible to connect so deeply with someone without saying a damned word, without spending months getting to know each other to build a bond? How had they skipped the fragile dance of dating, to instantly trust each other?

She'd trusted no one this quickly. Her idea of trust meant opening herself to someone. And she hadn't done that in a very long time, because when you'd lived with the sting of abandonment, you learned not to trust in a hurry.

Yet, it surprised her how easily she'd tumbled. To then battle her own will to leave him in bed. But she needed to finish this trek. Today was the last day.

'Any luck?' Lottie asked.

'No.' Teà pushed off from her chair and went to make another coffee. 'Your turn.' Because she'd been hoping if they worked out the puzzle, they'd hit the road and she'd never have to see Devin again. Awkward confrontation avoided. 'Want a coffee, Patrick?'

'I'm good, luv.' He waved from the far end of the room, methodically moving his mop from side to side as if in some form of meditation.

'My son's name is Patrick. We call him Pip,' said Lottie.

'You told me last night, luv. A couple of times.'

'Oh, right?' Lottie blushed behind her coffee cup.

'How are you feeling this morning, Lottie?' Teà returned to her seat, opposite.

'I'm good.' Lottie picked up the map pieces.

'Really?' Considering the mess her sister had been in.

'I am.' Lottie placed her hand on Teà's. 'Thank you for what you did. For not only finding the car, but for telling me to get out of my comfort zone, which I'll admit was scary. But if you hadn't pushed me, I'd never have ridden a camel and won the cup.'

'Did you tell Adrian?'

'I think I drunk dialled him. But I made so many new

friends last night and heard so many amazing stories about Dad. It was good.' Lottie's dainty hands deftly shifted the pieces around the table.

'You look like you know what you're doing with those maps. Puzzles were never my thing.'

'It reminds me of a dressmaking pattern with its necklines and hemlines. See …' Lottie traced her fingertip down the lines of the hand-drawn map. 'The place of the fold, notches, the X is for buttonholes. The broken line is the stitching lines and darts.'

Teà sat forward. 'Did Dad know these symbols?'

'I'm pretty sure he did.' Lottie nodded with excitement. 'Dad was married to my mother for over twenty years. He was always nicking materials or thread from my sewing room, teasing me about some morse code for a frock. We need scissors, paper, pens, and sticky tape.'

'Patrick, can I raid your office supplies?' Teà asked the publican who was still dancing with the mop.

'Just help yourself, luv. Door's open.'

Teà dashed behind the bar and soon returned with hands full of gear, dumping it on the table. 'What do we do?'

'First, we make a copy of the originals and trace over them.'

Together they traced over the maps, then cut out lines, folded, and bent the pages, even sticking some folds into sections. It reminded her of a time when they were children, making Father's Day cards from scrap paper. Only now, Teà and Lottie sat beside each other to build a map that was almost three dimensional.

'Is it a table?' Lottie asked.

'A box for something?' Even though she was impressed with Lottie's skills as a dressmaker, they were truly stumped. 'Hey, Patrick, what do you think this is?'

Patrick put down the last of the chairs on his now-dry floor and sauntered over. 'What have you girls got there?'

'We don't know. I think it might be a hat box or

something,' said Lottie. 'It's cute.'

'Nah, luv, I reckon that's Tree Stump.'

Lottie turned the paper model around on the table. 'It looks like a tree stump, with the rings on top of the paper design from the maps.'

Teà didn't know what it was. She wasn't that imaginative. 'Is there some other significant tree in the area, like the other Gregory tree on the Murranji Track?'

Patrick chuckled, pointing at their tacky paper model. 'Not *a* tree stump. That's Tree Stump Mountain, it's part of Tree Stump Station.'

'How do we get there? I don't remember seeing it on my map.' Lottie dragged her colour-coded map closer.

'Ask your mate, Devin. He'll tell you where you need to go.'

'Why would I be asking Devin about Tree Stump?' It's who Teà wanted to avoid.

'It's his station,' said Patrick.

Teà sucked in hot air. 'But Devin's a truck-driving, helicopter pilot.'

'I thought Devin was just a truck-driving cowboy,' said Lottie.

Patrick laughed loudly, slapping his hand against his belly. 'We consider Devin Asher royalty around these parts. That boy is a bachelor who's worth billions, so they reckon.'

The air got flew out of her lungs as her stomach dropped in a sickening freefall. 'You're kidding.'

Lottie tapped at her phone's screen to wave a Google page listing articles all about Devin Asher. There was even a Wikipedia page with Devin's sullen stare, among the headlines proclaiming him a cattle baron and more.

'Now we know why the barmaids were lusting after Devin so much. Way to go, sis. You scored big.' Lottie playfully nudged Teà's arm.

She just didn't believe it. The internet was known to have fake news, right?

'Patrick, do you have any idea why our father is sending us to Tree Stump?' Teà needed to stay focused. This wasn't about Devin. This was for family.

Patrick rubbed the back of his neck. 'I believe your father worked there.'

'I know he worked on a few stations. But why Tree Stump when this entire area is cattle country?' No way did Devin own a station. He'd said nothing, just that he had a job to deliver the helicopters before the weekend. The same ones he'd pointed out to her, yesterday, as they whizzed over the crowd in for the Pussyfoot Cup, giving rides to tourists.

'Oh-oh-oh, I remember now.' Lottie wriggled excitedly in her seat like a schoolgirl. 'While you were chasing down the car, the older stockmen were telling me stories about Dad. A few of them remembered Victor Voss working at Tree Stump Station with his best mate. His name was um ...' She waved her hand in circles with her lips pressed together, obviously thinking hard. 'Neil, Noel ... No, it was Niall. Niall Asher.'

'That's Devin's old man. Niall married Janice Bowman, whose father owned this area. But since Devin's been in charge, buying out his parents and his brother, Mason, he's quadrupled the size of their property, buying out overseas investors. They reckon Devin's looking to build an abattoir, with plans for a solar station. It'll be a massive bonus for the locals if he does.' Patrick tapped a stubby finger on Lottie's colour-coded map, showing them the area. It was bigger than some European countries she'd visited.

'Teà knows about solar stations,' said Lottie.

Helping the poor—not millionaires! 'How far away is Tree Stump Mountain?' Teà wanted to leave and now.

'About an hour away. There.' He tapped at the map's contours for elevation. 'The track runs from here. You'll pass a few cattle grids along the way.'

'Is that why the stockmen kept calling Devin *boss*?' She

had to know, was he like her—working class. 'Isn't boss the nickname they give for team leaders, like workshop supervisors?' Like all the other dirty, sweaty, hot workshops she worked in.

'Nah, Devin's the *big* boss. Not one of the mustering bosses. It's a rare thing for him to hang around the place, like he has been, helping you girls out.'

'But we met him on the road,' said Lottie.

'You know, that got us mob all wonderin' about that...' Patrick paused to rub the back of his neck. 'There had to be something in it for Devin Asher to drive his truck from one end of the country to the other, when he's got a team of trucks and drivers on the payroll to do the dirty work for him.'

What the hell!

Teà rummaged through her daypack and pulled out a fistful of cash, which she left on the bar. 'Patrick, this is for you and Pearl, for your amazing hospitality.' Making sure she left a big tip.

'Nah, luv, your lawyer paid us five grand for the privilege. Pearl was telling me that the lawyer paid Rusty the same. Victor Voss wanted to make sure you girls made it.' Patrick pushed the money back into her bag. 'You keep that, and we'll keep your room for the night. You can come back when you've delivered his ashes.'

'Thanks.' The hospitality she received from strangers was amazing. 'Lottie, let's finish this, huh? I bet we'll be hiking that mountain, and we need to be there by four. So ...' Did she dare say have some decent boots? 'Do you have anything else to pack?'

'All I need now is Dad and my Camel Cup.' Lottie pointed to the urn sitting on the top shelf behind the bar. She started putting the office supplies away with Patrick's help. 'You just need to grab the duck and your bag.'

'I'll be right back.' She was done being treated like a fool. She was done with this game her father had her playing. 'Get ready to go, Lottie. Let's finish this.'

Twenty-two

Teà stormed down the corridor of rooms. She should have gone to her room, instead she was in search of answers, and hammered her fist on the motel door. 'Devin. Open up.'

With his dark hair tousled and damp, he was wearing only a towel and a smile. 'Hey, you snuck out.'

She strolled past him as he closed the door behind her. 'Why didn't you tell me your father was BFFs with my father and that you owned Tree Stump Station?'

'Oh.' He rubbed the back of his neck.

'Oh. Is that all you have to say? Oh.' She crossed her arms over her chest, with her foot tapping in annoyance.

'I was wondering when you'd find out.' He pulled out some jeans from his duffel bag, spilling some paperwork onto the floor. He turned his back to her as he dropped the towel and slid on his jeans, leaving them undone and dangerously low on his hips.

She dropped her eyes to give him some privacy, and not perve and forget her train of thought, when her eyes landed on the paperwork. 'Are you freaking kidding me?' She snatched the paperwork off the floor, recognising the letterhead. It was from the lawyer. She spotted the names *Victor Voss*, *Loretta Voss* and *Teà Voss* on the page.

Her entire universe tilted, then rolled into a world of fury.

'You knew about us and this road trip, just like Rusty

and Pearl did?' She waved the lawyer's paperwork at him, ill to her core. 'You knew!'

He shrugged. 'What do you want me to say?'

'What was your part of the deal?'

'To make sure you two made it.'

They'd paid him to help! 'To get us to *your* station?'

'I guessed it was Tree Stump, but I don't know where. My father arranged it, as soon as he got the call from the lawyer after your father had passed. I only learned about Victor Voss a few months ago.'

'Why didn't you tell me?'

'I couldn't. I wasn't even supposed to meet you, but when Lottie hit that duck, then at Rusty's—'

'How much did you get paid? I know Dad's been generous to those involved, because he paid Rusty and Pearl five grand each, and we had a travel allowance of ten. So, if you followed us from … where?'

'Port Augusta.'

She crumbled to the end of the bed. Her mouth opening, then closing. It couldn't be true! 'You've been following us through two states? That's over two-and-a-half thousand kilometres.'

Devin said nothing, sliding down the wall to crouch directly in front of her.

'I trusted you.' Annoyed at her falling tears, and at herself for letting him in. 'I rarely trust anyone, but I trusted you.'

'I think the word you're looking for is connected. We connected, Teà. Far more than I've ever connected with anyone.' He reached out to her, but she pushed him away. 'I wasn't trying to hurt you or use you. I didn't want to ruin what we had.'

'You kept this from me. The entire time. I hate secrets. And now, I don't know if you helped me because of who you are, or because you were paid to do it!'

'I helped you.' He patted his bare chest. 'That was me. It was nothing to do with the money. Ever since I first saw you, I've wanted to help you, Teà. I'd do anything for you, just to be near you.'

She pulled back from him as if he would burn her. And she'd been burnt too many times already. 'What do you think this is?'

He shrugged. 'I don't know. I don't do relationships. It's always been easier to avoid the dramas.'

Hmph, she agreed with him on that point. 'And here I thought you lived in that truck travelling from station to station doing the musters. I hate secrets. Especially ones that involve me!'

'I couldn't tell you; it was part of the rules. You two had to find the maps yourselves. I was never meant to get involved.'

'Yeah, me neither.' She moved for the door.

But Devin was quicker, blocking her path. 'I didn't mean to hurt you, Teà.'

'How long did you know about this? About Dad's plans?'

He sighed heavily. With his head lowered, he lifted his eyes to meet hers and she was swimming in the world of sorrow filling his caramel-coffee-coloured eyes. 'It wasn't my job to do this trip, I was never a part of it. I manage the station, I rarely leave. My father was supposed to do this trip with Mum. But my brother's having a baby, so they drove to Sydney to help Mason with my nephews. My parents are grey nomads, towing a caravan these days. They would've matched Lottie's speed perfectly on the highway. They were supposed to do this job, not me.'

'Just a job, huh?' She crossed her arms over her chest. 'Did you spend the money, not that you need it, so I hear?' Christ, the guy was a millionaire. Not that she knew any, but he didn't dress like a millionaire, just a cowboy in his comfy jeans with a body made of working-man's muscle, complete with an outdoors tan and a down-to-earth working-class personality.

She was working class, too. Not a pinkie-raising

polished princess, but a girl in lace-up boots. And she'd believed Devin was working class too. Not rich!

'I used the money towards the helicopter.' He pointed out the window, to where the small chopper rested on the back of the truck. 'But I wasn't supposed to get paid. This road trip wasn't my job. I only did it as a favour to my folks — not for the money.'

'Yeah, right?' Why should she believe him now?

'My parents had been waiting for months, with their caravan packed and ready to haul butt to cross paths with the Voss sisters in Port Augusta. But then no one could find you. We didn't think this entire Sister Trip was ever going to happen. But then you showed up. How?'

'My sister put out a missing person's report to find me. Which wasn't hard as I'd registered with the Australian Embassy in Botswana to work in the Kalahari.' But her sister had searched for her for all the wrong reasons — because it was the rules of this stupid trip. Lottie had made that loud and clear when she'd first arrived, that if Teà hadn't shown up they wouldn't have needed to do this drive across the country. 'Is that why the lawyer made us stay five days at the farm? To let everyone — you — get into position?'

He barely nodded.

'Where?'

'I watched you guys fill up at the truck stop the morning you left Port Augusta. The Ford was easy to spot. I then waited around, did some tool shopping to give you girls plenty of time to get ahead of me. Same in Coober Pedy.'

She gasped. He'd been following her all that time. 'To do what?'

'Help if you needed help.'

'Which you did,' she said coldly. 'Thank you very muchly. I'll be sure to leave a glowing reference of the service you provided.' She leaned in with a sneer. 'It was real value for *money*.'

He frowned back at her with his square chin raised. 'Are you even going to ask me?'

'Ask you what?'

'If you can drive across my land to visit Tree Stump Mountain.'

She narrowed her eyes at him. 'Why should I? When we've already paid our toll fare that's sitting on the back of that truck.' Livid, she tried to open the door, but he snagged her wrist.

'I heard you last night, Teà. Telling me I felt like home. You held me so tight, like you didn't want to let go.'

She heaved in air, pressing her back to the door. That wasn't true. It couldn't be. It'd be a nightmare if it was, because she'd be breaking an oath to herself to never get attached to anyone again.

'You felt it as much as I did.'

'Just like I heard you asking me to stay.' She couldn't. Pulling herself free, she let the door slam shut behind her.

Twenty-three

Lottie's phone rang as she sat at the table in the bar just as Teà disappeared around the corner to pack. Recognising the number, she answered immediately. 'I'm sorry, Adrian, if I butt dialled you, or is that drunk dialled you last night?'

'You had a reason to celebrate. Pity I wasn't there to share it with you.'

'I thought of you.'

'Which is why you kept ringing me so many times.' His laugh was forced.

'We found the last clue, Adrian, and we're getting ready to go.'

'Um, yeah … Look, Lottie, have you talked to Teà about what she plans to do with the farm?'

'No. Teà's been busy finding the car. I think she hooked up with Devin last night—'

'I don't know who you're talking about, and it doesn't matter. Lottie, what do you know about your sister?'

'Why? She's my sister.' Lottie shrugged.

'Do you trust her?'

She leaned forward, resting her elbows on the table. 'Adrian? What aren't you telling me?'

'You know how you asked me to talk to the lawyer about contesting the will?'

Her eyes darted around the room to ensure Teà wasn't around to eavesdrop. 'Um, yeah.' She squirmed in her seat, filling with guilt for being so deceitful.

'It turns out if we contest the will, Teà gets everything.'

'What? How? Why?' She gripped onto her ponytail as if to get a handle on this conversation. 'Why would Teà get everything? She doesn't even live there.' Never once did Teà call it home, just the farm.

'There's a caveat on the property that should Victor pass away, it returns to Teà. Teà's grandparents put it in place. Apparently, they were looking after Teà when your father had abandoned her, after her mother had died. Is that true?'

She blinked but didn't see, barely hearing Adrian's voice that seemed so far away. 'Dad was heartbroken. Teà told me this. She told me he wasn't gone long, that Dad returned with my mother and me.'

'Did Teà tell you that Victor Voss was only the caretaker of Tucknott Flats? This farm.'

'What?' She felt the floor pull out from under the chair into a massive sinkhole of darkness.

'They only gifted Victor a few acres. The back shed area is his, a measly five acres. The other four hundred acres, including this house, belongs to Teà. It's always belonged to Teà.'

'But—but—it can't be true? Teà's been the driving force behind all of this, she climbed for clues on the windmill, she kept us going when we were stranded on the Murranji Track. Teà found the car, the maps …' It was Teà, first on the job at the table trying to work on the puzzle before Lottie arrived.

'I've never lied to you, Loretta. I'm not making this up either.'

She sat taller, nodding at the phone. Oh, bless him, he was a man of many faults, but his most admirable trait was he never lied to anyone. His integrity was flawless. 'What else did the lawyer say about the inheritance?' The lawyer who'd been in deep conversations with Teà a few times, behind closed doors, well before they started this journey.

'Victor cashed in some bonds and used the balance of

his life insurance policy to cover any of his debts, but mostly to cover the costs for your road trip to the Northern Territory. The lawyer did say the Ford is yours. What's left of Victor's inheritance is only the removable assets like the sheep and the machinery—not the land. That's why the appraiser was here, to see what was of value.'

'Do you mean I've been putting myself through all of this for junk!' The harvesters were on their last legs, the tractor a relic, with her father hiring equipment if they needed it. 'It's not true. The lawyer told us we had to drive all the way out here, to scatter Dad's ashes to get our inheritance or he'd donate it to some charity. It's why I put myself through this, for us. For our home—'

'That doesn't even belong to us,' said Adrian. 'It never even belonged to Victor Voss.'

Her father was a man of many secrets, but this couldn't be true. 'But the bills are all in Dad's name!'

'He's been the caretaker. Never the owner.'

'Why didn't Dad say anything? Or Teà?'

'Teà hasn't been there for seventeen years, but she's there now and it's time you asked her.'

Lottie scrunched up the map in her hand. Her eyes landing on the handwritten letter she'd received from her father, lying in her open handbag. 'Adrian, I'm going to finish this. If I do exactly as Dad's instructed us—to the letter—we'll then have a legitimate right to claim it as ours. Teà left seventeen years ago. She has no right to it. We'll fight it in court, because that property is *ours*. Dad worked on it, slaved away at it. We all did.'

'No, Lottie, listen …' Adrian sighed heavily. 'I've been thinking long and hard about this, ever since I learned Victor's secret.'

Her father's last line of his handwritten letter read: *… find it in your heart to forgive me for my secrets …* 'When did you find out?'

'Yesterday. I just didn't want to ruin your good mood, Lottie. You were the happiest I've ever heard. I'm so proud of you for having a go, too. The kids loved the video of you racing on that camel. They've watched it countless times.'

Sadly, all of yesterday's exuberant joy had shrivelled into dust.

'I now understand why Victor never let me work on the farm,' he said. 'It all makes sense.'

Yet, none of this made any sense to her.

'Victor didn't want us working on the property because it never belonged to him, or to our family. It's all Teà's.'

'And if Teà didn't want it?'

'She's there, isn't she?'

'That bitch!'

Twenty-four

Devin sat heavily on the bed, staring at the lawyer's paperwork. The letters shifted, moved, and rolled on the page, frustrating him to no end. He kicked it aside.

Can you spell b-o-t-c-h-e-d up, son!

It was never his job, he'd never planned on meeting the Voss sisters. His contract was to just watch them from afar. If they got into trouble, he'd play the part of a truck driver.

Which is exactly who Teà thought he was. She'd treated him like an ordinary person, never using him or sucking up to him, or being insincere towards him. And he'd been having a lot of fun with her, too.

Never once did she take advantage of him.

He'd seen his brother, Mason, simply smile at a girl, who'd then found out who he was to then suddenly want to move in with him.

Hell no, Devin wasn't going to make that mistake with women.

Yet, Teà had been different from the start. Bantering with him over duck dishes, while rescuing a duck. Teasing him in the bar over dinner, telling him up front from the start that nothing was going to happen. Answering his questions truthfully and straightforwardly. She'd seen him for who he was, and not for what he had.

She had walls up. He got that. He'd never judge her for that, because its what people did to survive. The heartache she must have gone through as a child, losing her mother to cancer, and now this trip for her father. But his gut was telling him there was something else holding her back.

He'd never lied to her either. He just didn't tell her the truth. And he'd been an idiot for not telling her sooner. He'd wanted to, but never found the right time.

But was Teà the right person for him? And this was just the wrong time, the wrong place in the wrong situation?

Hey, she knew now how he felt about her and still slammed the door in his face.

Dammit.

He shoved the last of his gear into his bag. The disappointment and ache of being so close to something so real, only to lose it, made him feel cold and empty inside. It shouldn't be like this. Not over someone he'd just met.

Aw, who was he kidding? This is why he didn't do relationships. Hook-ups were so much easier. Relationships that lasted more than a day were far too hard.

But this …

It had come so easily these past five days.

Working side by side with Teà had been an intense, emotional rollercoaster ride of fearing for her, to effortlessly care for someone in such a small space of time. He'd been part of a team with Teà, who'd included him in everything. Normally he was the one in charge, running a multi-million-dollar business, making all the decisions for mustering teams, stockmen, station hands, bore runners.

Yet, with Teà he was just a simple man, watching sunsets in silence. The pleasure of holding each other while covered in muck after facing a dust devil, and her relief and exuberant joy when he picked her up from Murranji. There were so many layers to the woman, from the mischievous way she hustled money at two-up, tipping him for what he'd lent her, to her fearless sense of adventure.

And the way she'd claimed that simple chipping hammer, as if it was a diamond, had completely done him in.

He was a fool to have not told her sooner.

Can you spell l-o-s-e-r, son?

Tossing his bag over his shoulder, he headed down the hallway to head home. Even if home felt like the loneliest place on the planet.

He opened the back door, the sun blinding. A wave of heat washed over him, but it failed to defrost the numbness in his bones. He unlocked the truck's cab, threw his bag on the seat, and began checking over his trailer. It was time to take his new helicopter home and put his investment to work. Even though he fought with the need to sell the thing because it'd be a constant reminder of Teà.

Nearby a set of wheels ground in the dust as a car took off, and fast.

It was the blue Ford, leaving in a stream of dust. No doubt Teà making a fast getaway. And she drove a helluva lot faster than Lottie ever did, and with ease. She was a woman who liked her own company. A strong woman who needed nothing she couldn't get for herself. Just one of the many traits he admired about her.

Damn, he'd stuffed up! Where was he going to find someone like that again? He doubted he could have found a better match for himself if he had been looking.

'Lottie, wait for me!' It was Teà.

From behind the truck, he spotted Teà carrying her backpack over one arm with the duck tucked under the other. Her face was pure horror as she crumpled to her knees in the dirt with her head hanging low and shoulders hunched over.

'Teà?' He jogged over to her. 'What's wrong?'

'My sister …' Her eyes were full of fear and hurt as she stared down the road. '… abandoned me.'

'Lottie wouldn't leave.' He helped her to her feet.

'She did.' She held out a piece of paper. 'See.'

'I, um …'

'See.'

'I see the paper.'

She scowled, shifting the duck to her hip as if carrying a child. 'Are you playing with me?'

'No. I can't read it.' He winced as his words echoed around him, the shame of his greatest weakness revealed.

Her frown fell as her defiant stance softened.

'I have trouble reading. I'm not dumb, I'm dyslexic.' He rubbed his eyes, preparing for either the pitying look or disappointment for a guy who had flaws bigger than the road train standing behind him. 'Neurodivergent.'

She stepped back from him with her head tilting. Her eyes used to measure him up as a worthy contender—only to learn he wasn't the man she thought he was.

'I'm not a moron.'

'I know that.' She shifted the duck to her other hip. 'That's why you kept asking us what the maps said, getting us to read it all the time.'

Damn, she was quick. 'I can read.'

'You'd use apps and stuff, right? Or glasses.'

'Apps. Font styles, sizes and colours, help. I spell words out in my head, a habit from my dad who'd challenge me daily to spell words to help me read.'

'But it hasn't stopped you …' She pointed to the helicopter strapped down to his truck. 'Is it hereditary?'

'No. I had an accident playing footy as a kid.'

The corner of her mouth slightly curled. 'Is that why you're such a grump to barmaids grunting out orders, telling them you'll have the usual, so you don't have to read the menus? And why you're still single?'

For someone who had admitted he'd been obsessed with watching her, he hadn't realised how much she'd noticed about him. He narrowed his eyes at her. 'It's not the sort of thing you bring up in a conversation. But you seem to know a lot about it?'

Teà gave a candid shrug.

'Aw, come on! That's all I get as your reaction?' He'd been building himself up for this.

'What do you expect—' She slow blinked, stepping back from him as if the penny had finally dropped. 'You were teased at school, huh?'

It was his turn to shrug.

Can you spell b-u-l-l-i-e-d, son?

But Teà never looked away, tenderly stroking the duck's neck. She didn't make fun of him. Keeping those dark eyes steady on his. 'I had an apprentice who had hereditary dyslexia and ADHD. Nobody would take him on. As a girl in a man's world, you bet I took that kid on. Simon does underwater welding now, sings really badly to me on my birthday, and sends me an annual tacky Christmas card. I never got a friendship bracelet out of him, but I got an invite to his wedding. And he's a total adrenaline junkie. You?'

'Um …'

'Dude, you own a helicopter and drive a big truck.'

'I can help you catch your sister. Lottie doesn't drive that fast.'

The smile left her face. 'Your job is done. I won't bother you.' She went to move away.

'This is not a job!' He caught her arm. 'I'm sorry I didn't tell you about the deal between our fathers. I never lied. I just should have told you sooner. But I don't want you to go.'

The breeze danced over the dust, but she never turned away. Her eyes remained steady, as if digging deep behind his shields. And he'd let her see. He had nothing to hide from her.

'Are you one of those people who hold grudges?'

'No, life's too short to hold grudges. But I understand the heavy burden of keeping a secret.' Teà stared down at the road. Pain flitted across her face with her shoulders heavy.

'You look like you've been carrying one for a while?'

'For seventeen years. Now, I'm tired of keeping secrets. You?'

'I don't normally have any, and I was only doing this as a favour to my father.'

'Like I'm here because of mine.' She inhaled deeply. 'Fathers ...'

'You can ask me anything. I'll tell you whatever you want to know, Teà.' He didn't want there to be any more secrets.

She gave such a sad smile that dulled the shine in her eyes. 'I didn't come out here to start a relationship. I told you that in the beginning, I'm here for family. And I'm sorry if you thought something else, I'm just ...' She winced as if in pain laced with fear. 'I'm working class, practically a drifter, and I don't know if I'm ready or even deserve to be with anyone.'

'Hey, I'm a simple guy, too. Give me a pair of denim jeans, boots, and an outback sunset over wearing a suit in the city any day.' He gently grabbed her upper arms to hold her in place. 'We can work something out, Teà. If you can forgive me for not sharing my secrets with you.'

'Can you forgive me? Because I doubt my sister ever will.' She stared down at the note in her hand.

'What does the note say?'

'*Liar.*'

Twenty-five

L ottie howled with tears streaking down her cheeks as she clung to the steering wheel following another dirt road. Her sister had lied to her. The entire time, driving from one end of the country to the remote Northern Territory outback.

Teà had kept secrets.

What was she, some joke to Teà? To snigger about with Devin in some game of *let's watch Lottie make a fool of herself*.

She should have known better than to let her guard down around Teà. After all, they were strangers. Sure, they may have shared a childhood together, but in all honesty, it was only the first ten years of Lottie's life.

People changed. She believed that, feeling her own changes from the confronting situations she'd faced this past week. Lottie had come to realise she didn't like parts of herself—but she thought her big sister had cared for her. Warts and all!

The liar!

She savagely wiped at the tears as she drove around a long sweeping bend and out of the dust rose Tree Stump Mountain. It reminded her of Uluru. Yet flatter and smaller. It really looked like a tree stump rising from the soil.

The car whizzed over a cattle grid, heading further inland. She was going to do this. Patrick had told her where to go. She didn't need Teà, who wasn't even part of her family, and this was for Lottie's home.

Her father didn't mean to trick her. She could explain it all to the lawyer, following the instructions to the letter. And if she got to her father's final resting place before Teà, and met the four o'clock deadline, she would own all of it.

Fwhomp-fwhomp-fwhomp-fwhomp-fwhomp.

Lottie ducked behind the wheel as the underbelly of a helicopter flew low and fast, straight over her car. She slammed both feet on the brake, blinded by thick swirls of dust.

The helicopter landed in front of her, its noisy engine silenced, and the long rotating blades slowed to a stop, allowing the dust to settle.

She recognised the helicopter. It was from the back of Devin's truck.

Devin was a liar, too.

Everyone was a liar.

Teà and Devin made a good couple, both liars.

She could hit reverse, then drive around them. But then that'd be silly, because Devin could just land that helicopter anywhere he liked.

'UGH!' Lottie screamed. Trapped, and treated like a fool.

'What did you mean by this?' Teà waved her note in the air, while Devin leaned against the helicopter with arms crossed, all smug like, with the duck balancing on his big shoulders.

That duck was a traitor, too.

Teà ripped open the driver's door and took the keys. 'Get out and explain why you deserted me back at the roadhouse and called me a liar.'

Lottie's hands shook with fury, as she faced enemy number one. *'You're a liar.'* The word *liar-liar-liar* echoing across the open plains.

'About what?'

'That you own the farm!'

'The only way you'd know about that was if you were going to contest the will.' Teà crossed her arms over her chest. 'Which means you were going to cut me out. Which you proved, by deserting me back at the roadhouse.'

'You *deserted* me seventeen years ago.'

'I did that for you.' Teà shook her head.

'Sure, you did? What did I get out of it? I don't see no pay-off. Leaving me to stay behind to look after Dad. The farm. The bills.' She wagged her finger at Teà. 'Don't you dare look at me like some know-it-all! Thinking you're better than me.' Lottie wanted to thump her sister for treating her like an imbecile. 'You kept this from me because you're jealous I have a husband and made a home with our father. And you have nothing and no one. Do you even know how to love?'

'YES. I DO. More fiercely and more loyally than you'll ever know.'

'You're lying. You just don't commit to relationships —'

'*I'm a widow!*' Teà's voice was strong, but the hurt was all over her face. 'I was married to an amazing man. It wasn't perfect, and we fought way more than we should, but we loved each other.'

'You're making this up. Why should I believe you?' Lottie waved her finger dismissively at her sister. 'If you'd been married, weren't we good enough to come to your wedding?'

'We didn't have a wedding. It was just a ceremony at a courthouse in Hawaii. The night before we caught a helicopter to meet an oil tanker to do some urgent repairs on the hull.'

So Teà didn't get a honeymoon-holiday either. 'Your husband was a welder?'

'His name was Silas Knowles. Half-Irish, half-Texan. His specialty was underwater welding.' Teà sighed, kicking her boot toe in the dirt. 'Silas said underwater welders rarely made it to forty. He was right.'

'How old was he when he ...'

'Thirty-seven.' Teà aimed a sour smile at the sky, her

eyes glassy with tears. 'We both loved riding, did bike tours in between gigs. The company we worked for gave us a sweet deal where we'd work one month on, two months off, leaving us plenty of time to explore. We rode our bikes across Europe, then from South America up to Texas to meet his family. Silas had just ducked down to the shops for his mother and …' The breeze dropped barely to a whisper to match her breathing, that was slow and deliberate. 'At least Silas didn't feel a thing when that soccer mum, staring at her phone, cleaned him up in her minivan.'

'How long ago was this?' Devin stood closer than she'd realised. His open care for Teà was so much deeper than what was written all over his face. Her husband had never looked at her like that.

'Two years ago.' Teà shrugged.

'Is that why you went and worked in the desert, and not back at sea?'

Teà nodded, barely looking at him.

Then she raised her heavy head and looked at Lottie. 'I was searching for something. I didn't know what. Too scared to get close to anyone because when you let someone in and then have them go so swiftly, it's heartbreaking. I tried to live with the grief, but the loneliness was suffocating …' Teà wiped at her nose, the tears spilling down her cheeks. 'To me, home isn't just four walls or a roof, it's a place you share with someone. It's that feeling you get inside,' she said, tapping over her heart. 'That no matter where you go, it's the memories you make together, and it's where you can be safe to be who you truly are underneath. I had that with Silas, and it's a very rare thing.'

'Have you ever felt like that with anyone else?' Lottie asked.

Teà dropped her heavy head, rubbing at her eyes.

Devin just stared at Teà.

It was another one of those long lingering stares—only

this time Teà wasn't looking at Devin, and the silence dragged on.

'*Peoples*, what's this got to do with the farm?' Lottie frowned, remembering they were arguing.

Teà raised her head, her eyes red and her cheeks stained with tears. 'When the police said you were looking for me, I came back. I didn't come back for the inheritance, or for the farm. I came back because you were looking for me. *You* lodged a missing person's report.'

'I only did that because I had to, not because I wanted to.'

Teà tossed her hands in the air. 'How stupid of me, to have such high hopes of finally being able to reconnect with my baby sister.'

'You could have done it sooner.'

'Lottie, I was miserable at the way I was treated in that household. Leaving that place just made it more comfortable for Dad and Lauren, which made it a happier household for you with me no longer in the picture. I wasn't meant to stay away this long, but then time just got away from me, thinking you'd contact me one day ... I've been waiting for you to find me for a very long time.'

Lottie almost collapsed under the burden of those words, pressing a hand against the car. 'I don't believe you. You ran away when I was ten. This is nothing to do with me.'

Teà inhaled heavily. 'For the record, I didn't run away. Dad drove me to Port Lincoln, where I started my apprenticeship with that welding company on the docks.'

'That can't be true. Dad said he didn't know where you were.' And Lottie was never allowed to ask again.

'Dad would visit, but I didn't want to see him.'

'Why?'

'Because our father is not who you believe him to be. It's because of Dad I left.'

'Bull. Don't say it's another secret. I want to know the truth!' She was sick of being kept in the dark about things.

'I deserve to know.'

Wearing a sneer full of hurt and hate, Teà glared at Lottie through hot tears. 'Let me warn you now, Lottie. Once it's out there, it can't be unsaid. Are you sure you want to hear it?'

Twenty-six

Teà waited, her shoulders tense as the breeze stirred the dust at their feet. It was like a showdown in the wild west. Which gun-slinging outlaw would draw blood first?

It felt like Teà had taken the first hit, with a wound so deep it had re-opened to bleed pure heartache.

Worse, she could feel Devin watching her, but she was too scared to face him.

It's because of Devin, revealing his secrets and how she'd felt knowing she'd been kept in the dark, that she'd finally found the courage to share hers.

She had nothing to lose. Her sister had already made up her mind they were never going to be a family.

'Do you want to know the secret I've been carrying for seventeen years, Lottie? The real reason why I left and haven't returned?'

Lottie crossed her arms over her chest in defiance. 'The truth. No more lies.'

'You need to say you want this.' Because it was going to crush Lottie, and Teà knew it.

Lottie faltered. 'I-I …'

'Louder! Say it like you mean it.'

'I want to know why you left.' Lottie gritted her teeth.

Teà responded in a rapid round of machine gun fire. 'I caught Dad cheating on your mother!'

'What?'

'But that wasn't the first affair, Lottie. Your mother,

Lauren, had an affair with our father while my mother lay in bed dying of cancer.'

'That's not true.' Lottie stabbed her finger in the space between them. 'You take that back!'

'And Lauren was my mother's best friend.'

Devin sucked air so fast it was as if he'd been sucker punched.

It made her wince at the hurtful truths she was finally releasing into the atmosphere. 'My mother died three months before you were born, Lottie. I couldn't tell you as a child, you were too young to understand. But I knew, and your parents knew.'

'I... I...' Lottie shook her head.

'You must have realised at some point because when I visited my mother's gravesite, waiting for us to start this road trip, I spotted your mother's gravesite only a few places over, filled with fresh flowers. The same flowers you grow in your front yard. You would've worked out the dates from my mother's passing date and compared it to your birth date.'

'It's not true.'

Talk about denial! Or her sister was living like an ostrich, always keeping her head stuck in the sand. 'Wake up and smell the red dust, sister. You were a child conceived out of wedlock to a man whose dead wife's body wasn't even cold!'

Lottie just blinked at the dirt, taking it in. It'd have to hurt. Lottie's rosy picture of their father was ruined.

It had crushed Teà, too. 'You'd think that bastard had learned his lesson. But no, Dad had to go and cheat on your mother too.'

'How—who was ...'

'The other woman?'

Lottie nodded, blinking furiously as if desperate to understand. Just like she'd done on the Murranji, first came the show of defiance, then the realisation of a helpless situation that led to despair.

Teà had to give her sister credit for finding the courage to continue. 'Her name was Ruth Oxford.'

A spark of recognition shifted in Lottie's eyes. 'You mentioned her before. Something about collecting Dad's papers from the newsagency and pharmacy.'

'Ruth Oxford worked at the pharmacy. She would fill out my mother's prescriptions, letting me take a lollipop from the jar on the counter. Do you remember her?'

Lottie thought for a while.

'She had red hair, freckles, and this annoying laugh. Your mother said it reminded her of a hyena.'

'Did my mother know about the affair?'

'Yes.'

Lottie gasped, her hand to her cheek as if bitch-slapped. She had to lean against the Ford for support.

'I'd caught Dad and Ruth in the back shed where we played two-up. I thought it was some trespasser. But it was Dad and Ruth in a very compromising position. It made me sick.' Teà screwed her face up. How could one incident ruin it for so many people? Her father had a lot to answer for. But then Teà was the fool, too, in all of this. She was the one who'd lost the most, losing her home and her family.

'Did you keep it a secret from my mother?'

'No. I liked Lauren, I really did. It's because I cared for her that I believed she deserved to know what I'd seen. I would've if it had been me.'

'What happened?'

Teà exhaled heavily. This was going to hurt. 'Lauren said she knew about Dad and Ruth's affair—'

'Nooo!' Lottie's face fell in sheer horror.

Teà couldn't stop now. 'Sitting at the kitchen table, sewing your party dress for your tenth birthday, Lauren told me she knew. She didn't even react. I was the only one reacting.'

'You wouldn't care—'

'I felt like Dad had broken my trust. Not to Lauren but

to us, to our family. I was so angry and mortified at what Dad had done. Instead, it was Lauren who made me feel guilty that I'd discovered their dirty little secret!'

'No, it can't be true. My parents were so good together.'

'Your mother said it was karma for her cheating with our dad when my mother was ill. I don't know if my mother knew about Lauren and our dad, because she hadn't lived at home for a year. Its why Dad left me behind—to deal with the shame of what he'd done. What sort of arsehole does that to their wife, dying in a hospital bed?' Teà scowled, no longer feeling the tears stinging her eyes. 'I was so angry at them; I didn't get it. To me it was a pathetic cesspool of lies. Why be with someone if you're going to cheat?'

'Why did they stay together?' Lottie asked.

'Why did you leave?' Devin asked.

She looked over her shoulder at him, the concern and worry worn in his eyes. Hell, she may as well scare him off so he could find something better. 'Because I was invisible.'

'Not to me.' Lottie's childlike voice was so tiny. 'You left me.'

'Because the longer I stayed, the more I ruined your happy family bubble. They were getting ready for your party like nothing was wrong. That year they gave you a pony, it was nothing more than a smokescreen to hide their lies, to help you forget I even existed. Lauren begged me to never tell you.'

'Why?'

'Pretty obvious, don't you think, Lottie? They loved you. We all did.'

'That still doesn't answer my question.'

'Because I was miserable, made to feel invisible in that household where they'd forget my birthday. To then find out Dad was cheating on Lauren, *and* my mother hit hard. I was also old enough to be on my own and start work. I also knew that once I was out of the picture, Dad could be this perfect figurehead, and your mother could smile again without feeling ashamed every time she looked at me. I was ruining everything for everyone because I saw the truth. So I left.'

'And this Ruth Oxford?'

'She left town soon after I did. I have no idea where she went. I didn't care. I just wanted you to be happy. Sadly, the longer I stayed away, working in some pretty remote locations, the harder it became for me to make that first move, to contact you...' She heaved in the air and let out a slow breath. 'Honestly, I was the one who was being a chicken, because I didn't want to answer the hard questions, I knew you were going to ask.'

Lottie just stared wide eyed at the dirt.

'I know it's a lot to take in.' It used to keep Teà up late at night.

Lottie lifted her head, tears staining her eyes. 'You left so I could have …'

'The perfect childhood, with parents who you believed to be flawless.'

They stared at each other. Teà had nothing more to hide. It was now up to Lottie what she did with that information. Huh, the world really did revolve around Lottie! Well, back then it did.

'You sacrificed your own happiness for family,' said Devin, placing his hand on her heavy shoulders.

She dropped her head. Was the heartache and loneliness worth it in the end?

'If you could do it all over, would you do the same? Leave?' Lottie asked.

'I wanted to believe that you had a good life, Lottie. I know I had some amazing adventures. But when you put that missing person report out on me, it ignited this deep desire I never realised was inside me.'

'What?'

'I wanted to be part of a family, again. I want what you have now, to fight for something so fiercely, which is what you've been doing, Lottie. Fighting for your home for your family. Your sheer determination and courage and the love you have for your family is admirable. Your amazing level of commitment to your family is something I want too. I don't want to live the life of a drifter, always being the first to leave, so I'd never be the one left behind again.' The duck brushed against her leg, she picked it up, not realising she was crying.

'That's why you didn't want to abandon the duck on the side of the road, like that,' Devin said, 'After your father doing that to you after your mother died, only to return with another wife and baby after your grandparents passing ... then your husband...'

And what Lottie had done just before at the roadhouse. You'd think Teà would be used to that nasty sting of abandonment, always being the one left behind. 'It's a horrible feeling.'

'I know,' said Lottie, her eyes full of fire, angrily stabbing at her own chest. 'You left me without saying goodbye. No word. No Christmas cards. Nothing. For seventeen years. Did you ever think that with you leaving like you did, how it would have affected my world too.'

'How?'

Lottie pointed at the car. 'All family trips in this car stopped. Everything to even show you existed was gone and I was never allowed to talk about you.' Lottie patted her own heart, the tears streaking down her cheeks. 'When you left all the fun in my childhood died and I was left to grieve for my sister who I thought didn't want me.'

'I did want to reunite with you.'

'But you never did.'

'You could've contact me, too.'

'How was I supposed to know that when *you*...' Lottie pointed a shaky finger at Teà. 'You made no effort.'

Teà cupped her mouth, almost doubling over with

pain, holding the duck to her chest. How selfish was she? To not realise the pain she'd put her sister through. She had no idea what to do or what to say, while struggling against the guilt gripping her rib cage.

'Hey …' Devin's fingertips gently brushed her arm that cuddled the duck. 'How about we take that duck home. I know the perfect place. But I'm driving.'

Twenty-seven

Teà sat in the front passenger seat holding the duck, while Lottie sat low in the back seat. Both girls were positively shell shocked from the info dump Teà had laid out on the table. The level of devastation from the secrets revealed was colossal. They both needed a pick-me-up, and so did he.

Can you spell s-e-c-r-e-t-s suck, son?

Devin steered the square-bodied Ford down a narrow corridor of trees. On either side, the turkey bushes' tiny flowers made them seem pink. Only to be overshadowed by thick blooms of yellow balls of wattles, along with the banksias, abundant with orange honeysuckles that scented the air.

Then the scrub fell back to open to an infinite blue sky and a wide clearing surrounded by brushland. In the centre, a sea of white, wild lotus flowers stretched to follow the sun's path, amid the calm waters that reflected the sky. Long-legged black storks, herons, and royal spoonbill water birds waded along the water's edge as pygmy geese floated on the shimmering surface of the spring-fed billabong.

'We're here.' He opened Teà's door, while Lottie stayed put.

'What is this place?' Teà asked, carrying the duck.

'One of my favourite spots on the station. It's a billabong that's fed from a natural spring, so there's water here all year round and no crocodiles. Look ...' He pointed to the far end where peeling paperbarks stood like soldiers towering over the elegant reeds. 'Do you see them?'

Teà stepped closer, the duck wriggling in her arms. 'Are they Burdekin ducks?'

He nodded. 'We'll take Quacker to the other side.'

Through the soft grasses, moss, and damp soils brimming with assorted wildflowers, they followed the edge of the billabong, to find a shady place among the ghost gums. Their pale leaves fluttered in the breeze that barely caused a ripple in the water.

'This will be a good spot.'

'What do I do?' Teà held the duck closer.

'We should take off that bandage first. The duck doesn't need to wear plaid anymore.' He held the duck as she unwound the plaid material, working like a team like they'd done the moment they'd met.

Teà gave the duck a gentle hug. His little legs and web feet paddled in the air as if already swimming. 'Goodbye, Quacker. Be safe.'

At first Quacker stumbled, then waddled, to hop and stand as he fluffed up his feathers. And then he duck dived into the water. His excited bursts of snorted quacking noises filled the air as he splashed around like a toddler in a bathtub full of toys.

Devin had to smile. 'We can watch him for a bit. See him settle in.'

'Um, yeah.' Teà was like a parent, watching their child go to school for the first time.

On the far side, Lottie sat on the grass, her back resting against the car.

Devin patted his pocket, checking he had the car keys, so Lottie wouldn't leave them behind.

'Did you mean it, what you said before?' Devin asked Teà.

'I said way too much. Lottie's a wreck.'

'She needed to hear it, and you needed to stop carrying those secrets to protect her. I know it's earth-shattering stuff, especially about your dad—'

'I hated sharing it.'

'I know. I could tell.' He shuffled closer, admiring the delicate hair strands framing her face. 'But I understand you more. Especially why you weren't looking for anything, being a widow.' But two years was a long time to heal, was she ready? 'Have you been with anyone else—'

'No. And I'm not like that. I wish I was. I'm just one of the boys.'

'Not to me, you're not. After seeing the damage your father had done, you'd be loyal to your family, to your partner.'

'Pfft.'

'You are.' Beyond anything he'd ever expected. 'Teà, you have been carrying this secret for seventeen years, for your family. Hoping for a family. It's something I would do too.'

'Yeah,' she said with a sneer, 'so why does it hurt so much?'

'Because you care so much.' He pointed over to Lottie, sitting cross legged in the grass, pulling up the wildflowers. 'I can also see what Lottie is going through, too.'

'Huh?'

Maybe it was the fresh air, or this billabong that was always his safe space. Maybe it was this weird magnetic pull that kept drawing him to Teà. Whatever it was, he was suddenly whispering secrets he'd never told another soul, hoping to help Teà. 'My older brother, Mason, was pretty damned perfect in my family.'

'I don't believe it. Look at you. Look at what you've done for yourself.'

'It's taken me a long time to get there, too, Teà.' He still struggled, like how much he'd struggled to tell her about his defects. Yet the more he talked to her the easier it was to find that freedom from the shame, choosing to avoid

getting hurt. Hell, why not put it all out in the open...
'After my accident, before I got diagnosed with dyslexia, I sucked at school. Mason got all the honours, became school captain, and was everything my family hoped for. Me, I was failing miserably.'

'When did they diagnose your condition?'

'Not for a long time. We did school of the air, where our lessons were read out to us over the radio, which was an advantage for me. But when it came to reading and writing, I was considered slow. I'd get so frustrated. Words sucked, but numbers I'm good at. It wasn't until I was at boarding school, a teacher picked it up.'

'Did you and your brother have some sibling rivalry?'

'It was more to do with my jealousy of Mason. I came to resent my older brother every time my parents would ask why I didn't get good grades like Mason, especially when I knew the answers, I just couldn't write them down. I didn't know something was wrong with me, I just thought I was stupid.' He tugged at a clump of wild grass, long and green in his hand.

'You're not.'

'Thank you. But when they did some tests, the only person who sat with me in the corridors of the hospital was my brother. My parents were here at the station, and I wasn't sick. They just saw it as tests.'

'Must have been scary?'

He shook his head, ripping the seeds from the stem of the wild grass. 'I was terrified of what they'd find. But my brother didn't tease me, he truly supported me. Didn't think he would, but he did.' Like Teà had done for Lottie, but in the most extraordinary way.

'And when you got the results?'

'After they explained it to me and told me how to deal with it … I was relieved.' He pointed back at Lottie. 'Tearing off the bandaid, like you did with your sister. Lottie may be angry with you now, but before that, she was jealous of you. Have faith that in time she'll thank you for your honesty.'

'I'm not so sure. Would you handle that about your father?'

'My father wouldn't do it to my mother. And I believe you wouldn't do it either.'

'Not after I've seen it destroy families.'

'I've seen what happens to good men when their partners cheat, too. But I have to ask something …'

'Do I have to answer it?' She winced, like she knew it was coming.

But he'd been dying to know, ever since she's said it earlier.

'Is it true what you said, about a home being more than just four walls and a roof? But a place you share with someone, that feeling inside?' He tapped his chest as he spoke, his words filled with the heavy emotions he felt for her. 'Where you can be safe to truly be yourself?'

She barely nodded.

'Last night you said I felt like home to you—' He caught her hand before she walked away. 'I felt it too. I've never been like this with anyone. Believe me, I avoid it. You said you weren't looking for anything; neither was I.' He grabbed both hands to stand in front of her. 'Teà, I honestly believe we were meant to meet each other.'

She arched an eyebrow, stepping back, but he held her fast. 'Yeah, right, like fate?'

'Hear me out.' He blew out a hot breath from a heavy chest. 'Times like this, I wish I had the fancy words, like my brother. But what I can give you is the truth and how it is. You'll get me—the real me.' He tapped his chest. 'I've never truly let my defences down around anyone, until I met you. To think of how many things that could've stopped us from ever meeting. My father was meant to be doing the drive from Port Augusta, not me. But you're here now, and I want you to stay.'

'And do what?'

'Anything you want?'

'And stay where?'

'With me. I have a house, it's big and empty. And a housekeeper, so you don't have to bother with anything. Being as independent as you are, I'd give you a job.'

'Doing what?'

'I've got a workshop full of machinery in dire need of welding repairs. I have these plans to build a solar station. Or I'd love to teach you to help with the musters.'

'I can't ride horses.'

'On ag bikes.'

'Hmm …' She arched an eyebrow. 'Would you teach me to fly?'

'Baby, I'd give you the world—and it's a pretty big world out here—if you decide to stay.'

She swayed; the wind clearly knocked out of her.

He tenderly re-gripped her hand, her strong slender fingers entwined with his. 'Look, I'm not some fancy suit guy. I'm the sunset and dust guy because I'm working class too. My brother's the snob in Sydney.'

'Doing what?'

'He's a lawyer. He's happy. Me, I'm happy here on this station.' He waved at the scenery.

'You said you don't like people.'

'Except you, Teà.' He gently tucked her hair behind her dainty ear, craving one of her full-lip curving smiles that made his heart warm.

Can you say you're in l-o-v-e, son?

'I want to be your guy, the one who'll never leave you behind. I'll never leave you hanging during a dust storm. I'll be the guy who'll come looking for you first, because I'll be the guy who will never desert you, I swear it.' He cupped her cheek, watching her dark eyes so soft and sorrowful. 'I know you're scared to let anyone in, and I get why. So believe me when I say I'll take it as slow as you want. I just don't want you to leave, especially when I know we'll be so good together.' He pointed back at the duck, floating on the billabong, already making friends with the other Burdekin ducks. 'That way you'll be able to check on Quacker, and maybe use those maternal instincts you have for animals towards your own family. The one you desire. Maybe one with me.'

A small squeak escaped her throat. 'We've only just met.'

'I know. But what have we got to lose?'

Twenty-eight

Without a word to each other, Teà and Lottie climbed the rocky path along Tree Stump Mountain. It wasn't that steep a climb, but the mountain was wide and short, like someone had chopped off the top, leaving a stump.

The blue Ford waited below, Quacker's new billabong home was just beyond. Devin, in the helicopter, was long gone on the distant horizon, leaving Teà reeling over Devin's suggestion. She had to be wearing the same shellshocked expression worn on Lottie's face.

Lottie huffed and puffed, stabbing at the dirt with the first hiking pole Teà had made her, not speaking a single syllable. Nothing. Compared to the constant chatter along the Murranji, this silence was unnerving.

Halfway up, they stopped at the lookout to take in the enormous view, with the world stretching on forever like a carpet of pure country. It's where red roads ran like ribbons among the trees, and open plains.

'How much of this land belongs to Devin?' Lottie asked.

'As far as the eye can see in all directions.' She'd never met anyone who owned that much land.

'The farm we've been fighting for is nothing, a mere four-hundred acres.'

'Devin has paddocks that are bigger.' It kind of put things into perspective.

'So, what do we do now?' Lottie leaned against her

pole, the world at her feet, still drowning in sadness. 'Do we just climb to the top and throw Dad's ashes out? I'm tempted to just smash the urn and go.'

'I think we're meant to look for another letter.'

Lottie removed the worn map from her bag, the one she'd proudly put together with sticky tape, now crumpled and worn. 'Saint Teà is right, again. As per usual.'

'Stop that.' Teà scolded her. 'Can't we at least be friends?'

'I don't have any friends.'

'Any wonder why.'

'Is that your form of an apology?' Lottie's eyes narrowed at her.

'Hey, I honestly believed I did the right thing hoping you'd be happy. Look, I'm sorry it wasn't a perfect childhood, it's not what I'd wanted for you. And you're right, I selfishly didn't think about the impact it would have on you.'

'I missed going on those road trip adventures with Dad after you left. I spent all my time trying to make Dad happy.'

'Sounds like your life was all about Dad. What about you? What makes you happy, Lottie? Because I remembered the sweet little child you were. You were so happy chasing the adventures found in each day. You had such a huge thirst for adventure, so much bigger than I ever did. And don't blame your family on that, because I recognise that same spark in your children.'

Lottie stepped back blinking hard as if she'd been slapped.

'You can't blame me for your unhappiness, and I'm sorry I didn't contact you sooner. I really am sorry.' Maybe then Lottie wouldn't have turned out the way she did. 'But would you have believed me then? Can you imagine how awkward it would've been having this conversation with Dad about all of this?'

Lottie swayed as her eyes closed. Was she trying to control her anger or come up with a smart-arse comeback?

'I warned you —'

'I know, I know.' Lottie patted at the air. 'I just didn't think it was this.' With her back turned to Teà, her head dropped. 'I was in denial over being born only a few months after your mother's passing. Do you blame me for that?'

'No. Not at all. You were a baby. I adored having a little sister.'

Lottie sighed, her voice heavy with her confession. 'I didn't have you … It would have been nice to have my sister around.'

'Yeah, right, like a hole in the head.' Teà sipped on her water, even grinning at Lottie doing the same. Obviously she'd learned the lesson on staying hydrated, even wearing decent shoes for the climb, along with a hat and sunscreen.

'I'm serious,' said Lottie, resuming their walk up the hill. 'I would have loved you there when I got engaged and to have you be a part of my wedding. I even told Adrian I wanted you to come to our wedding.'

'It would've made it very uncomfortable for your parents if I did show up.'

'I know that now. And if we're confessing dark secrets, my wedding wasn't perfect, either. Dad got drunk and gave this really embarrassing speech. Adrian's sister got even drunker and slipped on the dance floor, putting her back out. We had to get an ambulance because she'd slipped her disc. It was a mess.'

'I'm sorry to hear that.'

'I'm sorry about Silas. Was he a good man?'

'You probably wouldn't have liked him. Silas didn't have patience for people.' But it was two years ago, a long time to hold on to something she could never recapture. Not when the path was so newly laid out before her, climbing a mountain with an uninterrupted view of the world.

'You like Devin, I can see it.' Lottie playfully wiggled her finger at Teà as they continued higher on the wide path in the mountain's shade. 'You two have this incredible chemistry—now *that* is something to be jealous of. Are you going to keep seeing him?'

'Devin has asked me to stay. He's even offered me a job, if I want it, with a promise to take it slow.' She also believed him about not deserting her, because he'd proven himself a few times already. He'd been her hero. But was she ready? 'What about you, Lottie? What do you want to do?'

'Well, I have no home, do I?' Lottie speared her hiking pole into the dirt.

'Hey …' Teà tugged on her sister's arm to face her. 'I have always planned to give you half of the farm.'

'Really?'

'It's what family does, right? Share.'

'But—'

'Call it my gift as a way to make up for not being there for you sooner.' Lord knows she had a lot to make up to her sister, especially for the time lost.

'For real?'

'Want to make a pinkie promise like we did as kids.' She held up her pinkie finger hoping to get some smile out of her baby sister. 'Lottie, you lived there. I didn't. The place holds very few happy memories for me, so I'm okay with selling my half. But what do you want, Lottie?'

'What do you think I should do?'

'It's your life. You just need to do what makes you happy.'

'Isn't that what you're meant to be doing? Is wearing black a sign to show that you're still in mourning? For two years …'

Teà hesitated, her eye caught by the rich depth or redness in the rock that made up the walls of the mountain, and the sheer strength of the trees that grew among the steep inclines. 'Look.' It was a rock painting of sorts. 'Is that meant to be a V for Voss?'

It looked more like an off-white arrowhead pointing down at the rocks.

'That's subtle, not.' Teà grinned with Lottie as they scrounged among the rubble.

'Found it. Oh, look peoples, we have another plastic bag.' Lottie screwed her nose up at the white envelope.

'I'm hating these notes.'

'Me too.' They shared another smile that came much easier this time.

Lottie opened the bag, taking out two envelopes. 'This one is for you.' She held out the envelope bearing the name *Teà Eliza Voss.*

With shaky hands, Teà tore open the letter and sat on the nearest rock.

'I'll give you some privacy.'

'No, stay. I'm done keeping secrets in this family.' Teà cleared her throat and began reading aloud …

'To my darling daughter, Teà.

Hey, kid, it's Dad here, writing the toughest letter of my life.

I've been staring at this empty page for months, trying to find the courage to write.

Heck, what can I say? There's no map for being a grieving husband, and no guide to being a father, but we both know how much I failed you as a father. So for that, I am truly sorry.

What happened between us is the biggest regret of my life. Letting you walk out the door, without telling you how much I loved you, is something I have always regretted.

I've lost count of the many times I picked up the phone to call you to say come home. But then time and distance spread more dust between us, and you seemed so happy from the travel photos on social media, I lost my nerve.

I was also sorry to hear about your husband passing. I wished I had the spine to be there for you, but I didn't feel strong enough to reach out and unearth all that pain between us.

But, kid, you must know you were my greatest joy, and sadly, my greatest regret.

If you haven't already, I want you to tell Lottie what I've done and your reason for leaving. I was weak and had no excuses. Just know that with your mother, Eliza, I truly loved her in a way I never thought possible. I also loved Lauren. And I also love my daughters, all of them. Including you, kid.

Now, you being as smart as you are, you'd be wondering what my feral brain has been planning, why I chose this outback adventure? There were a few reasons. Lottie needed to get out and get a taste of what went on in the world—who better to accompany her than the world traveller you are.

Crikey, you're a strong woman to admire and respect. It's a damned shame I never had the guts to have a beer with you and hear your stories, the way you used to listen to mine.

Anyway, kid, the reason I chose Tree Stump Mountain as my resting place is that it was the place where I'd found myself at my loneliest, completely alone in the world. It's on top of Tree Stump, where I made a promise to myself. You see, I thought I'd fallen in love with a woman who didn't love me, because she loved my best friend, Niall Asher.

Heck, we were like brothers who'd been through a lot together, mustering through the Territory.

Niall knew I cared about Janice Bowman, the station owner's daughter, and it nearly broke us as friends. But he was a brother to me, Niall was the only family I had, and he deserved his happiness.

So, I quit my job, packed up my swag, and as my final hoorah, I stood on Tree Stump Mountain and made a promise that I'd find someone special to create my own family with.

It was like I'd made a promise to God.

Funnily enough, not long after that I met your mother, and found the true value of what love was—what I'd felt for that other woman was nothing, compared to Eliza. I just clicked with this cheeky jillaroo, with a wild spirit and thirst for life so pure, I was a goner. There was no way I was letting something that precious go, so I followed her home.

Her sickness killed me.

I wanted to be strong. Kid, I wanted to be strong for you. I just didn't know how.

Instead of comforting my daughter, I found comfort in the arms of another woman, Lauren. The guilt of what I'd done was soul crushing for me.

And when I lost your mother, who was my entire world, my soulmate, the shame of what I'd done to her ate me alive. I couldn't look at you without drowning in shame for what I'd done to our family. I didn't deserve your love.

It's why I left, believing you were better off with your grandparents, who truly adored you.

I returned to the Territory, back to my old stomping grounds, until Lauren reached out and told me she was pregnant with Lottie. To me, it was like I'd scored a second chance at having that family again. To keep that promise I'd made at Tree Stump.

When we returned to the farm, we were truly happy. I was once again living the dream and you doted on your sister.

I don't know what happened then.

I always did love large. Or it was me being weak again, that you found me with Ruth Oxford? I have no excuses.

But I can honestly say, after you left, I never touched another woman besides my wife. Heck, I was lucky Lauren stuck with me after what I'd done.

But then, Lauren was always a soft soul. She said it was karma for what we'd done to Eliza, who, as you know, was Lauren's best friend. And we were both grieving the life of a wonderful woman.

You look just like your mother. That woman had a smile that would bring me to my knees, making my soul feel alive. It was that feeling of finding home in your heart that I recognised her as my soulmate.

I hope you find that kind of love one day, you deserve it. If you do find that depth of love, hold on to it as tight as you can. Be sure to cherish every moment you can with them because every second is a precious gift.

You too were my precious gift, a result of something

wonderful — the love I shared with your mother. It was priceless.

I'm so sorry I failed you on so many levels, in ways a father shouldn't. I deserve the hatred that you showed me when you found out what I'd done, it still pains me. I honestly don't know how to tell you I'm sorry.

It's why I put so much thought and effort into planning this trip. You see, I wanted you and Lottie to travel to Tree Stump Station, hoping you could be sisters again. I want you to be a part of the family again.

Making you two travel alone for seven days, I hoped you'd learn not just about me, but more importantly, about each other. And kid, I know you left because of how much you loved your baby sister.

Be good to my little mate, Lottie. She misses you. She probably won't admit it, but there were moments I'd see her smile fall when she'd spot something that reminded her of you.

Heck, there were countless moments I thought of you, wishing I could turn back time. But then I'd see your smile in some far-off destination on social media, that I'd only joined to follow you, to see if you were happy.

I hope one day you can forgive me for what I did to you, to your mother, to Lottie's mother Lauren, and to my little mate, Lottie. I'm sorry I did this to all my girls.

I love you, kid, I've always loved you and I've always been proud of the amazing woman you are today.

Dad.

Teà wiped at her tears and shared a soft smile with her baby sister.

'So it's all true?' Lottie used her plaid scarf to dab at her tears.

Teà nodded.

'What do I tell my children? My husband? Our father was a rake.'

'Pearl called him a rolling stone with the ladies,' said Teà. 'Still, it's no excuse.'

'Yeah, but …' Lottie winced, wearing the same level of

shame Teà had spotted in her mother, Lauren.

Teà patted her sister's hand. 'We don't need to advertise it. You can keep it a family secret just between us: you, me, Adrian and the kids.'

'Our family secret.' Lottie put her arm over Teà's shoulders. 'We're sisters, right?'

'That we are. Reckon we can hug it out without killing each other?' Crinkling the letter in her hand, she stood with arms open wide.

'Yeah, why not.' Lottie hugged her, both wearing smiles.

'So, what did the other note have to say?'

Lottie opened the single page. *'Congratulations. I'm proud of you both for making it this far. As much as you may hate me, there is one more surprise waiting for you. Please climb to the top and wait. I promise, this is the last stop. Love Dad.'*

'Wait for what?' Teà checked her watch. 'We've got an hour to four o'clock.' It was a race to get here, now they weren't in a rush. They had time.

'I'm sick of waiting. Can't we just finish this?'

'Yeah, let's do this.'

Together, they climbed to the top, where the view was truly spectacular. The land disappeared on the curve of the horizon, topped off with a cloudless azure blue sky.

They dumped their bags, sipping water and took in the endless view unmarred by anything man made.

'Do we throw the ashes now?' Lottie removed the urn from her bag.

'I don't see why not. The instructions didn't say not to. And I'm done waiting, Lottie. I've been waiting seventeen years for this, to be with you. I'm sorry for being so harsh with you on this road trip.'

'Hey, I needed it. I'm sorry for being such a ...' Lottie waved her hand in circles as if searching for the words. 'An egotistical, narcissistic, ponytail-swinging prima donna.'

'Yikes.' Teà winced.

'I'm thinking of cutting my hair shorter.'

'Not on account of what I said?'

'Nah, but this ringer in the bar showed me what a Karen was on TikTok.'

'Oh …' Teà rubbed the back of her neck, remembering calling Lottie just that.

'I refuse to be like that.'

'Good.' There may be hope for this sister bond to grow yet.

'Do you forgive our father for what he did?'

Teà stared at the urn, her father's final letter in her pocket. Realising she was just like Lottie, holding her father to a higher standard than he could attain, the guy was human, too. People made mistakes; she made plenty of them. And her father did have many good points that she couldn't ignore. Both father and daughter, had stubbornly allowed time to slip by to not make amends with each other sooner. She would've liked to have had a beer with her dad to share their stories.

And to think of all that time she'd lost for not connecting with her sister sooner. Foolishly holding onto the hatred for something that happened a long time ago. It was time for her to let go.

Her father may be gone, but he would never be forgotten, as his story would live on through his legacy. As to how much they'd share with others outside of the family … Well, that was another story.

'What are we going to do after this?' Lottie started peeling off the tape that secured the urn's lid. That urn had been through a lot this past seven days, travelling from one end of Australia to the other. Babysat by a protected duck, carried to a stockman's boneyard, stolen from Knockabout Stockyards, and had rum and beer spilled all over it as the guest of honour to a rowdy mob of stockman at the local roadhouse.

Her father, the rogue he was, would've loved this adventure to Tree Stump Mountain.

'Anything we want, Lottie.' Teà gazed out of the

enormous uninterrupted view of an extraordinary country. It was breathtaking yet scary, staring out at the outback with so much still to be explored. 'It's like we're on top of the world here.'

'It is. It's a good place to make promises, you know.' Lottie cradled the urn to her chest. 'Dad has truly fulfilled the promises he made here, because here we are, his family bringing him back to where he made that promise.'

'That's true.'

'So, in honour of my father making his promise, and his wish for us reconnect as a family,' said Lottie, with her chin raised, smiling at the view. 'I promise to keep in touch with my sister. I'll want your phone number so we can call each other regularly. I'm not sure what we'll do about Christmas.'

'What about the farm?'

'It's a big world out there, isn't it?' Lottie pointed to the vast horizon.

'Yeah, but it's a beautiful world, too.' She'd seen many wonders and was looking forward to more.

She spotted a road train stirring up dust in the distance, coming from the direction of the roadhouse.

Her heart rose with the spiral of dust, thinking about Devin's offer. Did she, or didn't she?

With the sun streaming over the land that effortlessly spread before her on top of this mountain. It was like standing at a crossroads where you knew deep inside your soul that in this one moment, if you didn't take a chance, it was going to haunt you for the rest of your life.

Instead of shielding herself off, she chose to embrace it. It was time to finish her mourning. It was time to live again. 'I'm going to take up Devin's offer. So, I promise to try to learn to love again.' Although the way her heart felt, she already was in love.

'Good.' Lottie practically gushed. 'I'll make the wedding dress.'

'Steady on, we're going to take it slow.' She nudged her

sister playfully. 'So, what about you?'

'I want to learn to let go. The first thing to let go of is the farm. We'll sell it, and do what Adrian wants.' Lottie sighed, still smiling, with none of that control-freak brashness to it either. 'My husband has stuck by me, and we're going to do what's right for us.'

'That is?'

'Go on a road trip, so I can learn to be a fun mum. To have some crazy fun, like go in a camel race and hear tall tales in an outback pub, with my husband beside me. I want to see the wonder in our children's smiles as we camp under the stars and create our own amazing memories, making family day everyday like our dad did with us on Sundays.'

'Well, it looks like we both have lots to look forward to and lots of stories to share.'

'Weekly?'

Teà shrugged. 'If we're in phone range?'

'I'll need to check in with someone if we're on the road. You know, probably someone resourceful enough to make me get up and keep moving forward in the worst of times. Someone to put me in my place when I become that Bossy Lottie, again.' Lottie tossed her arm around Teà's shoulders and squeezed. 'Who knows? I may even let Adrian drive.'

'The Ford?'

'Hell, no. I want a car with air conditioning, decent suspension, and a sound system.'

They both grinned at the blue Ford waiting below.

'Are we ready to do this? Let Dad's ashes go?' Lottie asked.

'Yeah.'

They stood on the edge of the world, with Lottie holding the urn in their hands.

When a roar came up from behind them.

They came face to face with a helicopter.

Was it Devin?

It was the exact same helicopter he'd carted on the back of his truck. But it was the twin, with a different pilot. 'What now?'

They hid their faces from the dust as it landed on the far end of the plateau and waited for the engines to stop. The silence eerie.

A young woman, about eighteen, jogged towards them, holding a business-sized envelope.

'Please tell me that's our golden ticket or something, and she works for the lawyer.' Teà whined at Lottie. They deserved a win after what they'd been through.

The girl brushed her red hair behind her ears and smiled at them. 'Hi. Are you Teà and Lottie Voss?'

'I'm Lottie, this is Teà. Who are you?'

'Naomi. I got this letter from Victor Voss. Is that him?' Naomi pointed at the urn.

'Yes. Did you know Victor Voss?'

'No. But my mother did.'

'Who was your mother?' Teà asked Naomi.

'Ruth Oxford, and according to this letter, I'm your sister.'

The urn slipped from Lottie's fingers. Its hard porcelain shell smashed against the rocks, releasing the ashes of Victor Voss to scatter on the breeze, and disappear over the outback, leaving his three daughters staring at each other. *Bloody hell, Dad!*

Twenty-nine

'I'm your sister!'

'That doesn't mean I have to like you,' Teà said to Little Miss Lottie Voss, the middle sister, who was steering the 1970 XY Ford Falcon 500 down the dirt track. In the back seat, Teà wriggled in her dress. 'You made this too tight.'

'No, it's fitted. Don't you dare wreck my best work!' Lottie slapped Teà's hand. 'I hand-sewed that gown on our drive over from Queensland.'

'You made this too low. I'm all boobs.'

'Honey, you look great. You're just not used to wearing dresses. Devin's going to die.'

'I'm going to die from not breathing—*Watch out, Lottie!*'

Lottie's little feet slammed on the brake, and the car slid in the dirt.

Only this time, Teà was ready for it and jumped out of the car.

'You'll get your dress dirty!'

The gown's delicate hem dragged in the dust, as Teà made her way to the front of the Ford. 'Quacker, how many times have I told you about this?'

The duck honked, flapping its wings, fluffing up its feathers in the middle of the dirt track.

'I can't believe the duck is still doing that,' Lottie said.

'Every time you come near the place Quacker likes to play chicken with cars like it's his own pelican crossing.'

'Did you ever find out where Quacker came from?'

'Devin thinks someone poached Quacker and he became someone's pet.'

'That's how we found him in the middle of nowhere.'

'And why he's so friendly.' Teà scooped up the duck. 'I guess we can't do this without you being a guest of honour.'

'Talking about honoured guests, the bride needs to show up preferably before sunset or Devin's going to chase you down in his helicopter.'

'I got one too.'

'What?'

'A helicopter.'

'No way!'

'It was my wedding present. I help with the musters. It's a total buzz.' She carried the duck to the car, remembering that road trip less than a year ago, watching the world from the front seat of the blue car. The family car.

Tree Stump Mountain rose in the distance, with the billabong before them.

'You didn't want to do this on Tree Stump?'

'No. Devin and I spend a lot of time here. We like watching the ducks. Quacker's got his own family now.' She nuzzled into the neck of the white-headed duck who practically purred.

'Here we are ...' Lottie pulled up to a small oasis among the land of red dust and sunshine. It was a place where soft grasses blended into a green carpet dotted with soft pink and blue wildflowers. The shady canopy of sturdy gums was home to a spectacular collection of flourishing wild orchids in full bloom, and the vibrant fragrance of wild jasmine and wattle filled the air.

Pushing up his glasses, her brother-in-law, Adrian, met them at the car. 'I was about to send a search party for you pair. You didn't pass any speed cameras on the way? Your sister's developed quite the lead foot on the highways.'

'Only on bitumen highways. Adrian's the king of four-wheel driving. But I'm better at backing in the caravan these days.'

'So proud.' Adrian kissed Lottie's blushing cheek. 'So, do I cue the music?'

'There is no music. We wanted this day to be as simple as possible.' After all, they were simple people. Teà waited for Lottie to finish fussing over the dress, while she cradled the duck instead of a bouquet of flowers, because she wasn't that kind of girl.

And she smiled.

Because Devin was the type of guy who'd understood why she'd bring a duck to their wedding.

'I'm getting married.' Teà gasped in her tight dress; not from fear, but from an overwhelming feeling of blissful joy. She wanted to do cartwheels down the grassy aisle, to jump into the arms of the man who'd accepted her for who she was. Boots and all.

When she'd made her promise that day on Tree Stump Mountain, she let Devin in. Fully. Completely. With all her soul. They hadn't spent a night apart since. Why fight what felt right, and felt like home?

And when he'd proposed to her, in the same place where they were getting married, where he'd hidden her engagement ring inside a toolbox, giving it to her on one of their picnics while watching the ducks. It was a no-brainer saying yes, because the dusty-denim-wearing cowboy with the sexy swagger took her breath away every single day.

Only a few had gathered for their special day, including the roadhouse proprietors who'd become firm friends—Rusty, Pearl and Patrick—having a rare day off.

Devin's brother, Mason, was the best man. His wife and three children were with Devin's adorable parents who'd welcomed the Voss sisters as if they were their own.

Lottie was the matron of honour. Her husband, Adrian, held their daughter Sophie's hand, while Pip, their son, sat on the shoulders of their new aunt, Naomi.

It was a mixed batch of people, all sharing one common trait—they were family.

And for a girl who'd struggled with abandonment issues and grief, being too scared to find a family of her own, she smiled at the man daring to take on that challenge.

Devin.

Her heart bloomed, unashamedly and without fear. She got to be a bride, walking towards him in a gown handmade by her sister. Holding a duck.

Devin grinned at her as he met her before the celebrant. 'Why am I not surprised you brought Quacker?'

'He walked in front of the car.'

'Your sister didn't hit him?'

'You know how slow she drives on dirt.'

'On this occasion, I'm glad of Lottie's slow driving. She is carrying my most precious cargo. You.' He kissed her nose, then took the duck from her hands. 'Quacker, you can hold the lady later, it's my turn.' He gently placed the duck on the ground, took Teà's hand, and gave it a gentle squeeze. 'You look beautiful.'

'You, too.' The guy was in a suit! *Can you spell S-E-X-Y, sister?*

His eyes met hers and the rest of the world fell away, and like magnets their lips met, mouths meshed, and she was in heaven. Crushing her to his chest, he wrapped his body around hers as if to shield her from all the bad, and she deserved something good. Hot. Muscular. Wrapped neatly into the heavenly temptation of the glorious male that he was.

'*Excuse me, peoples!* You're meant to kiss *after* the ceremony.' Lottie said, as the group chuckled.

'Ready to do this?' Devin smiled at Teà.

'Yes. Are you?'

'Hey, I would've married you the day you walked

through my front door.'

The day they'd come down from the mountain, after spending hours learning about Naomi, Teà had knocked on his open front door and cheekily cried out, 'Hi honey, I'm home.' He'd met her with open arms, and she'd introduced him to their new sister.

A lot had happened since then.

The farm was sold. Lottie cut her hair and became a brunette. And she and Adrian invested in a caravan and a fancy four-wheel drive and began their slow tour of the country. Together, they home-schooled the children, got odd jobs here and there, sharing pictures, and weekly phone calls with updates of their adventures on the road. For them, they got to be the fun parents living family day every day.

The blue Ford never went back down south. It stayed with Teà, tucked up under protective tarps, safe and secure in a shed on Tree Stump Station, only coming out on special occasions, and for family days like today's wedding.

With Tree Stump Mountain in the distance, it was a reminder of those promises she'd made with Lottie. At times, it felt as if her father was watching over her in this land he'd loved. Somehow, her father had given her the greatest gift. A husband. A new circle of friends. A growing family. And sisters.

As the sun set across the outback, the billabong's calm waters reflecting the sky, Devin and Teà exchanged their vows.

An incredible warmth filled her with a deep and true love. Her smile radiated from the inside out; she knew she had to be glowing. Devin's smile was just as wide, as his hands tenderly caressed her belly, preparing to share the good news as their gift to their guests. Their family was growing.

Teà got to live in a place where her dreams did come true. She'd found a home in this alien outback world, sharing her life with those she loved. She had her tribe, her village, gathered in this valley of love where she now understood that love comes in many layers with friends, family, lovers, brothers-in-laws, and sisters. It was a family worth fighting for.

As she hugged her sisters, preparing for the photos, she knew that no matter what, they'd have each other's backs, that they had formed an unbreakable bond. Sure, they'd argue, cry, laugh, shout at each other, and slam doors to end a conversation. They'd borrow clothes, swap recipes, playlists, and even makeup tips. They'd make memories together, singing badly to each other on birthdays, share gifts at Christmas, while creating embarrassing moments that they blamed on the wine. But they would also share many secrets without any form of judgement, because that's what sisters did in this family. How about yours?

The End...

Because you read the story....

See the Voss Sisters' Photo Album

it's your free gift.

For details visit: https://melarowe.com/tstgift/

Did you like the story?

If so, your opinion matters to me!

It's true. A good reader's review is worth a lot to this author.

So, if you enjoyed this book, please leave a review & recommend it to your friends.

I'd appreciate it.

With much gratitude,

mel
A . R O W E

ACKNOWLEDGEMENTS

Thank you

Thank you for reading this story and to those who have helped me on this amazing journey to get here, I wish I could name you all.

No secret I love road trips, all kinds of road trips. They clear the head, and I get to sing loudly, and badly—because no one is around, luckily. That's because I live in the Northern Territory, where we're able to explore its vast outback regions. No wonder these adventures ended up in this story.

So I'd like to thank all of my amazing road trip buddies of the past, present, and future adventures to come. To the Handbrake for suffering along with my singing. To my singing, playlist-sharing partner Vicki Bates, who helped me concoct this road trip story while on a road trip! True story. But do spare a thought for those many men and women who did perish along the notorious stock route, The Murranji Track.

Thank you to my online writer friends and to the amazing editing Deb team at DNP. Thank you to Clare Burns for having a sharp eye, and to the Fabulous First Readers team for their support, I am truly blessed to have you all join me on my writing journey.

Lastly, to you, dear reader, thank you for taking the time to read this story. It means the world to me, and I look forward to sharing more with you in that *'Escape to Happily Ever After'*.

Until next time,

Mel

A. ROWE

ABOUT THE AUTHOR

Australian bestselling author, Mel A ROWE, creates escapes for today's busy women to enjoy from the comfort of their home.

Delivered with a dash of drama, witty humour and quirky family units, Mel is known for reinventing romantic versions of home, taking her common characters on uncommon journeys that lead from boardrooms to billabongs as they try to find their own HAPPILY EVER AFTER.

Living in Australia's Northern Territory, Mel enjoys random outback road trips, fumbling with her camera, annoying her family with her bad singing, and making new friends in the middle of nowhere—except for water buffalos. She's been chased by a few.

Find Mel at

MelAROWE.com

Receive exclusive insights, book gifts, news
of upcoming releases by joining:
https://melarowe.com/newsletter/

Also by MEL A ROWE

ELSIE CREEK SERIES:

The ART of DUST

DIAMOND in the DUST

CAKED in DUST

XMAS DUST

MUSTER in the DUST

ROLLED in DUST

WRITTEN in DUST

OASIS OF THE OUTBACK DUOLOGY:

The Station - Volume I

The Station - Volume II

Standalone Stories:

Avoiding the Pity Party

Unplanned Party

The Football Whisperer

USA Bestseller—Winter's Walk

Run Beautiful Run

The Sister Trip

For story exclusives & more visit MelAROWE.com